San
Santos-Febres, Mayra, 1966-
Sirena Selena /

HARRIS COUNTY PUBLIC LIBRARY

W9-CIG-120

CYF $21.00 ocm43599003

Sirena

Selena

Also by Mayra Santos-Febres

Urban Oracles

Mayra

Santos-

Febres

Sirena

Selena

Translated by

Stephen Lytle

Picador USA   New York

SIRENA SELENA. Copyright © 2000 by Mayra Santos-Febres. Translation copyright © 2000 by Stephen Lytle. All rights reserved. Printed in the United States of America. No part of this book may be used or reproduced in any manner whatsoever without written permission except in the case of brief quotations embodied in critical articles or reviews. For information, address Picador USA, 175 Fifth Avenue, New York, N.Y. 10010.

Picador® is a U.S. registered trademark and is used by St. Martin's Press under license from Pan Books Limited.

Book design by Victoria Kuskowski

Library of Congress Cataloging-in-Publication Data

Santos-Febres, Mayra.
  [Sirena Selena. English]
  Sirena Selena / Mayra Santos-Febres ; translated by Stephen Lytle.—1st ed.
    p. cm.
  ISBN 0-312-25227-7
  I. Lytle, Stephen A. II. Title.

PQ7440.S26 S5713 2000
863'.64—dc21   00-025261

First Edition: August 2000

10 9 8 7 6 5 4 3 2 1

Sirena

Selena

C *áscara de coco, contento de jirimilla azul, por los dioses dí, azucarada Selena* . . . Coconut shell, melancholy and restless, from the gods you came, sweet Selena, succulent siren of the glistening beaches; confess, beneath the spotlight, *lunática*. You know the desires unleashed by urban nights. You are the memory of distant orgasms reduced to recording sessions. You and your seven soulless braids like a *selenita* bird, like a radiant bird with your insolent magnetism. You are who you are, Sirena Selena . . . and you emerge from your paper moon to sing the old songs of Lucy Favery, Sylvia Rexach, la Lupe, sybarite, dressed and adored by those who worship your face. . . .

2

*I*n the airplane, sitting next to la Martha, who is a real lady, a veteran of thousands of footlights: El Cotorrito, Bocaccio's, Bachelors. She once did shows at La Escuelita on Thirty-ninth Street in New York City. She even had a devoted husband who set her up in an apartment in El Condado. "Just like you now, *niña,* as you begin your zenith. I was his decent little wife when he came to Puerto Rico from Honduras. He was a businessman, my husband. And since I have a businesswoman's blood, I learned from him how to keep books and sneaked as much as I could to set up my own little business. Don't think that I was going to end up broke and alone when that businessman grew tired of it. Me, in the street again? Never, never, never. I went through too many police raids to get these implants and the hormones that make me so fabulous. Sorry, *nena.* I've gotten used to the good life."

Martha, *toda una señora,* her guide, her *mamá.* The one she never had, the person who pulled her from the street and put her in the Blue Danube to sing. She was tall and peroxide-blond, with a portentous pair of silicon breasts and incredibly smooth skin in the cleft of her bosom. She was tanned and long-legged; her nails were always painted garnet red, like a drop of coagulated blood on the tip of each of her fingers and toes. Not a single hair showed to betray her. Only her height and her voice and her very feminine mannerisms, too feminine, studiously feminine. Her teeth were perfect, no nicotine stains, though she smoked incessantly. Maybe that explained her grainy voice, as if millions of sand particles had lodged in her throat, in her long, well-moisturized neck, already a little wrinkled, but still elegant, stretching up in a proud curve to her permed hair and down to a back that was a little too wide, but nevertheless still appeared to be the delicate back of a woman of a certain age who had already lived many lives.

Vampiress in your novel, the great tyrant . . . : la Sirena was practicing on the plane as they flew toward the Dominican Republic. They were traveling on business, he and Martha. It's his first time flying in an airplane, his first puddle jump. The second will be to New York, he imagines. To try his luck there as who he really is.

Before he met Martha, Sirena hadn't always been a wanderer. La Selena had once had a roof overhead, but when his grandmother died from cleaning too many rich people's houses, there was no one left to take care of him. Uncles: dead or emigrated overseas. A mother: whereabouts unknown. Social Services wanted to send him to an orphanage. But for la Sirena there wasn't much difference between an orphanage and hell. He knew he would be abused by the stronger boys; they'd hit him, rape him, then leave him bleeding and half dead on the dirty floor of some storeroom. So Selena preferred to make the street his home. First with Valentina. And later with Martha, his new *mamá.*

Now they were going together to the Dominican Republic on business. Martha had taught him how to save money. And where to go for really cheap wigs and makeup. Martha had made him get rid of the cocaine habit that was wrecking his nasal passages, making them bleed. "*Loca,* that's not where a young lady is supposed to have her first period," she said, and gave him an alternative to hustling men in European cars. She cleaned him up and helped him find the sweetness in his voice again. "You sing like the angels in heaven," Martha had told him excitedly one day, the day Selena was collecting soda cans around the Blue Danube and, without realizing it, softly singing one of his grandmother's favorite boleros. He sang it with his whole voice, as if he were going to die when he finished, he sang it to feel his misery—like a wounded dog, a purebred, but one with leprosy, dying beneath a dismantled car.

Las dragas, the drag queens, listening to the bolero just stood there with their mouths hanging open. They were working the street, negotiating with clients, when suddenly they heard a sorrowful murmur, a heartbreaking agony that invaded their flesh and kept them from being sufficiently alert to negotiate prices for their couplings, or for quickies with husbands escaping their homes. They couldn't do anything except remember what made them cry, and their false lashes began to come unglued from their eyelids. They spun around on their high heels and loosened their wigs to hear better. Then, in a daze, they called for their manager, Miss Martha Divine, to come hear this street hustler with the voice of a holy angel.

It was Lizzy Starr, shouting at the top of her lungs, who got Martha's attention. She stood closest to the door of the Blue Danube, that little bar of derailed *travestis*, where the splendiferous Martha Divine reigned as sole proprietor. Lizzy merely swung open the door, stuck her head inside for a second, and shrieked, "Martha, hurry, come see this!" Martha emerged quickly from the Danube, preparing herself for the worst. She thought she was going to have to fight with some policeman looking for a bigger take who was beating up her girls, or clubbing some client. But that's not what it was. As soon as the door closed behind Martha, she heard a subtle melody that held the entire street in suspended animation. Martha's gaze sought out the origin of the voice. And found it. It was coming from the throat of a young boy who, drugged way beyond unconsciousness, was singing as he collected empty cans. Martha just stood there, like all the other *dragas*, like all the *clientes*, stunned, like all the people driving cars along the street. When she recovered, her businesswoman's blood started pumping through her veins. She walked over to the boy and invited him into the bar for a Coca-Cola. She ordered him some food, took him to her apartment, and before long helped him kick his habit and taught him how to dress like a bolero singer. Little by little she helped to transform him into who he really was. And now she was personally taking him to the Dominican Republic, because la Selena had never flown in an airplane before. They were going on business, to see if they could sell his show to a hotel. They both had the blood of businesswomen running through their veins.

Young Selena was nervous, perhaps because of the emotional impact of her first trip, or the hope of a new life through this plan of performing in another country, even though it was just a neighboring island. She had already done her little show at Crasholetta. She had already sung privately for the most glamorous *locas* in the city's gay scene. But she was still too young to be able to get a contract in the tourist hotels. "Even if you lie about your age, they can't hire you, *mi amor*. Federal laws prohibit child labor. Didn't you know that? So, instead," said her new mother, "we'll go to the Dominican Republic, where they don't care about such things." And now, thanks to the federal laws, Sirena Selena was about to become the diva of the Caribbean. She would awaken the yearnings of a whole new public with her songs. Her show would make her the brightest star in any four-star hotel. She would have a dresser and lights and wardrobes made of the finest fabrics. She would finally be able to display the full glory of her voice. *Oh.* Her voice, please don't let it fail now, Virgen Santa, don't let it change, let it stay just as it is, sweet and crystalline. The girls she worked with at the Danube never tired of telling her how a trickle of tarnished melancholy flows from the center of her chest, but it was always fresh, as old and as fresh as the perennial pain of love on the face of the earth. So many people had told her so many things about her voice. "Your voice smells like honey. Your mouth is a piece of fruit," an admirer once murmured into her ear as he tried to kiss her. She had just finished singing and was exhausted from being onstage, so she let herself be kissed. She allowed the man to wiggle his eager tongue past her exhausted lips, caressing them to see if he could loosen her up a bit. She let his tongue explore her mouth, sip the dense saliva of a night of cabaret. But in the middle of the kiss, Sirena noticed that the other mouth was seeking something more than is normally sought in a kiss. That mouth wanted to swallow a melody. That kiss was trying to devour her voice.

When the admirer finished kissing her, he looked at her victoriously. Sirena resumed the role of mysterious woman and walked away without a word toward the back room that served as a dressing room

5

for all the *dragas* at the Danube. Her slight hips swaying, she held the foreign saliva in her mouth, without swallowing it, suspecting sabotage. When she arrived in the dressing room, she rinsed her mouth with water from the faucet and Listerine. Afterward, when she arrived at Martha's apartment, she gargled with a mixture of rose petals, magnolia petals, and garlic to rid herself of any envious bacteria that might have remained hiding in her mouth.

And that's how she felt now, wanting to put a handkerchief full of herbs around her neck, drink a shot of brandy with honey, orange blossom water, and cinnamon, swallow a raw egg yolk, pray to San Judas Tadeo. She wanted to protect her voice. It's a good thing that Sirena knows it. Her voice is the only thing she has that can get her anywhere in life.

In the airplane, Martha didn't notice her nervousness. She gazed at Sirena, who was seemingly deep in thought, never imagining that she was praying to Santa Clara, or to la Virgen de la Caridad del Cobre. Martha thought she was going over the words of the boleros she had selected for the audition. It amused her to think that others might see them as a family, her the mother with her fifteen-year-old son, who seemed like, but wasn't exactly, any other boy; his too-meticulously-cared-for nails, his high arching eyebrows, the slender waist, all indicating something else. And she, who was, but not really, the doting mother, a *doña* of a certain age who never allowed herself to be conquered by motherhood, someone who had been a young mother, a friendly confidante, and a support to the family. La Martha Divine, a little too tall, a little too strong in the lines along her chin, a little too smooth and round here and there . . . But even so, anyone would think, at a casual glance, that the woman and her son constituted a family going on vacation in the Dominican Republic. She gazed lovingly at her *hijito,* touched his head, and Selena responded with the usual smile, distant and almost imperceptible, still engrossed in the whisper of words, prayers, and songs that was throbbing in his mind.

You, María Piedra de Imán, enchantress and touchstone, who walked with the seven Samaritans and gave them beauty and recognition, bring me luck and fortune, bless your Sirena, so that I can sing, Piedra Imán. You were magnet and compass: you will be my protector, with me always. I ask of you that my voice come out filled with needles, dense, that it enter the breasts of those who listen to me and wring longing and applause from them. I ask for gold as my treasure, silver for my house, and I want you to be the sentinel of my home and my personality as you were the guiding light for the Holy Virgin Mary. You know, Santísima Piedra Imán, that drinking egg whites helps, gargling with seawater and Listerine helps, practicing the recorded exercises of maestro Charles Monigan that Martha bought me from the television and that I put on the videocassette player in her apartment helps; but they don't assure me of anything. Your protection is what I seek for my assurance. . . .

That is why I entreat you to make my house prosperous and happy and to let your star guide me and illumine my path. Lend me your beneficent magic. I want you to lend me your talisman, I want to have power and dominion to conquer my enemies. I want you to guide me, Piedra Imán, on the opposite path, opposite to when I was working the streets. To be able to sing as if nothing had ever happened, as I did when I was a child and had a home and a family. We were poor, sometimes we had to eat cold Chef Boyardee and bread, night after night, but we were happy. There was no need to succumb to evil, to grow desperate, and to sing just to survive. To pour all the anger into a song. And now, Piedra Imán, I don't want to sing like that anymore. I want to sing from a new mouth, as if newly born when the lights shine on me. Free of memories.

In return for what you give me, I will give you amber, onyx, coral, so that you will free me from all envy and evil. I will give you pieces of steel so that I will have more than enough of what I need and to assure my path to success. I will give you wheat so that I may triumph over my enemies, incense and myrrh for the gift that the three kings brought to beloved Jesús, and I will give three *potencias* for the virtue of Piedra Imán: three *credos*, for the first; seven *salves*, for the second; and five *Padres Nuestros* and five *Ave Marías* for the third, praising the Lord on this holy day and saying Glory to God in the Highest and peace on earth to all men of goodwill, blessed bread of Holy God who satisfies my soul and cleanses my sins.

Cleanse my sins, Santísima Piedra Imán; the sins of this faithful believer, the most fragile of all the hustlers on the street, the most screwed-up fifteen-year-old in the whole barrio. And not by uncles, or godparents, or neighbors enamored of an innocent gaze, but by people who came and went and never came again, by grown men who from a distance somehow realized something that I only felt vaguely. They came and opened their car doors already knowing I would get in, I would sit there staring coldly at them, I would let the trembling hand go wherever it went, knowing that what always happened would happen, the swelling, the delicious fear, the urge to cry, the burning saliva, the tear in my eye, the yearning to die right there. They knew I would permit the tons of liquids pouring onto the interior of the car, dampening the rugs, the vinyl seats and even the steering wheel, staining them with their smell. Then came the hardening of their faces, after discovering, but not saying, what they had discovered. They paid me twenty pesos, Piedra Imán, twenty pesos pressed with their own hands into the pocket of my sweaty pants, as if that were the price of my secret, of what was contained within my skin. The price of my sins and of my beauty.

But if I sinned, they were worse sinners, they were my worst enemies. I never saw those men again, María Piedra Imán. They disappeared afterward, as if swallowed up by the earth. You, who put them in my path, from my path you will take them, you who gave beauty and recognition to the seven Samaritans, to this child who lies prostrate before your feet, give him the name that you choose, protect his voice so that he may pray to you and ask for your protection. And he will offer you that same voice as his greatest offering if you guide him and illumine his way, Holy Ember, light of my home. This I give to you, Holy Stone.

4

*M*artha grips her armrest. She feels almost as if she could rip it from its fixture. They are only a few moments from landing. For some mysterious reason, takeoffs and landings always make her nervous. But not flying: hanging there suspended in the sky didn't make her the least bit uncomfortable. Being up there was like being in a movie, and she thrilled at the idea, requesting service from the thin, elegant stewardesses. Indeed, she remembers occasions when she came across stewards who recognized her from the bars, remembered her cabaret shows, when she imitated Barbra Streisand and Bette Midler, and they would even ask for her autograph. But takeoffs and landings always provoked anxiety in her. And there was no anxiety in this world that didn't prompt Martha to think about her body.

Oh yes, her body, this disguise that was her body. She trembled just thinking that someone, in the middle of takeoff, might point a finger at her and shout, "Look at that. That is not a woman." And they would turn the aircraft around and force her from it, throwing her suitcases to the ground. Her bags would open, suddenly spewing high heels, gauze and tape, depilatory creams, and thousands of other cosmetic items, lending themselves, the bitches, as evidence. The captain himself would deplane to insist that she had no right to enjoy the comfort, the airborne luxury, the dream of traveling to other shores. Not her, she's an impostor.

But with the money that Martha can make on this trip, she will finally be able to pay for the operation, which will be a very difficult change for her. She doesn't mind the sacrifices. Having the operation isn't the same as dressing up—this was something she knew deep within herself. To be able to take off her clothes and see herself, finally, from the waist below the same as from above the waist, with tits and candy. Together. To finally be able to rest in a single body.

The operation would liberate her from her worst fears, cure her subconscious nightmares. That was the diagnosis of a girlfriend who had a degree in psychology, but never practiced. After the operation Miss Martha would feel much relieved. There would be no more dreams in the middle of the night of sleeping naked in a circus tent while everyone paid to look at her, the main attraction, chained to a pink post adorned with Christmas garland. Never again the fear of being kicked off an airplane in the middle of takeoff. Customs agents everywhere would welcome her with courtesy and respect. She would be able at last to rest in a single body and to take care of her girls and this child that the Exterminating Angel himself had sent her. Able finally to finish paying her debts and release the karma for what she did to her husband. But it wasn't all her fault. As much as she had begged for the money for her operation, he would never give it to her. What else was she supposed to do? What indeed, if wrinkles were already appearing in her voice and the hormones had already reached her soul? What, when she could no longer meet the stares of the neighbors in the apartment building where her husband had sent her to live, and when she no longer had the desire to go to restaurants with him? But by helping this child she was protecting, she would be able to help them both. Then she could finally turn herself into a real lady, have a single body, airplanes, cars, in one body, hotels, husbands, in one single body, and moneymoneymoney.

They had landed. Now, the bitter pill of going to look for suitcases, lining up for customs, paying entrance taxes, showing birth certificates, and finding a taxi to take them to the hotel. As soon as they arrived she would call the manager and the person in charge of entertainment. The presentation was ready—her singer was rehearsed and ready to dazzle them. And, just in case, there was a comfortable wad of bills gently pressing against her skin in the small purse that she always wore beneath her blouse. She had taken this precaution in case Contreras, the hotel administrator who had invited them, failed them somehow. He had told her that he would take care of all their hotel expenses. But for Miss Martha, seeing was believing. She and la Sirena would be in Santo Domingo for a week, and in a week you can spend a lot of money. Experience had taught Martha that it's better to be a safe *loca* than a sorry one. Besides, of this she was certain: during that time, she was going to sell the show, whether to Contreras's hotel or to another of perhaps lesser category. Then the bonanza would come: success, the end of her agonies. Money would flow, money for her unified body, money for her shining star and for the Blue Danube, two Blue Danubes, branches of the Blue Danube in all the gay sections of this wanton Caribbean, where the people fornicate as if the world were about to end.

Now the passengers had formed a line to deplane. Miss Martha waited for Sirena to remove her belongings from the overhead compartment, checked to make sure that they weren't leaving anything behind, then looked for a place among the tourists, salesmen, and families who had accompanied them on the flight. She began to feel eyes on her and her adopted son. "Please, Jehovah, God of the armies, give me strength. This is what I hate most about landing." Despite her attempts to calm herself, Martha again felt the anxiety turning into a living tumor in her stomach. The doubts came back. What if they noticed something strange around the edges of her makeup, and if what happened to Maxine happened to her? They figured Maxine out as soon as she got off that 747 and put her through shame after shame in the customs office. Almost twenty hours they detained her, the guards making fun of her, dumping out the contents of her suitcases, breaking jars of makeup on the floor. Expensive hydrating creams, smeared all over her dresses—Alfaro's, Anna Sui's—copied from magazines and made especially for her. "A nightmare," Maxine had told her. "I will never get on another airplane as long as I live." What if the same thing happened to her?

The line started to move; then they were climbing down the stairs and walking toward customs. Martha noted that her charge was equally nervous. Sirenito's forehead was sweating and he was so pale that it seemed that he might faint at any moment. The crush of people, the noisy airport, and the fear of leaving home for the first time were confusing him miserably. Messages echoed from the loudspeakers: "All arriving passengers must pay arrival tax. Please proceed to the arrival tax window before passing through customs." At the same time another loudspeaker blared, "Money exchange to the right. Please proceed to the cashier's window. . . ." And outside, across the barriers, the taxi drivers shouted, "Where shall I take you, *señora*, where shall I take you?" It would nauseate anyone. The child in her care didn't know where to look and clung to his suitcases as if they were flotation devices.

Martha's maternal instinct kicked in. She took Sirena's face between her hands and said in her most tender voice, "Don't worry, *mijito*, this will soon be over." She wiped her hand across his forehead, clearing away the cold sweat. She straightened his shirt. She wasn't going to let anything happen to her adopted son, her good-luck charm. Nothing was going to interfere with the plans she had cooked up for the two of them. By helping la Sirena, she was helping herself; by helping this little jewel that had fallen from the sky, she was at long last going to be able to reconcile herself with her own body. She had to control herself, to be careful not to let la Sirena see that she, too, was scared silly. She murmured to herself, "Always remember, *mamita*. You are Miss Martha Divine. Where there is a will, there is a way. So just keep moving forward and don't look back." She breathed deeply, thrust out her chest and, with her face set more precisely in the manner of a *mujer elegante*, set off to look for their bags.

They paid the arrival tax, showed their birth certificates, exchanged some dollars into local currency. Nothing to declare. Luckily they didn't have to open their suitcases. If they had, how would she have explained the three sets of sport shirts and shorts and the array of dresses and wigs that were not the *señora*'s size? Thank God they didn't open them. That proved to Martha that someone was protecting them. Definitely, some unseen power was guiding them. And that same beneficent force waited for them just beyond the glass doors where the heat, the bustle, and the daily struggle welcomed them to this other godforsaken island, floating as well as it could in its ample ocean.

Outside they found swarms of taxi drivers and without looking back they climbed into the first car and sped off toward the hotel. The Hotel Conquistador was pure luxury. In front was a majestic fountain spraying streams of water over a statue of a woman playing a flute shaped like a seashell. There was a brick driveway. The lobby featured works of art and a reception counter of dark mahogany and cut-glass lamps that brightened the room nicely. Thick marble columns that stretched up twenty feet to the ceiling anchored the space. The floors were waxed, and plants and small seating areas with couches upholstered in brightly colored fabrics were scattered around the room. Next to the carved-mahogany tables were matching floral-patterned Chippendale chairs. To the right were doors leading to the casino and in the rear was an expansive swath of green crisscrossed by well-tended paths and the plate-glass windows of two restaurants, one Chinese, the other French, something for every palate. Beside the elevators was another counter where the bellboys waited to be called to serve the hotel guests. That's where Martha was looking now, studying the hotel's cleanliness and elegance. What Contreras had told her on the telephone before she decided to come was true: "It's a five-star hotel. The guests are mostly European tourists looking for adventure and entertainment. Until now we haven't offered more than an occasional pianist in the bar. Maybe a singer would brighten things up and grab the guests' attention." *Ay* Contreras, will it ever! You'll see what happens when the guests hear Sirena Selena sing.

They checked in. Everything went smoothly with the reservations made by Billy, a friend who worked at a travel agency in Hato Rey and the agent who had taken care of all of their travel plans. La Billy had been in Martha's care a long time ago, but was no longer very involved in the *ambiente*, the scene. What he had always wanted was to earn enough money to pay for a course in travel agenting, so he could work legally. He didn't care much for life on the street. Martha herself noticed that and took the trouble to advise him, with a great deal of tact so as not to hurt his feelings. "*Papito, fíjate,* I don't think this life is for you. You are the shy, relaxed type," she said, "and all this stress is going to embitter you, *corazón.*" "You're right," agreed Billy, and he thanked her warmly for the advice. Martha did him another favor. She gave him a tip about a job and gave him some money to buy an Yves St. Laurent shirt to impress them at the interview. "Billy, always remember that image is everything. If you look like a professional, you are a professional. The rest is choreography and acting." And that was how she gained the unconditional loyalty of her former charge, though with *locas* you never know. But you have to trust someone. And in this scene you need to develop contacts, just like anywhere else.

Eleventh floor, Room 1105. The bellboy accompanied them to the room. He opened the door for them and waited for the tip, which Martha gave him to get rid of him as soon as possible. The room was to die for. Two double beds with mahogany headboards and matching night tables, peach-colored duvets to complement the room's décor. The floor was covered with wall-to-wall carpeting. In one corner stood a cedar cabinet containing a fully equipped twenty-one-inch television with Surround Sound, next to an air-conditioning unit, gently whispering its breath of cool air. The bathroom was impeccable, the walls covered in white tile and the towels embroidered with the hotel's emblem. When Martha walked over to pull open the curtains, she discovered a view that was almost as fabulous as the room itself. From where she stood she could see all of Santo Domingo— the cathedral, the streets of the colonial district, the alleys of shops, the houses lost in the distance beyond other hillside hotels.

All that luxury made the child in Sirena come out. As soon as they got rid of the bellboy, she ran to play with the curtains, flipped the air-conditioning on and off twenty times, trying out everything in the room. "*Nena,* don't jump on the beds like that. I don't want any problems with the management," warned Martha sharply, but she was laughing inside to see her young daughter so happy and carefree. She had seen her like that only a few times, shouting playfully, playing with the water faucets, the pillows, laughing uncontrollably, letting herself be the child she was.

Martha walked over to the telephone on the night table and called the front desk.

"Operator, I would like to speak with Mr. Contreras in administration."

"One moment, please."

"Señor Contreras? This is Martha Divine. We've just arrived and are a little tired. No, the trip was divine, no problem in customs or here at the hotel. I was just calling to let you know that we're here, all rehearsed and ready to accept offers. The audition? You name the time and we'll be there. We're professionals, you know, very punctual. Tomorrow at six? Perfect, Señor Contreras, we'll see you then. *Ciao . . .*"

Miss Martha Divine took her time in hanging up the receiver. She remained quiet for a few seconds, feeling the saliva glide down her throat, moistening it, preparing it for the words she was going to say to her student and charge. She smiled to herself, almost ready to turn to look at Sirena, who she knew was hanging on her every movement. Then she turned, enigmatically, toward Sirena.

"Tomorrow at six, Selena. Tomorrow at six the magic begins."

Sirena burst out laughing. She was amused by her adopted mother's melodramatic air. She applauded playfully and threw herself on the bed, shouting *"Bravo, viva!"* Somewhat offended at not receiving the reaction she had expected from her adopted daughter, Martha walked over to her purse. She searched for her cigarette case and the lighter, then sat beside the nightstand, ready to light up. "So we have the rest of the day free?" asked Sirena mischievously as she sat on the bed beside Martha. "Yes, dear, with all expenses paid by the hotel management. We are their special guests."

"Then there's no time to lose," Sirenita shot back. Now it was the younger woman's turn to be melodramatic. Martha watched her walk to the nightstand and reach for the telephone. She lit a cigarette as Sirena lifted the receiver with the mannerisms of a jet-set girl, then dialed the front desk and cleared her throat so that her voice would sound calm. "*Servicio?*" she heard Sirenita say. "Yes, please. I would like to order two filet mignons with roasted potatoes and a green salad. Oh, and a bottle of Champagne. Do you have Veuve Clicquot? Perfect, then send up the coldest bottle you have." Suddenly she remembered something else. "Oh, and an order of fresh strawberries, no whipped cream, please. I have to watch my figure, you understand." She giggles. "Room eleven-oh-five. *Muchas gracias.*"

Sirena kept her back to Martha, who was still sitting there watching the whole little number with a raised eyebrow.

As soon as the telephone conversation ended, the singer released her pose. Her body relaxed; her shoulders fell forward over her torso. It was as if when Sirena replaced the receiver a great weight had been removed from her. She remained quiet, pensive. Her guardian didn't want to disturb her. She was waiting for a reaction from her adopted daughter, thinking that Sirena was searching for the appropriate words before turning to face Miss Martha Divine, before responding with another silly act like the one she had performed moments before, when Martha had finished speaking with Contreras. But as she waited for the laughter, the air in the room became charged with another energy. For a second, which seemed like a century, a heavy silence filled the air. It was so pervasive that she could hear the whirring of the air-conditioning as it cooled every corner of the space, the muffled steps of someone walking along the carpeted corridor, and the still breath of the objects adorning the room. Sirena turned toward the corner from which Martha sat watching her. She hugged her chest with both arms and in the near ecstasy of relief she whispered to her mother:

"Oh, Martha, laugh at me if you want, but I have spent my whole life waiting for this moment."

Martha didn't laugh. She understood perfectly.

I tell you, Sirena, Luisito Cristal was a trip. The diva of the seventies. We called her Cristal because she always went to the discos dripping in lights and rhinestones, in gowns of glass and beads. She loved glitter. I had known her for a long time, from when she did shows at the Flying Saucer, standing on the platforms for go-go dancers, dressed in silver leotards, capes of translucent plastic, and boots covered in glass. *Un escándalo* la Luisito. In that disco I met a bunch of friends from the scene for the first time, when I was launching my pretty self as Miss Martha Divine. Kiki, for example, who tells anyone who'll listen that when she was younger Luisito Cristal saved her life. She had gone to the Flying Saucer to dance with a girlfriend, because she hadn't realized her true inclinations yet. But she was curious. And when she saw Luisito Cristal dancing on the platform, dressed with all the glamour of this world and bathed in the aura of a decadent rock star, she said to herself, 'That's it. . . .' She became bolder and started wearing more androgynous, more daring clothing, until one fine day she arrived at the Flying Saucer dressed in a silver miniskirt that the girlfriend had lent her. 'We had broken up by then, of course, but we had become best friends,' said Kiki. That Kiki is so divine—I introduced you to her, didn't I? There's nobody who can cut hair like her.

"The atmosphere at the Flying Saucer was relaxed. There were lots of teenagers there, just getting into the disco scene, and couples dancing salsa, looking for a place to show off their urban choreography—everybody went. Luisito came and hung out, but it wasn't where she really let go. Where she really let go was in the gay bars in Viejo San Juan. One night, I think it was at the Lion's Den, where the baths on Calle Luna are now, she arrived all wrapped up in tiny Christmas lights. She said hello to everyone, did a few spins on the dance floor, and then started to look all over the place for an electrical outlet where she could plug in this creation of electric lights. She searched and searched but couldn't find anything, because the disco was super dark, and the strobe lights were flashing, making your eyes crazy.

"Everybody had taken Quaaludes and acid that night and they were tripping to the max. That was the style back then. I didn't know what Luisito's drug of choice was that night, but she was flying, off in her own world. She looked like a model on the runway, even though she was still desperately trying to find an electrical outlet. Every now and then she would take a break from her search and would settle into a corner of the bar, by now full of sweaty men and fashion girls caked with makeup. Even then she looked fabulous, veiled in her own glamour. She was a diva from beyond, honoring us with her luminous presence, a goddess who had descended from Mount Olympus to mingle in the dark with us mortals in the hidden bars of gay San Juan. And there were a lot of bars in those days, not like now, there are only two or three left. The only ones that have survived from that time are Bocaccio's and Villa Caimito. I don't know how Dulce and Amelia managed to keep Bocaccio's open. It's more like a museum than a bar, frequented now by old *locas*, like me, the ones who outlived the country, AIDS, and all the ravages that a body in exile must suffer in order to survive. . . . Those two big lesbians are strong—Dulce isn't as sweet as her name, let me tell you! Before, they had another bar, what did they call it? Page Two, *sí*, Page Two. It was the only hot place to go. And there were other places, like the Abbey, where Bobby Herr was a featured performer. And El Cañanga and the Annex . . .

"But besides the Lion's Den, the club I liked best was the Bazaar. You entered the Bazaar through a dark labyrinth, painted black. That's where the most futuristic *locas* stationed themselves, with punk makeup, lots of eyeliner, lip gloss, and dark eye shadow. I think

Luisito Cristal's ordeal with the lights was at the Bazaar, come to think of it. That's why it was so hard for him to find an outlet that night. The Bazaar was like a cave. Super dark. If you looked in the corners, you would see couples entwined in the shadows like serpents with two heads. Tongues, hands inside pants . . . Total debauchery, I swear to you, not like now. These kids just go to a disco to watch drag shows, take a few hits of cocaine, and maybe dance. Everything's so controlled now. But in my day, *nena*, in my day you went to the bar to get trashed. And Luisito Cristal was the queen of getting trashed.

"But that's not what she was doing on the night of the gown with the lights. Luisito was on a mission. She spent hours searching, running her hands with their freshly painted fingernails along the walls, listening intently to cracks in the walls. It was like she was tripping on acid. But la Luisito maintained her elegance. She kept on searching, disturbing couples, slinking around in the dark in the Bazaar. Finally, around midnight, she found the damn electrical outlet. Relieved, *la loca* plugged herself in, back in a corner of that disco, and her gown of lights shined like a Fourth of July parade at Disney World. We all cheered and applauded insanely. And Luisito started to dance, she danced the whole night plugged into her corner, taking the room's décor to a whole new level. A gift from the gods. A scandal, that Luisito Cristal. I think she works in a florist shop in El Condado now, and in her free time she runs an agency for erotic dancers. She is just as fabulous as before, but the years pass mercilessly.

"Now, Luisito wasn't what you would call a performer. She was more like a nocturnal diva. Her thing was to dress up like those jet-set models, Bianca Jagger, Margaux Hemingway. They were her idols— she loved to emulate them, because that made her divine, splendiferous, opulent, too, in her fantasy—a Caribbean *loca* trying to be something else. We all wanted to be something else, to be somewhere else, Studio 54, Xenon, walking down Fifth Avenue in Manhattan without anyone noticing the dark blotches from the mosquito bites on our legs. The thing was always about denying our miserable reality, to disguise it with . . . glitter. Or, better still, to invent a new past, dress ourselves up to the hilt, head out, and be someone new, among the spotlights and the dry ice, mirrors and strings of lights, to start out fresh, newly born.

"That was what Luisito did best. But she wasn't a performer. There were others who were, though. Pantojas, Barbara Herr, Renny Williams, Milton Rey—I haven't heard anything about Milton lately, since I saw her imitating I don't know who, I can't remember now, in a piano bar in El Condado, the one they call the Penthouse. What Milton liked to do was go to the bars for the tourists who came to this island in search of the mythical Latin lover who would jump their bones in a night of glorious passion under a palm tree. That's what Milton liked, the gringo bars. She only went out with blue-eyed blonds who had a lot of Ben Franklins in their wallets. And she plucked them like hens. They ended up not knowing what hurricane had blown over them, with their pockets plundered, their flesh burning, and their brains intoxicated to such a degree that it was a miracle they remembered their names. Milton was heavy duty. You had to be careful with that *loca*. Getting mixed up with her was like jumping right into the fire. The thing is that Milton Rey's art, besides lip-synching the divas of the seventies, was seduction through words and conversation. She was a true artist at coaxing and wheedling.

"Renny was a *transformista*. He did a Diana Ross to die for. Copied her costumes, her poses, her wigs, perfectly. And the physical similarity was shocking, because Renny was a dark, skinny kid, almost tubercular, with huge eyes and streamlined features, exactly like Diana. His study of the diva was exhaustive. He knew her songs by heart, the pauses, breaths, repetitions, the high notes and the low ones. Renny imitated everything about her perfectly, so well that anyone not from our crowd could easily have confused him with Diana, making a secret appearance in some bar in Old San Juan. But he spent too much time at Arcos Blancos, the baths, where half the community was infected with AIDS. He used to go there for just one thing. And since they had rooms one could rent, it was easy to go to the bar for a few hours, flirt a little, hook some unsuspecting tourist or local, and run downstairs for the first lay of the night. Then the second, the third, well, we all thought we were invincible and untouchable at those moments of happiness, even if it was all a lie.

"Renny got a case of AIDS that made her lose a lot of weight in a matter of months. One day I saw her on the street, accompanied by a *señora*, maybe it was her mother. She already had wasting syndrome, the poor thing always had been slender. She looked like one of those children from Biafra that you saw on television. I looked away and crossed to the other side of the street to avoid running into her. The wonderful, the fabulous Renny Williams, converted into that scrap of fuzz and bones. I couldn't even say hello to her.

"There was another famous performer, I can't remember her name now, a *cubana* who did her show at Bachelors. I shared the stage with her on several occasions. Her performance was unusual, because she told lots of different types of jokes. She always dressed like a little girl and wore a wig with two braids when she went onstage. A blond wig, with long braids like a Dutch milkmaid. And, in contrast, her skin was the dark color of mahogany, with a pair of *bembas* that trembled every time she lip-synched Carmen Delia Dipiní. She didn't have to do anything more than come out on the stage and the audience would die laughing. I asked her once why she dressed like a child and not like a woman, since that's where the glamour is. *'Ay, vieja, qué se yo!'* she answered, and told me stories about Cuba, of the plays that used to be performed in the town where she lived, always featuring the characters of a *mulata*, a Spaniard, and a black man.

"Growing up, she went to a lot of those shows. Her whole family would go to the theater, they all loved theater and music. One of her aunts played in a women's orchestra for many years. She told me they always entertained themselves by organizing impromptu musical performances, or by dressing up like characters on television or from the theater. I didn't know whether to believe her or not—who knows how people in Cuba entertain themselves at night? You know those republics. They probably don't have many movie theaters or bars or anything. . . . If you could have seen how that *cubana*'s eyes glistened every time she described the theater's footlights and its heavy burgundy velvet drapes, drenched in color, like the blood of a bull. The *cubana* always identified with the black man in the plays, but since she turned out 'backwards,' her costume was always that of a little girl.

"The Cuban told me about the braids one night as we were leaving after a show. Said she had always wanted to have long blond hair, to be able to make two braids that would fall halfway down her back. One day when she was about nine or ten, she found a wig in an old trunk belonging to one of her aunts. The aunt's name was Mercedita and she loved to dress up like a mermaid in their little plays. . . . So the *cubana* brushed out the wig as well as she could and put it on. Then she marched right into the living room and did a little routine based on what she remembered from the theater. Well, her father was angry as the devil, but her mother and aunts defended her: 'Don't you see, Dámaso, he's just playing theater. Leave the boy alone, he doesn't mean any harm.' The father kept grumbling from the balcony. 'You keep on laughing at how cute the boy is, but don't come crying to me when you have to face the consequences.' He must have had some idea of what was to come. . . . You know how parents are. They always know, even if they do everything they can not to face it.

"*Dios mío*, what was her name? Matilde, Maruca . . . It's as if I were looking at her, with the little light blue dress, the ruffled cotton underpants, and the two blond braids down her back. She acted as if she had been frozen in time, as if leaving Cuba had returned her to her childhood. Her repertoire consisted of the songs of Toña la Negra, instead of the copied poses of American singers. To me it all seemed very strange. She was the only one in the group who didn't want to look like Marilyn Monroe. Her crowd was of older *locas*, or émigrés who had come to the city to escape from different *pueblos* on the island. I learned a lot from that *cubana*, because my thing was humor too, making people laugh, interacting with the audience. On her advice, little by little I started singing less and acting more, making jokes to entertain the crowd. . . . How can it be that I can't remember her name? I never asked her when or why she left Cuba; I only know that she wasn't like the other *cubanos* who'd lived here for years, closed off in luxury developments and controlling the economy. She obviously wasn't from that group. First, because she was dark-skinned; second, because she was *pata*; and third, and even worse, because she dressed and did the bars like any other Puerto Rican drag queen struggling to survive.

"One night as we were waiting for them to organize the sequence of acts for the night, we heard from the bouncer that she had been shot in an overgrown lot in Bayamón. We didn't dare to go to the morgue; we weren't about to be arrested and interrogated. At that time for us to deal with the police was no little joke. I don't know if she had family in Puerto Rico, or what ever happened to the body. That night we dedicated the show to her.

"Why can't I remember that *cubana*'s name?

"Well, that's how things are sometimes. As hard as one tries, the mind always chooses what it remembers and what it forgets. . . ."

6

A *ver*. Let me see. Where did I leave the keys to this house? Skirt pocket, apron pocket, purse? Here they are, *abuela*, said Sirena. Don't you remember, you gave them to me so you wouldn't lose them? *Ay, sí, mijito*, my head's all mixed up. Getting old is the worst thing in the world. How about some light in here? Let's open the windows. This place is as dark as a bear's den. These people live all closed up here like hermit crabs. It's because of the central air, *abuela*. What do you mean, "central air"? The air circulates everywhere. No, *abuela*, I mean air-conditioning in the whole house. They must pay a lot for electricity. More than what I charge them to clean this mess. It looks like they had a party. Look at all the cigarette butts and empty bottles. And this powder? *Abuela*, I think it's cocaine. That can't be, *muchachito*! These are decent people, lawyers both of them. Their being lawyers has nothing to do with taking a hit now and then. What kind of talk is that, "taking a hit"? How do you know so much about those things? I don't really, *abuela*. Cuqui, Doña Tanín's boy, told me once that's what they call it, since he's in the business. . . . I better not catch you around that Cuqui again, or I'll skin you alive. You hear me? Now go and get me the broom so we can start to clean up the mess. Virgen Santa, look how they've left the living room. They even stained the rug. How are we going to clean that, *abuela*? I think the *señora* bought one of those machines that looks like a vacuum cleaner, but that you can put water in through a tube and it gets rid of stains and odors. Go look for it, *nene*; it's in the closet beneath the stairs.

How many bedrooms does this house have, *abuela*? I think it has six. No, there are four bedrooms and two bathrooms. But there is another room out by the pool. You see that little door next to the bar? That's the entrance. *It's midnight and you're not here by my side . . . holding me now in your arms . . .* Can you imagine, so many rooms? I would be happy living just in the one outside. I'd get up in the morning and dive into the pool just to wake up. *Ay, abuela,* I would be so happy there. Who wouldn't, *papito,* who wouldn't? Wait until you see the bathrooms, they're bigger than our kitchen. *Ay, abuela,* don't exaggerate. You know we live in a matchbox. I'm not exaggerating. There were so many children in my family that we couldn't all fit inside the house, even with all the girls sleeping together in one room. Geño, the oldest boy, and two of the younger ones slept outside in hammocks, we were so poor. When she got older, Crucita was sent to the Déliz house as a servant. We only saw her on weekends. Angelita, the oldest girl, had taken off with a laborer who was passing through town and gave birth to two children right away. Papá didn't want us to go visit her, because he thought she was a bad example. I always arranged it so I could escape to the little house where she lived alone with the children, because that boyfriend of hers had left town to go back to where he came from and abandoned her with the babies. Sometimes I went with messages from Mamá, who sent a little something whenever she could to help out, but Papá never knew about it. *Feeling my hand in yours . . . and my kisses searching for yours . . .* Mamá washed and ironed for other people, that's how we survived. I helped her for as long as I can remember—that's how I learned how to work. Papá and my brothers worked in the fields, from sunup to sundown. When the owners of the *finca* sold it, we all moved to Campo Alegre. That's how it was. No, *nene,* don't turn on the air-conditioning. It's better to open the windows and let in some fresh air. I don't understand how these people can live so closed up in here.

What's that about Campo Alegre, *abuela*? I mean the neighborhood around the Plaza del Mercado. But isn't that called Parada 19? That's what it's called now, but when we moved there it was called Campo Alegre. It was where all the poor folk from the countryside went.

Most of us came to the city to sell our produce in the Plaza anyways, so when we left our town, we just ended up staying there. It was a familiar place. And the most wonderful man, Don Chago, had a stall at the market. He helped all the farmers and the new arrivals. Don Chago bought from us at fair prices, told us how much things were worth so we wouldn't be cheated, and even helped Papá find a job and a house. Look at all the dirty clothes in this hamper. You take that basket and I'll take the colored one. We'll put the laundry in yours and the dry cleaning in mine. *When two hearts separate, when they say good-bye, and then forget* . . . I loved living in Campo Alegre. The school was nearby. And all the luxury stores, spread along the avenue. It was an easy walk in the shade. Casa Cuesta, Padín, La Giralda . . . I'd go to those stores to buy fabric and make myself some beautiful dresses. What were they like, *abuela*? The dresses? They were very tailored at the top, with rounded collars, and they had big skirts with crinolines or starched cotton slips so they flared out wide below the waist. I looked like a queen in them. I was always thin, with a wasp waist. Don't laugh. I was a beautiful girl, and even prettier when I wore those dresses on Sundays. With Papá's permission, we'd go for a ride on the trolley. Crucita, Angelita and her children, Fina, and me. Sometimes we went all the way to Viejo San Juan. Back then it was a shantytown, not like it is now, looking like a wedding cake with all those restored colonial buildings. We'd get off the trolley in the Plaza de Armas and would sit there to look at all the people. *Mijo,* that was the good life. Not like in Caimito, where there was nothing to do once the sun went down. Should we send this with the laundry, *abuela*? No, I think we can wash that dress by hand. But what if we damage the embroidery? What embroidery? Look closely, *abuela*. You see how there's another thread sewn on top of the fabric? My goodness, *muchacho,* you have such sharp eyes. How do you know so much about clothing? I don't know, *abuela*. There was a program about fashion on television the other day and I watched it. Who knows, *nene,* maybe you'll be a tailor or a designer. What program was it? *Mañana en tu Mañana.* Oh, I love that show, they prepare such wonderful dishes. Why don't we make one of those dishes at home one of these days, *abuela?* If these people pay me today, tomorrow we'll go straight to the *supermercado* to buy the ingredients for the recipe they give on the show. We'll eat like rich people. Just wait.

> *. . . and far away you've forgotten me*
> *so very far away*
> *my thoughts fly to you*
> *and so sorrowful*
> *are the sighs*
> *of my heart . . .*

You have a beautiful voice, *papichulo.* You sing just like a *sirena.* If you were a girl, that's what I'd call you, Sirena. *Ah, mi sirenito?* May God bless you, child. You remind me of your mother. If she hadn't gone astray, she would be a first-rate singer today. *Ay, abuela,* don't exaggerate. I'm not exaggerating, *nene.* Your mother sang like an angel. Once when she was a little girl I took her to Channel Two, for a program that came on at noon. They had a talent contest and your mother won first prize in the children's category. Those people at the show told me to get her a teacher for voice, one for diction, and I don't remember what other mess. But, *mijo,* how was I supposed to pay for all that? And you sing just like she did. Besides, talent like that runs in the family. Papá Marcelo had a voice like you've never heard. In Caimito all the neighbors would come to our house and ask him to perform at dances and give *serenatas.* Even in Campo Alegre he was famous for his *parrandas.* We had so much fun there at Christmas. . . .

7

Sirena reluctantly picked up the towel and the magazines from the ground. She had fallen asleep on the chaise lounge. She didn't remember what she had dreamed, maybe it had been about her grandmother, but it was a beautiful dream, because she awoke rested. This was the third time Martha had sent a waiter to get her. The waiter had said that Martha insisted that she come up to the room, that it was time to get ready for the six o'clock audition. She wanted to stay by the pool a while longer, but she knew that Martha wouldn't leave her in peace. La Sirena walked to the reception desk and dialed the number of their room. Martha answered the phone.

"*Chica*, let me stay down here a little longer. It's still early and the water is so enchanting. . . ."

"Fine, *nena*, the water will still be enchanting tomorrow. Just come up here now."

"We stayed up so late last night talking that now I'm tired. Just give me ten more minutes."

"*Nonono, mamita.* There'll be plenty of time to rest. Right now we have to get ready, because it will be six before you know it, and you know better than anyone how long it takes to prepare. So let's get to work, baby, and lift those spirits. Hurry on up, we've got to get the hotel manager in our pocket."

"If I had known that you weren't going to let me rest today, I wouldn't have listened to you babble so much last night."

"You sure do complain a lot, young lady. Stop fussing and come up here, we're almost out of time."

Sirena had spent most of the previous night listening to old stories about Martha's youth. The session started just after room service arrived with the filet mignons and Champagne. Martha and her adopted daughter sat down to eat and talked until dawn. At first, la Sirena thought she wouldn't be able to sleep in a room that was so different from her own, and with her chest so tight from anxiety about her audition the following day. That was why she let Martha go on and on with her endless string of memories. But curiously, Martha's quiet voice had a tranquilizing effect and she slept peacefully the rest of the night.

When she awoke in mid-morning, la Sirena had to hurry in order not to miss what was left of the breakfast buffet. Martha sat with her for a while, then decided to return to the room. Sirena preferred to spend the afternoon at the pool. The water looked so fresh and clean, as if it came from a spring. And there was always an attentive waiter to cater to her every whim. They brought her drinks, little ham sandwiches, fruit salad. . . .

But Martha was right. She did have to leave all that behind and get up to the room. If everything turned out the way they hoped, there'd be plenty of time for luxury and rest later, in Santo Domingo, New York, Paris, Tokyo. Just as Diandra has plenty of time for luxury, so would she. And Lypsinka, doing private shows for businessmen on Fifth Avenue. If all her forerunners have time for luxury and glamour, why shouldn't she? You just need a little talent. A little talent and a lot of businesswoman's instinct. Sirena bets that she has more than enough of both ingredients. So she'd better get going. *Hay que trabajar.*

In a matter of seconds, Sirena's young, playful face was transformed into a rock-hard billboard. Selena walked slowly, with resolve, toward the elevator and pressed the button for the eleventh floor. When she arrived she put down the magazines and towels and stepped into the bathroom. Before closing the door, she looked at her *mamá* with one of the looks that she used to bewitch her nocturnal public at the Blue Danube. Martha never knew what Selena was hiding behind those looks of innocence combined with ferocity. She never ceased to be shaken by them, as if she were always seeing them for the first time. When Selena finally closed the bathroom door, she broke the spell holding Martha's eyes, and her mentor was able at last to rub her arms and recompose herself. If the hotel manager and the rest of the public were as affected as she by a simple glance, if they felt somewhere between frightened and seduced, between dying for more and crazy to get away from that overwhelming gaze, then success would be hers and Selena's, she felt it, success, money, and respect for both of them, for her, Miss Martha Divine, who deserved it so utterly.

Sirena spent hours in the bathroom. While she filled the tub with bubbles, she gargled with warm water from the sink mixed with orange-blossom water and a little crystallized salt she had brought from the other island. She shaved her legs and calmly shaved her chest, arms, and chin—not that there was much to shave in those regions, but it was preparation for the artifice that she would soon undertake. She rubbed her skin thoroughly with a loofah sponge to remove dead cells. And then she soaked in the tub with her eyes closed, reviewing in her mind each line of each song that she would sing at six o'clock.

After drying her entire body vigorously with one of the hotel's embroidered towels, Selena discreetly splashed on some perfume, behind her wrists and her earlobes, at her décolletage and her ankles. She didn't touch her eyebrows; those had already been plucked. She rinsed her jet-black hair in the sink, then applied fixing gel and gathered it with a band into a bun at the back of her head. Finally she called Martha to begin her transformation.

The master of illusions entered the bathroom with her case of bases, powders, disguising makeup, and magic. She sat the towel-wrapped Sirenita in front of a mirror illuminated by rows of bright lights lining it. She took out the blow-dryer, plugged it in, and dried the gelled hair to fix the bun that Sirena had made. Then she scrutinized her disciple's face to see whether it was completely smooth. After she was certain there were no lingering unshaven hairs, Miss Martha Divine, master among masters, applied a reddish-brown Pan-Cake base to cover the areas darkened by the shaved beard. She applied the base thickly to cover the large pores that, responding to the call of traitorous hormones, were already preparing themselves for a man's beard. The base was a fundamental weapon in the war declared against nature. Selena didn't like to see the foundation plastered on her face and all the way down her neck to her chest. She looked like a clown, a ridiculous lie that denied her doubly.

"Close your eyes, *mamita*, I'm going to apply the powder, and if it gets in your eyes it won't be a very pretty picture, darling." La Martha always hurried through this initial step. She, too, felt uncomfortable applying the red base. Innumerable times she had made up girls who, upon seeing their faces disfigured by the harsh color, broke down in tears over old problems or changed their minds about going through with the transformation. They got so caught up with confessions, with the pain of uncertainty, and with pleas for advice, that when they went out into the street or onto the stage completely finished, their faces showed bitterness. Instead of seductive smiles and vampiress eyebrows, their faces displayed the sour grimace of someone suffering the untimely surprise of her own transformation. Applying the base was always like rowing in a tumultuous ocean. Only the seasoned *loquitas* or experienced divas could regard their half-made-up faces without danger of falling apart in front of the mirror.

"*A ver, nena,* close your lips so you don't crack the Pan-Cake," ordered Martha, after applying the first coat of translucent powder. With a sponge already coated with another, flesh-colored base, she started applying makeup along the hairline from Selena's forehead all the way down to her chest. She rescued Selena's nose from the ridiculous red hue, prepared her eyelids for gradual layers of shadow, and readied her cheekbones to receive the blush. Playfully, Martha dabbed around the shaved area above Selena's upper lip, tickling her and pretending to be annoyed. Later she would cover everything, including the lips, with a flesh-toned base, in effect completely erasing the adolescent's distinctive facial features. Then she would begin to redraw Selena's lips with black liner, then with red, fill them in with the matte tones of raspberry-wine lipstick, cover them with a fine layer of more powder, and finally paint them with another layer of glossy lipstick so they would sparkle in the stage lights. Today she was going to apply silver sparkles to achieve a feeling of fantasy, the perfect setting for Selena's love songs.

Now she had to apply the corrector. Light on the tip of the nose, under the eyes, and on the cheekbones. Darker along the sides of the nose and along the jawline to soften the angles. Another layer of powder, and a lot of rouge in the hollow of the cheeks and at the temples. More powder to avoid beads of sweat and to fix the work. Now only the eyes were naked. Martha had already chosen the gown, shoes, stockings, slip, and wig. After arduous deliberation while Sirena was bathing, the tutor had determined that the happy winner would be the long evening dress, in a pearl-colored imitation raw silk, embroidered with pink jewels and white sequins that formed raised arabesques around the bosom. The neckline of the dress was round, discreet, close to the neck; the arms were left uncovered. At thigh level there was a deep slit that revealed the right leg, which would be sheathed in translucent hose just a bit darker than Selena's skin. The pearl-pink high heels matched the embroidery of the dress. They were closed at the toe, with a delicate strap that wound chastely around the ankle and supported the heel. On her left wrist, la Sirena would wear a bracelet of three strands of cultured pearls with a gold clasp, the final gift from Martha's ex-husband before he left on a business trip never to return. The zirconia ring gracing one of Selena's manicured and perfumed fingers completed the ensemble. The fake rosé-hued nails determined that the eye shadow to use was definitely the Lancôme that Martha had used to make up the girl who got married a few years earlier in the Botanical Gardens. The girl was marrying a gringo—a sweet, handsome, rich, blond American with blue eyes. A tremendous catch for the child, who was as black as a telephone, but fine-featured and very pretty, though she was heavy in the hips. She had a gaggle of friends who were *locas* and who recommended Martha to do her hair and makeup. From time to time

Martha had seen her at the Blue Danube, supporting her friends on-stage. So she did the girl a favor. Later Martha found out that the gringo and the girl divorced. "Not even death could separate me from a husband like that," thought Martha as she dug around in her cosmetics case in search of the remembered shadow and for some adhesive for false eyelashes.

Shadow applied, brows and lashes blackened with pencil and liner. There was still the ritual of the gauze and tape for the privates, which wasn't anything easy. It's not that Sirena wanted to boast, but she had enough down there to share and then some. Every time they got to this point, Miss Martha laughed and said, "*Ah mija*, I can't wait for you to start taking hormones to see if that thing shrinks a little. I'm going to have to start charging you more, to cover the cost of the extra tape." Even as they shared the joke, they both knew that Martha was trying to cover her gluttony and surprise at the size of her daughter's genitals. Stunned, she couldn't imagine how from that thin, fragile body such a thing could hang. Sirena's penis was immense, a little grotesque because it was so disproportionate to the rest of her body. If Martha hadn't been looking at it through the eyes of a mother and a businesswoman, she would not have hesitated to find a place to put that hunk of meat, just to satisfy her curiosity about feeling it inside, in all its magnitude. For this reason, Martha Divine always hurried through the binding ritual. She didn't want to tempt herself with a hunger that she might not be able to control.

Once around, twice, done with the gauze, filling out the breasts with synthetic foam inside the brassiere, and, finally, the long, glittering dress. The disciple almost converted into *una damisela elegante*, demure, enveloped in a theatrical melancholy. Only the wig was missing.

When Sirena passed through the door of her room, at exactly fifteen to six, she was the living image of a goddess. Each step, carefully considered, evinced the aura of a consummate *bolerista*. She was seductive, serene, with her head crowned with perfect black curls and her face framed by two curls that fell to the middle of her cheeks.

From each ear hung a spray of oval pearls surrounded by diamonds. Her slender form was sheathed in sparkling mother-of-pearl, from which a tanned, perfectly sculpted leg emerged with each step, as if from the sea at sunset.

La Martha wasn't far behind. She had retouched her own makeup, rearranged her blond hair, and changed into a cocktail dress of red rayon and a matching vest with a black border. Proud of her work, she walked beside her *ahijada*, her adopted daughter. Already savoring the conquest of the manager, she couldn't stop smiling, imagining the moment when Contreras saw Sirena appear in the hotel lounge. He would fall smitten at her feet, assuring them a one-way ticket to true fame. And that would be even before he heard Sirena Selena sing.

They descended in the elevator, entered the cocktail lounge, and waited fifteen minutes in complete silence. Martha didn't speak for fear of shaking her protégée's concentration. Sirena was completely immersed in herself. At five after six they saw a circumspect gentleman approach with another man, dressed impeccably in a white linen suit and wearing a thin wedding band of brilliant gold. You could smell his position and class from a distance. The two large men escorting them stayed at the door to the lounge to keep watch. La Sirena immediately looked down. Martha stepped forward. Surely one of the two was Señor Contreras.

"I brought a friend who has impeccable taste. I would like him to be present for the audition, if you don't mind."

"Not at all," responded Martha, smiling seductively.

"Then please begin whenever you like."

"We'll begin now, but first I'd like to introduce my artist to you. Sirena, come, I would like to introduce you to Mr. Contreras and . . ."

The other gentleman stepped forward at the introduction. He wanted to see this creature from close up, this fallen angel, this fragile, boyish girl, delicately made, who glowed with her own light in the darkness of the bar. Moving as close as he could to the singer, the guest introduced himself:

"Hugo Graubel, at your service."

Sirena noticed the guest's curiosity. Without realizing it, Hugo Graubel had given her a pretext to assume her character. In response, Sirena slowed her gestures. She lifted her eyes slowly until they were fixed on those of the gentleman who had come to hear her. During those moments Hugo Graubel couldn't prevent himself from blinking nervously. His chest refused to release the final breath of air occupying it. His heart forgot to beat for an instant, just an instant. Each of the hairs on his skin stood up. Sirena was aware of his guarded awe, and smiled capriciously. Then she searched for the perfect intonation, swallowed, and responded slowly.

"Sirena Selena; *encantada.*" And that was all the *bolerista* said, or rather murmured, before she turned slowly and walked toward the stage.

Sirena sang three boleros without pausing, and the bustling of the hotel disappeared for her. Contreras and Hugo Graubel remained quiet, not even daring to applaud at the end of each song. Only when everything was over, and only then, did they destroy the silence with their applause. Martha awoke from the melancholy stupor into which she always fell when she heard Sirena sing. She knew that her protégée had not given all of herself. Sirena must be nervous, Martha suspected, but she soon realized that the magic had been enough to cast a spell over the select public evaluating her. Hugo Graubel watched the stage eagerly, and Contreras was overflowing with compliments and praise.

"If I didn't know that it was an illusion, I would never know Sirena's *secreto.* She looks so fabulous."

"She is fabulous," corrected Martha, "and I guarantee you that's exactly what the audiences flocking to your hotel's lounge are going to think."

"What do you think, Señor Graubel?"

Graubel took a sip from his glass of whisky; then, after a short pause, he answered, "I've never seen anything like it," gazing at la

Selena, who skillfully avoided that and the succeeding glances, so as to remain inaccessible and desirable.

"I, myself, would sign a contract right now, but I have to arrange things with the central administration and finalize the terms of the offer. If that is all right with you, Doña Martha?"

"Finalize and arrange all you want. I'll be right here and won't move an inch until you make me a final offer. I assure you that if you allow this opportunity to pass, you'll regret it for the rest of your life."

"Of that I haven't the slightest doubt."

"You shouldn't, Señor Contreras, you shouldn't."

8

*L*eocadio, don't stray too far from the shore, *mijo*, the sea is rough
and you don't know how to swim."

His mother had taken them to spend the day at the beach. The
beach at Bocachica. Leocadio can count with the fingers on one hand
the number of times his mother has found the time to take him to
the beach.

He had spent the previous night alone. His mother told him that
she had to go on an unexpected trip to Monte Cristi, to visit his
grandmother. Leocadio asked her whether it was an emergency,
whether his grandmother was dying. "Child, she's too mean to die,"
his mother answered, as she made her preparations for the trip. "I
can't tell you what it's about now, it's a surprise." But before she
hurried out to the bus station, his mother promised they would have
a big celebration when she got back.

The following afternoon his mother returned, with a young girl
holding her hand. Leocadio walked slowly down the hill in front of
his house. Then he ran with all his strength when he realized who
was holding his mother's hand. It was Yesenia, his older sister, whom
he hadn't seen in over a year. Leocadio and Yesenia didn't sleep that
night; they just talked. They shared a bed. It felt so good to have
someone to laugh with, be scolded with by their mother in the middle
of the night, someone to joke with and howl about her constant
vigilance. It felt so good not to be all alone.

And now they were at Bocachica, Mamá, Leocadio, and Yesenia,
who was going to come live with them in the capital. That was the
surprise his mother had kept from him. His sister had grown so much.
She was already a little taller than he was, and two little mounds had

begun to emerge beneath her shirt. Yesenia looked a lot like him, with the same yellow skin and curly, honey-colored hair. But there was something sharp about her features, maybe it was the angle of her chin, or her eyebrows—something that caused Leocadio to look at her for long periods of time, as if he were the one who should have those features and she, his; as if their faces were on the wrong bodies.

His mother had prepared a celebratory feast that morning. White rice and a fricassee of goat that their grandmother had sent as a gift from the country. At the market she had bought *kipes* filled with meat, bottles of soda, and candy. Leocadio watched his mother prepare the dishes of food, covering them with banana leaves so that they would stay warm; then he watched her walk toward Yesenia and him, and she smothered them both with kisses. "Let's go, children, the beach is getting crowded," she said to them, as she took a few T-shirts and pairs of shorts from a chest. "We'll end up without any shade and I'm already too dark as it is," his mother joked, then laughed, displaying her perfect white teeth, teeth that announced a special happiness. Leocadio heard his mother laugh freely as never before, and he too became infected with laughter. Yesenia started to laugh too, without really knowing why. So, with their bellies bouncing joyfully, they left the house to look for a bus that would take them to the public beach at Bocachica.

They walked along the beach until they found a shady place to spread out. From a large bag, their mother pulled out a sheet that she had folded carefully so it wouldn't take up too much room. She hung the sheet between two branches of an Icacos tree, creating a colorful canopy. On the ground, which was uneven because of tree roots and sand, they placed a large beach towel that his mother had "borrowed" from the *patrona*'s house. Then, Yesenia and Leocadio ran to bathe in the refreshing ocean.

There were many things to celebrate. "The *patrona*'s daughter needs a girl and Yesenia is old enough to start helping out. They would pay her the same as a woman, because I assured Doña Imelda that, since Yesenia has grown up in the country, she's very skilled at housework. Her daughter only lives two blocks away, Leocadio, two blocks! So Yesenia can move to the capital! It's such a relief, child, because it was giving me terrible nightmares. With you having to stay home alone so much and your sisters having to live out in the country with Mamá, who's about to drop dead of old age. I just couldn't go on with so much anxiety all the time." As she talked, his mother ran all over the place searching for wood to start a fire. Seldom before had Leocadio heard her speak with such excitement. "Imagine, Leocadio, two paychecks. And who knows, maybe soon I'll be able to convince the *patrona* to give you a job, too. Then we'll bring Mileidi to the city and we'll all live together. The Holy Virgin is arranging everything perfectly. You'll see, Leocadio, it won't be long, you'll see."

Leocadio and his sister collected kindling to add to the fire his mother had built. "My children are not going to eat cold food today, damn it, so you better get going," his mother ordered the fire, as Yesenia and he looked at each other, covering their mouths so they wouldn't burst out laughing. Yesenia found a piece of cardboard and offered it to her mother for fanning the pieces of wood that had already begun to give off smoke. Leocadio went to get the food to put it on the fire, then took a walk along the beach.

The water was almost cold. Leocadio walked along the water's edge with the waves coming halfway up his leg. With the bottom of his feet, he tried to find a shell for his sister, uncover half-buried glass bottles, or feel the brush of a little fish passing by. Suddenly he felt a heavy gaze on his shoulder. It came from a large red man who was looking at him from a distance, farther out in the waves. Leocadio looked around. He was sure that man was looking at him, and smiling at him. Leocadio's face darkened. Even at the beach those men wouldn't leave him alone. He didn't know how they found him, how they tracked him down everywhere, how they saw something in him that made them drool over him and filled their eyes with trouble.

He had to go back to his mother. She was his savior, his touchstone. If they saw him with her, they wouldn't bother him and he could go back to play in the sea in peace. Leocadio held the man's gaze and returned it with all the hate he could muster. Then he turned away disdainfully. That's when he saw him.

There on the sand: a boy several years older than Leocadio, with a long, lean body sucking up the sun's rays. The boy stretched slowly and walked to the edge of the sea, glaring catlike as he tried to step around the trash washed up by the waves. The boy gingerly lifted his delicate legs to avoid the plastic cups and candy wrappers. Wearing a tiny bathing suit and a T-shirt, with a band holding back his jet-black hair, the being approached the sea seeking relief from the heat and rowdiness of a day at Bocachica beach.

Leocadio walked toward the apparition and looked at him with unmasked curiosity. It was a boy, a boy who looked like a girl. Just like him, just like his sister, but with light cinnamon-colored skin, extremely dark hair, and carefully plucked eyebrows. The boy returned the stare with open hostility. But then he smiled at Leocadio. And Leocadio smiled back. The younger boy even dared to wave timidly as he crossed the sand toward the flowered canopy. His mother was still fanning the fire with the piece of cardboard, reheating the feast she had prepared to commemorate their special afternoon.

os mil, doscientos pesos. Two thousand, two hundred pesos, first offer," one of the men said. They must be out of their minds, thinks la Sirena as she calculates the exchange to dollars. "How about three thousand?" Maybe. "Four thousand, two hundred." Well, that makes everything better. Selena bites her succulent lip and maliciously accepts the invitation extended by a group of hustlers on Bocachica beach. A private show nearby for a rich man from Juan Dolio—the rich man who had seen her at the Hotel Conquistador, at her audition. Three hundred and seventy-five dollars for just one show. Fortune was starting to knock at her door.

That morning, she had gone to Bocachica beach alone because— shitty country—the hotels in the capital were situated along a sea without a beach, along a *malecón* full of cars, beggars, and con men, trying to get as much as they could from the tourists. She wanted to rest a little at the beach. Martha stayed at the pool waiting for calls from the hotel manager. No offer yet. Sirena dressed irritably, caught a bus that took her to Bocachica, and the offer was made. Forty-two hundred pesos *dominicanos* for just one show . . . She would tell Martha. She would leave a note at the reception desk. Three hundred seventy-five dollars; her opportunity to go to New York to try her luck. "It's a deal. Take me to the hotel so I can get my things."

"Where are you from?"

"Puerto Rico."

"How old are you?"

"Eighteen," lied the fifteen-year-old, as she placed her perfumed derriere on the seat behind the driver.

Hugo Graubel III, in another car, was waiting for answers about Sirena, remembering seeing her enshrouded in a rapturous haze on the stage of the hotel lounge. Now, he didn't quite know how, he recognized her from watching her rest her androgynous body on the dirty sand of Bocachica. The *tigeritos* from the capital took the bus to the beach every Sunday. The families with their pots of *moro de gandules* celebrating birthdays, throwing beer bottles and paper and bags of garbage in the water. La Sirena sniffed in disgust, her "Why didn't I just stay at the pool," her disdain at "these people who are such pigs." Amid puddles of urine and shit floating on the waves, Selena walked along the edge of the ocean. Her hairless body, seminude, in a tiny bikini, made her look like a tomboy trying to be *un hombrecito* on the beach, but showing her femme side with her little jumps and squeals among the trash.

Hugo Graubel III recognized her as Sirena Selena. He saw her, the temptress on the sand, and thought of her dressed as a bolero singer, standing in the lounge of the Hotel Conquistador, singing as if her soul were going to escape through her mouth. He remembered her as fragile, as omnipotent, as dark-haired, as illuminated onstage by the spotlights, and as alone, absolutely alone. He desired her that way, so tiny, such a little street boy. He recognized her as the woman of his dreams. He gave immediate instructions to the chauffeur to park near the ocean so he could watch her, even in front of his wife, who watched him disdainfully from the car, glaring at him, complaining with a look about the dirty, disgusting beach where they always have to stop (she doesn't know why) on the way to their beach house for the weekend.

He never knew for certain how he recognized her, a feeling in the blood, a quickening beat of the heart. Hugo Graubel III had to stop to look at la Selena, had to bear his wife's complaints, had to send his employees on an errand while he continued on to his residence at Juan Dolio. As he watched the countryside through the window, he was pummeled with thoughts and a few crazy words that he couldn't help repeating silently . . . :

43

"I will love you, Selena, as I have always wanted to love a woman, as I have always wanted to love a woman, as I have always wanted to love a woman."

It had been a long time since anything like this had happened to him, Hugo Graubel III, who walked around dead inside, bored with his life as a businessman, married to a wife who no longer even remotely interested him, and trapped on this stagnating island. The business games he played with the continuous parade of government officials didn't inspire him, nor did his shopping trips to Miami and New York, nor his extravagant lifestyle, nor the rise or fall of his stocks on the international exchange. And now, precisely now, he found la Sirena on the shores of his weary boredom. How could he not try to lure her into his hands? How could he not search for the necessary strategies to draw his prey close enough to allow him to satisfy his hunger? Ignoring his wife's furious glare, as she barked something about what people would say if they saw his Mercedes loitering about the public beach at Bocachica, he picked up his cellular telephone. He had to make an important business call. "Hotel Conquistador? May I speak with Señor Contreras, please? Hugo Graubel speaking. I'll hold. . . ." And while he waited on the line, he lined up in his mind the words he would use to ask his friend a huge favor, that he delay as long as he could the offer to hire la Selena, to give Hugo time to make his move. He had to arrange it so that la Selena would stay in his house, outside, in the apartment by the pool. He had to hire her to give a show, on the pretext of entertaining a gathering of foreign investors, whom, conveniently, he was about to host at his home. Meanwhile, he would draw nearer, little by little, seducing her with doting attention, granting everything she asked for with that bewitching mouth. Contreras, on his part, would have to distract the other one, let her stay at the hotel, all expenses paid, or go out shopping, doing the tourist routine while she waited for the offer, which had been delayed due to unforeseeable matters. "Invent whatever you like, Contreras—that the cost of the show wasn't clear, the owner of the hotel is away on vacation, that they are trying to

44

arrange for available dates, whatever. . . ." This would give him a chance to gradually get closer to his Sirena's mysterious skin.

"What new trick are you up to?" muttered Solange, his wife, sitting as far as possible from him, next to the window in the backseat behind the driver.

"*Nada.* A surprise I am preparing for the investors who are coming to visit us."

"But didn't we agree that I was going to be in charge of entertaining them? I have already hired the pianist from the Hotel Talanquera, and made arrangements with the chef to design a special buffet."

"You don't have to cancel anything. My plans won't interfere with yours."

"And may I ask what your plans are?"

"I'm hiring a singer to perform two or three songs before dinner."

"That sounds nice. But still, you should have told me before now."

"I just thought of it."

"When? Just now, while we're sitting here staring at the trash in the parking lot at Bocachica?"

"Well, actually, yes. The sea always inspires me."

And that was the end of the conversation. He knew Solange was going to make a stink when she saw la Sirena, and he wouldn't have any argument to pacify his wife except that it was a whim. But he would cross that bridge when he came to it. For the moment, what should be occupying his mind was how to cross the abyss that separated him from Sirena Selena, that being of fantasy, who had awakened in him an agonizing yearning. He didn't know for certain what it was he wanted from Selena, or for her or with her. But there was no doubt that he wanted to have her near, at his side, no matter the cost.

45

10

Sirena's appearance beneath a fantasy moon in a mansion. Selena's foreign debut, across the Caribbean. The appearance of that melodious singer, her body transformed into the very essence of temptation, Sirena Selena, singing her ballads before those rich people, ecstatic in her presence. They would become her followers as soon as she opened her mouth, her eager fans wanting her only for themselves. But no, she wouldn't be able to favor them. A rendezvous with destiny awaits her in New York. . . .

She will have them in the palm of her hand, she always does, ever since she began to sing at the Blue Danube. "You are not of this world," Martha had said to her after her debut in the bar. Then he knew he was beautiful, as Sirena, *bellísima*, men dying at the door of her dressing room, giving her whatever she wanted for a night, just one, during which they could remove, one by one, the false eyelashes, the red of the cheeks, the color of the lips, lick the sequined dress and the décolletage, and, trembling, kiss the adolescent breasts, the exquisite waist, and then that which Selena hid beneath gauze and tape like an undersea pearl. Many have sworn they would give anything to see that naked body, not knowing whether it belonged to a man, a woman, an angel escaped from heaven, or an adolescent devil.

But now that he remembers, sitting in this car conveying him to his destiny, he was used to provoking stories before. . . . Before being la Sirena. He remembers how stories about him circulated at the Danube. It was rumored that even when he was a kept boy no one had been able to hang on to him, that at the precise moment when one penetrated him, melodies escaped from his chest and he began to croon with his ecstatic and glorious voice full of the Spirit of Light.

They said that even the most macho men wilted in his presence, and that later he would gently turn them, wet them with ceremonial saliva, and enter their hot, waiting bodies. The stories about her, the one who was now la Sirena, filled the house at the Danube every time she performed there.

And now another door is opening. "Opportunity doesn't knock twice," Martha had told her. Sirena was going to try her hand at a private show for these rich people. This is a prelude to New York. She would leave them as she always left her audience, astonished, vulnerable, dying of desire, at her feet. "You are not of this world," they would think, just as Martha felt on the night of her debut.

. . . but I'm not about to live as a mere kept woman. And I'm never, never going back to the streets.

"I beg your pardon?" said the driver.

Sirena hadn't realized that she was speaking her thoughts out loud. The driver's question brought her back to earth. Sirena smiled as if she were starring in a film, looking off into the distance, ecstatic. She kept absolutely silent, emptied her head of every memory, and concentrated on the route along which Señor Graubel's "employees" were driving her. On her side of the car, the sea roared and the *malecón* extended out into a salty mist, the hard sun bouncing off the shoulders of the people there. On the other side, giant mausoleums of marble and cement rose, the most luxurious hotels la Selena had seen in her life. Here were the Conquistador, the Quinto Centenario, with their fountains and carefully designed gardens, their multiple floors defying gravity and the dirt that sometimes remained visible, as when some beggar approached the tourists to beg for money to buy food. La Sirena felt like a movie star being returned to her hotel (a little more modest than the others, but not too) in her benefactor's chauffeured car. She looked disdainfully at the miserable pedestrians who spoiled her dream, then stared off into the distance, avoiding their illegitimate presence there, before the eyes of the recently discovered diva, eyes watching for the address of the hotel, ready to identify the luxury that will accompany her from now on.

"*Por favor*, turn to the right here. This is my hotel. Wait in the car—I'll be right back," she ordered with an elegant but firm voice, completely accepting her role as the star. She had to hurry up to the room, gather what she needed for the show, and go. Even while in the elevator, Selena selected three possible outfits for her private debut: the long-sleeved white dress encrusted with jewels, a red organdy gauze number, and the one with the pronounced neckline in gold moiré. The silver stilettos and the heels she wore for the audition (she still wasn't in a position to be able not to repeat a single piece of wardrobe) would complement the ensemble. She would borrow some cosmetics from Martha's magic box, and the bracelet with the three strands of pearls. She would buy Martha a real one soon, or send it from New York once she got there.

Luckily Martha wasn't in the room. That would simplify Sirena's plan, save her long explanations trying to convince her mentor. If she did this alone, she could prove that she truly did have the faculties to direct, promote, and administer her own affairs. And this way she wouldn't have to share the profits. She could start financing her dream. Better that Martha wasn't there. She would leave a note with the necessary information. Martha should just sit and wait at the pool or in the lounge; this wouldn't take long, three days at the most. She could use the free time to negotiate more money from Contreras, and to arrange more shows in the capital, look for a boyfriend to order around and to wait on her. She couldn't disapprove of this opportunity. "Businesswoman's blood," the diva said to herself, looking for a piece of paper and a pen to write the note for her mamá.

Bendición, Mami:

> I got a fabulous offer to do a private show at the residence of the gentleman Contreras introduced us to. If I don't act now, the opportunity will be lost. Besides, I think the guy has contacts for other shows here. Don't

know the telephone number where I'll be staying yet—will call you as soon as I do. Don't worry. We'll be in touch. You keep on working Contreras, while I work this other one from my end. We are going to be rich!!!

Kisses,
Selena

She left the note on the dresser and flew into the corridor to avoid running into her mentor. She didn't want to be caught with her bag already packed, because then Martha would throw a fit right there in the middle of the hallway, for sure. She'd have time to explain later, and she'd give Martha a figure much lower than the real one, so she could keep the difference for herself. And keep a few names too, to make her own contacts later. Back downstairs, Sirena walked toward the chauffeured car waiting for her on the boulevard.

"Everything is ready, *señores*, we can go now," la Sirena ordered, somewhat radiant at her recent success in escaping from Martha. Señor Graubel's employees put out their cigarettes, buttoned their jackets, and climbed into the car that would take the juicy prey to the boss's luxurious residence. The house was situated in an exquisite cluster of villas along the beaches of Juan Dolio. The area was part of a tourist consortium near the Hotel Talanquera, in which Graubel was a stockholder and partner. The magnate went there on vacation, from time to time with his family, or—less frequently of late—allowed himself an escape with some little bonbon of flesh that his employees brought for his enjoyment. Recently he'd preferred to go alone, to spend the nights by the sea drinking heavily until he fell asleep in a chaise lounge at the pool or in a wicker armchair on the balcony. In the morning, the servants had to shepherd him to his room, putting up with the stench of stale alcohol and his verbal and physical protests that he just wanted to be left alone, to be allowed to ruin his life since it was his fate, to sleep off his hangover in front of the sea, toasting himself beneath the sun, encrusted with salt like debris vomited by the waves.

Twenty minutes by car from San Pedro de Macorís, half an hour from the capital, Juan Dolio rose above the reefs, with its villas and luxury beachfront houses, its village of sugarcane workers and fishermen now transformed into hotel employees, its red earth and coral rock now used for the construction of souvenir shops, Italian restaurants, and golf shops for European tourists. That's where they were taking Selena, to alleviate the magnate's melancholy, to give him something to relieve his boredom and desperation—a passionate entertainment for which they would collect a fee. Maybe there would be something left of Selena for them, once Graubel had finished savoring his exotic delicacy.

The farther they drove from the city, the deeper Selena immersed herself in silence. She was nervous, anxious, but at the same time she felt as if she were accompanied by a hovering presence that calmed her soul. Maybe it was Valentina joining her on this adventure. Valentina Frenesí, her protecting spirit, the guardian angel who watched over her from above, guiding her to the doorstep of fame and fortune, to Señor Graubel's residence on the beach at Juan Dolio. So immersed in thought was la Sirena that she didn't perceive the employees' stealthy glances at her, as they tried to disguise the looks of men for hire written plainly on their faces. She wasn't even aware of their presence, their secret conversations, because they weren't Valentina, or la Martha, or el cliente. For Sirena no one had ever really existed outside of her world, even if their paths crossed. Besides, she remembered well: "When a fat pigeon comes on the scene, all the others become secondary. Nothing exists, only him and the array of strategies for the seduction of flesh and wallet." That was the first lesson she had learned on the street with la Frenesí, with Martha, with all those who shared her world and who now, alive or dead, escorted her on this adventure. That was why she didn't notice, wasn't even aware of, the masks and murmuring of the employees. It was the Absent One, the man who waited behind his disguise of host, there in the house, sharpening his desire. He was the Real Client. And if she arrived bruised and whining, these men would have to deal with Him, say good-bye to their salaries, their country too, for fear of reprisals—who knows, in these independent republics the powerful are more immune, more omnipotent than on her island. The desire of the client who is waiting for her, his impatience and his hunger, these are her protection. And Valentina, Valentina too, her guardian angel, her good-luck charm.

11

*T*hat night the street was slow," Sirena remembered Balushka telling one of her many stories about Valentina. "Fabiola, Lizzy Starr, and I were sitting there bored as flies at the bar with nothing to do. Every now and then we went out into the street to see if by the hand and grace of the Holy Spirit we'd find a trick. *Pero nada, muchacha,* it was like a holiday, Father's Day or something, and you know how the clients get on heavy guilt trips during family holidays. . . . Well, it looked like the whole Puerto Rican male population was performing an Act of Contrition that night, praying at home with their kids and wives—you know, 'The family that prays together, stays together.' And we went back in and came out again and then in again and back out of the bar. . . . On one of these trips Lizzy decides to ask me:

" 'Balushka, how much work have you had done on your face?'

"Can you believe what that *cabrona* asked me . . . ?

"I would have preferred to take that secret with me to the grave, but for some reason—I don't know why—I confessed that night. I told her my lips, cheekbones, and nose had been done in Venezuela.

" 'Everything at the same time, *loca?* That must have hurt a bunch.'

"You know that Lizzy can be very chic and very wow, but she's the dumbest *loca* ever born on this side of the Atlantic. I had taken an Altane and was relaxed and at peace with the universe. So I couldn't have insulted her if I had wanted to. I was most cordial.

" 'No, *chulita,* I did it in parts,' I explained. 'First I had my nose fixed because it was very coarse, too broad,' and I went on telling the story about how the more corrector and base I put on that nose, the more it seemed to take up my whole face. Ever since I was a child I dreamed of having fine and provocative, but delicate, features. Delicate, above all. One day I called a plastic surgeon in town, someone I knew from the *ambiente,* and made an appointment. I was so enthusiastic! Went as a civilian and everything, not a single drop of makeup, the most macho that I could on the outside, but so happy on the inside because I was going to an appointment with my plastic surgeon, just like Marisol Malaret and Ednita Nazario. I felt like an international diva. Very sure of myself and of my role in the world. Now, very macho on the outside . . . I was so excited that I even asked Papo, my neighbor, to take me to the doctor's office in his brand-new Mirage. And he took me!

"Everything went like a fairy tale. I got out of the car in front of the medical offices, entered, wrote my name in the book that the very nice receptionist gave me. I killed time reading magazines and looking at the delicate faces of the models, with their tiny noses and their softly molded faces. . . . I tell you, I got so excited and everything. When my turn came, I went in, greeted the doctor, and told him everything that I wanted to have done, beginning with the nose, which was a priority. He sat me in a chair, took a photo of me on the computer, and showed me the different types of noses that would go well with my features. I chose a small, sort of pinched one, which made me look so beautiful in the computer. Like a rich girl, I looked like the daughter of senators, going to an elegant dinner at the Caribe Hilton with my boyfriend who had just graduated from an American university. . . . But the dream ended right there. When he told me what he would charge for the operation, I couldn't believe it. It was so hard to believe that I erased the amount from my mind and left, as composed as I could manage to be. It was a good thing I had dressed as a man, which helped me, because dressed as a woman, I would have collapsed right there in tears. Such high hopes . . .

"But I took the image from the computer home with me and I couldn't get it out of my system. Me with that fine little pinched nose. I looked like someone else, someone I should be, someone I was inside since I was a little girl. I couldn't give up so easily, just because of the thief of a plastic surgeon who had given me the appointment. 'He who perseveres, succeeds,' I told myself, renewing my faith. And one night the miracle occurred. I was dancing at the Crasholetta, having a good time with the other girls from there, and as if by magic, I met this Venezuelan doctor who was hanging around here on vacation. 'Look, *chicas,* how God works his wonders,' I said to Fabiola and Lizzy when I told them this story, because you know I am a good Catholic and nobody can take away my faith, even though they don't accept me as I am in the Church. And so I'm dancing and the Venezuelan bumps into me and spills the drink I had in my hand. I was about to eat him alive when I see his worried expression. '*Ay, amor, perdóname,* you look so divine, and clumsy me, I've spilled your drink. Let me buy you another, *vale?*' I was so amused by the '*vale*' and the little accent he spoke with that I accepted. And we sat down to talk. He told me that in Venezuela the costs of plastic surgery, or 'corrective surgery,' as they call it there, are almost half of what they are here and that he has a lot of Puerto Rican clients. He gave me his card and assured me that he would give me a package deal, and I went with him and sucked him in his car out of pure gratitude.

"I worked and worked and worked for months, saved all my money. I didn't eat. I got so skinny, which helped me visualize a new me in an aesthetically improved condition. One fine day I took an airplane to Venezuela and had my nose done there. I took advantage of the situation and had my lips injected with silicone, since the first operation was so cheap, comparatively speaking. The cheekbones came later. It took me an entire year to save up, because I couldn't work during the three weeks it took for the swelling to go down. That set me back in my finances. When I got back to Puerto Rico after having my cheekbones done, I had to stay in a cousin's house for nearly a month, because I couldn't even pay the rent, I was so broke. *Pero, mijita,* it was worth it. It was worth the trouble and the sacrifice. Look at me now, finally stunning, exquisite.

"So that's what I told the girls that night. Afterward, we found out that things were slow because there were rumors of a bust. And us sitting there so pretty, at risk of the police arriving to make us go through some shameful ordeal at the Puerta de Tierra jail. But the dogcatcher never came, there was not even a single patrolman scouting the area. I said good night to Lizzy and Fabiola in a bad mood and arrived at my apartment without a dollar in my purse. The next day, when I am in a better mood, I find out. . . .

"When I wear my hair colored auburn, I look at myself in the mirror and I find that I look like her. . . . It must be the pinched nose and the high cheeks that I had done. Now I realize that they look a lot like Valentina's."

12

*J*ust look how careful he is. He's an exemplary child, always looking nice and well groomed. He's never given me a moment's worry. Not like the other urchins in the neighborhood, who are always causing problems. Not Leocadio. He just likes to stay at home or clean houses with me or spend hours fixing up the patio, sweeping leaves. Sometimes the *patrona* lets me take him to her house and he keeps himself busy looking at the plants and thinking up new ways to combine them in the gardens. Oh, how he bothers the gardener. . . .

"The thing is, he's always been very quiet, sort of timid, you see. But I can't keep leaving him alone in the room that we rent, because he is *muy delicado*. The other boys in the barrio come after him and shout filthy things when I'm not there, because he's different. Look at his hands, *señora*, see how delicate his fingers are, and he's a hard-working boy, always doing something. I have other children to support, and my husband took off from Barahona on a boat. He said he would send me money for tickets for me and the kids and I'm still waiting. I think he married *una boriqua*, a Puerto Rican woman, over there—they say they are sluttier than chickens. He's probably forgotten all about us.

"And my *patrona* tells me I can't bring the boy to her house. I asked her to give him a job. He's already thirteen, almost fourteen. He needs to learn how to earn money and the value of work. But I still haven't been able to convince the *patrona*. They bother him at school, *señora*, and they won't leave him alone to listen to the teacher or do his work or anything. He has asked me himself why he should even bother going. And I can't defend him, with everything I have to do to support us. I'm from Monte Cristi. My mother is there, taking care of the youngest girl. Leocadio is the only boy. But he doesn't want to go to the country. He grew up with me here in the capital and he really clings to me. It breaks my heart to have to leave him, but at least this way we'll be close. It's just for a few months, until I can convince the *patrona* to give him a job and I can take him home with me to live again. In the meantime, I can come visit him without any problem, can't I, *señora*? I'll give him a little money each month. Besides, this is a better environment for him. You give your pupils good food and treat them so well. And Doña Rosa tells me some of them are even enrolled at the public school and they get a good education. Maybe you could give my Leocadio what I . . . You see, *señora*, I have so many limitations. And besides, what am I going to do with such a delicate child in the barrio? One fine day the little terrorists over there are going to mess him up bad, I can feel it. You don't know how afraid I am each time I go to the *patrona*'s house, and leave Leocadio alone, that a group of them are going to get into the house and God knows what they'd do to him.

"But that's the way it's been from early on. He was born that way, I'm sure of it. Maybe because he grew up without a father . . . I don't know what this child has that makes the men crazy. They follow him, and they stand there looking at him in a way, I don't know, it's as if the devil has gotten inside them. Just because they saw him, *señora*, just because they saw him out of the corner of their eye. And I bet you that if I don't get him out of there, one day I'm going to find him in a pool of blood and really messed up. And then they are going to have to lock me up, because it's not his fault, he's an angel, just look at him. . . ."

13

*V*alentina Frenesí was her first mother. Better still, her big sister. They nicknamed her Tina in the street. Valentina loved her when she wasn't yet la Sirena. And took care of el sirenito just after his grandmother died, as he watched them carry his *abuela* off in an ambulance to the morgue and cried thinking of the burial he could never give her, how his *abuela*'s bones would always be rattling around the world, wandering, lost. Valentina loved him when Social Services threatened to take him to a state orphanage. She helped el sirenito hide from the police and social workers, taught him how to be a professional. It was she who informed him about the prices for work—"Ten for a blow job, eight for a hand job to climax, and if you can get it, twenty-five to forty for a lay. Don't let them try to bargain. You control this game. Rubbers are on the house." Valentina, a total businesswoman, but always so witty: "*Ay, nene,* if I had a face as beautiful as yours and such straight, shiny hair, I would be the sensation of the street," Valentina said as she brushed el sirenito's hair. Valentina nursed him after the accident, listened to him somberly croon the old boleros that his grandmother used to sing. Valentina Frenesí loved him as no one else did, and taught him how to survive.

He met her one slow night as he was working the street. La Tina stuck out among the other *dragas* on the block for her sense of fashion and her thin body with its soft lines. Impossible to tell that she was a man. Only by comparison with a real woman could her secret be detected. And even then it was difficult to uncover her lie, because she didn't overdo it like the others. Her face was a perfect balance of makeup and chimera. Valentina never seemed completely done up, she never exaggerated the tone of rouge, or lip pencil, she never wore wigs. Her midnight auburn tresses were all hers; the starved, yet well-muscled, frame hers; the risqué, but never clownish, sense of fashion, all hers. Every aspect, every detail was cultivated by Valentina Frenesí with infinite care. It took her years to obtain the happy transformation of her body into pure luxury; years leafing through beauty magazines, catalogs of haute couture, makeup manuals, years of studying the histories of the most fabulous divas of film and television. She wasn't stupid, either. In fact, Valentina was a certified stylist, a real expert. The most beautiful and daring of all the *dragas* on the coast.

Working kitty-corner to where the diva was strutting the runway, el sirenito wanted to know how Tina accomplished her perfect simulation. "Not yet, *nene*, as a rent boy you have more opportunities. You are beautiful. Among so much trash, to find something so pretty is a miracle." And in that instant they pledged friendship.

They started a partnership through which they would share corners. The arrangement allowed them to offer a greater variety of services to the ever-changing tastes of their clientele. El sirenito never told Valentina where he spent his dawns, after work. He kept to himself the days spent under bridges, or huddled in dismantled cars when he could no longer hide in his grandmother's house after the welfare officials had closed it while they looked for another federally subsidized family to assign to it. He didn't want to spend his money to rent a cockroach-infested room. He wanted it to go toward clothing, food, a little bag of *coca* here and there for the disco, where he could also latch on to some tourist to pay for the night or the entire weekend in a hotel suite. As he gained confidence in his partner, he asked small favors of her—would she keep some articles of clothing in her apartment; could he come eat a home-cooked meal . . . ?

"*Mijito*, don't you have anyone to cook for you?"

"The only person who ever took care of me was my *abuela*, and she died three months ago," el sirenito responded shyly, and then was silent. He didn't tell Valentina about his life, his dreams, or his interests. Maybe because he still didn't know what they were. But Tina figured what was going on.

59

"Social Services will be looking for you."

"Yeah, but you know how government agencies are. It's easy to escape them."

"*Nene*, you should have told me before. . . . Come to the house around three. I'm going to prepare a new recipe from the back cover of this month's *Vanidades*. Wait till you see the feast we're going to have. In memory of your *abuela*."

At three, the boy rang the bell at Valentina's apartment. He was eager to see what his new friend had prepared for him. When the hostess opened the door, the table was already set.

"We've done very well with our business. Today I counted what we've saved up and I said to myself, 'Valentina, diva, you owe yourself and your little friend the dinner of your dreams. You have both earned it.' "

She had prepared oven-roasted steaks in *chimichurri* sauce, roasted potatoes *alioli*, and watercress-and-papaya salad drizzled with balsamic vinegar and extra-virgin olive oil, "just like me *papito*, don't you be fooled. You know that appearances can be deceiving." For dessert his hostess had decided to serve tropical fruit sorbet. Tina had cooked way too much food, a gala feast for her *amiguito*, who, with his mouth full, stared timidly at the overwhelming meal. They drank wine and, after dinner, a mint liqueur. Then they sat down to watch the movies that Valentina had rented from the neighborhood video club.

"We're not working tonight. We're going to stay here watching movies like two *señoritas* at home."

"Which ones did you rent?"

"*Pretty in Pink* and one with Bette Midler. Have you seen how fat she's gotten?"

"Two movies? It'll be so late when we finish watching them. . . ."

"When we get sleepy, we'll just go to bed. You'll sleep here; don't think that after the meal I just prepared for you, I'm going to let you out of here to sleep under some bridge."

"But Tina . . ."

"You're going to spend the night with me. I don't want any discussion. We'll open the sofa bed and that's that. I have enough space here for both of us. As a matter of fact, *papito*, I've been thinking . . . wouldn't you like to be my roommate for a while? While things cool off a little, that's all. If it works out well, then we'll make long-term plans. But this is fifty-fifty, *negro*, you put up half of the rent and I'll cover the other half. You can't screw up on this."

The guest's only answer was to lean his head against Valentina's neck. Filled with emotion, Valentina kissed his cheek. After hugging him for a while with damp eyes, Miss Frenesí perked up, changing the tone of her voice and surprising her little brother. "And to finish off this real-life melodrama, a surprise!" she said as she pulled a joint out of the stuffed bra that she wore around the house, because even there Valentina's performance was flawless. "The honor is all yours." Valentina handed the *moto* to the boy, then rose from the sofa to turn on the television and look for the remote control for the VCR. "Besides," added the hostess, "who could go out to work the streets tonight on a full stomach?"

The following night they were back on their regular corner. Now Sirenito had to work to pay rent; he couldn't allow himself the luxury of wasting time. Besides, he couldn't count on things continuing to go as well as they had been until now. One slow night could set him back in the payment of his debts and damage his relationship with Valentina, maybe even cost him her friendship. Then he'd have to go back to wandering. Back to sleeping in boxes and on burned mattresses on the edges of the avenues—no, not him. Never, ever again. So he had to work hard because the night was long and there was a roof to pay for.

Things went on as usual; some nights were more successful than others. Every now and then they relaxed between clients by drinking orange juice in front of the café owned by the Dominicans. That was their favorite spot. They spent downtime there, talking about adventures with their clients, almost all married men, or about some couple of old *locas* looking for a thrill for the night. It was precisely there that, one cursed night, a gray Mercedes with darkened windows stopped in front of them. Sirenito remembers it well. He remembers how from the darkness of that car came the whitest hand holding a big wad of bills, showing it to the two of them. There were more than forty bills in the wad, lots more. Frenesí looked at Sirenito, maliciously, and let out a laugh. With this job the night was over, good-bye to aching feet and sloppy old men bargaining for a discount blow job. She coquettishly approached the driver's door, crouching seductively to begin negotiations with *el cliente*.

"*Nene,* he says he doesn't want both of us, only one."

"Okay, you go, then."

"No, *papito,* he wants you."

"How much is he offering?"

"A hundred and fifty." Laughs and more laughs. His share of the rent, covered by a single client.

"Tell him it's not for the whole night."

The boy fixed his hair and his shirt, finished his orange juice, and walked over to the Mercedes. Once inside, sitting in the passenger seat, he winked at Valentina—"I'll be right back"—and the car disappeared down the avenue toward San Juan.

"I'm not going to wait here all night," shouted Frenesí, and went to sit and wait for him in the bar.

But the night came and went on the street. Valentina rejected clients. She started walking from corner to corner, looking for Sirenito in the distance, biting her nails. "The little bastard took off with the hundred bills to snort up his nose all by himself. I hope he overdoses," she growled to herself, furious. She left the corner to see if she could spot him down the street. Nothing. Around four-thirty she heard dogs howling and felt a terrible shiver up her spine. "Why didn't I go, damn it, I have more experience!" And she took her brush and makeup kit out of her purse and nervously brushed her hair and fixed her face out of pure habit. Five o'clock came, and the sky grew lighter. The street began to awaken. Homeless people hurriedly picked through the garbage from businesses and residences, trying to stay ahead of the municipal street sweepers and the garbage truck in their haste to collect aluminum cans to sell at the metal plant in Trastalleres. The police on the night shift started to order breakfast at the counter in the café.

And Valentina—"Virgin of Mercy, don't let anything bad have happened to the boy"—distracted herself a little while longer listening to the bustle of patrons, the rattling of the Dominican waitresses, ordering ham, cheese, and egg sandwiches for the gentleman, two coffees, toast with butter, and three scrambled with onion *para el de más allá.* She watched the trucks come in with provisions for the day, plantains, cartons of eggs, bags of oranges, boxes of papayas, loaves of bread. She covered her face a little with her hair—"Daylight is not tremendously flattering to drag queens"—and ordered another orange juice to see if she could scare away the sour taste that was forming at the corners of her mouth. Five-thirty. "What the hell am I doing here, damn it?" Frenesí rose from her seat, went down an alley, down all the alleys in the area, calling softly to el sirenito. Then she didn't care, she started to call loudly. The dogs barked at her and threw their chests against the cyclone fencing, half-awake voices insulted her, ordered her to be quiet, or threatened to call the police. Louder she called out to the boy, her voice hoarse and broken. Furious, worried, feeling ridiculous, she called him as she turned the corners of that decaying labyrinth of old houses spruced up with paint, abandoned houses converted into shooting galleries, union headquarters, spiritual temples, cheap jewelry stores, pawnshops, bars. She turned down a small residential street that ended at an empty lot where stolen cars were sometimes left after being stripped. She felt a faint murmur of sobs, a slight movement among the boxes; then she saw him, with his pants pulled halfway down, his hands clenched, his underwear bloody. . . .

And she cried, cried with him. She lifted him up from the debris, laid him over her shoulder. Then she kicked off her shoes and ran to a public telephone to call a taxi to take them to the neighborhood hospital. She cried as she argued with the taxi driver, who didn't want to take them because they would stain his car with blood, and who was going to pay for the car wash afterward? With the boy still over her shoulder, she had to run to the Dominicans' café to see if she could locate Chino, who drove a gypsy cab and could take them to the hospital at Barrio Obrero nearby. There was Chino with his station wagon. As well as she could, Valentina explained what had happened, and they loaded the boy in the rear of the car. They sped to the hospital, then Chino said to Valentina, "This is as far as I go, *mamita*, if the guards start asking questions it could get ugly. You'd better prepare yourself. What are you going to say to the nurse when she asks you for the boy's papers?" "I'll lie," said Valentina; she'd lie like she had never lied before. Throw herself into the performance of her life to save her *amiguito*'s.

14

*E*l sirenito was kept there for five days. The people at the hospital called Social Services. At ten o'clock on the third day a social worker came with two policemen. Meanwhile, Valentina had managed to slip out of the hospital. Since the boy was taking heavy painkillers, they had to wait until the following day to interrogate him. During the interrogation he gave a description of the man who attacked him, told them his name, and gave them his grandmother's old address. The social worker reactivated his file and he was turned over to the custody of Social Services.

Valentina visited whenever she could, especially when she knew that the guards and the social worker had left him alone. She had to go dressed as a civilian, so uncomfortable, in pants and long T-shirts. She had to remove her fingernail polish, wear a baseball cap to hide her long hair, and put on glasses to disguise her plucked eyebrows. "I look like a wreck all covered up. *Nene*, this is more work than when I make myself up to go out on the street." Valentina made him laugh with her comments. She told him gossip about the other drag queens and hustlers in the area, trying to drive the memory of the attack from his mind.

When he felt better, the boy escaped from his room in the service elevator. He wandered around the streets for a while, then finally ended up at Valentina's apartment. When he arrived he timidly rang the doorbell. Valentina opened the door, a little startled. She invited him in and made him a cup of chamomile tea, and then they sat in the living room to talk.

"*Papito*, maybe it would be better for you to stay with the people from Social Services."

"Tina, don't tell me that, you know how their orphanages are. I'm never going to one of those places."

"*Pero, mi amor,* you are too young to run loose in the streets."

"Too young? What about Samito and Bimbo? They've been working the streets since they were twelve!"

"Yes, but that's them, not you. You weren't raised like that. Those boys have been alone since they were born. You had a home, someone to worry about you. . . ."

"*Pero se murió,* Tina. She died. No one else in my family has lifted a finger for me. So I just have to take care of myself. Use what I have to my advantage. And where else can I do that? Not in school. Not in Milla de Oro, as if I were a businessman. Where am I going to earn cold hard cash?"

"But the government will take care of you."

"How's the government going to take care of me? By locking me up in a home and treating me like trash? The only place I can make it is on the street, Valentina. On the street."

"To end up like you did last time? No, *mijito,* I won't go through that experience again. I'd look real pretty running from one end of the avenue to the other carrying a half-dead boy on my shoulder."

"If you want, I'll move out of your apartment. But I'm not going to a home."

"You're still not well, you little devil. Can't you see that you need to rest until you heal?"

"I don't care, I'm not going to a home. I'm as grown-up as I'll ever be."

"But *nene*—"

"I'm not going, Tina." He glared at his sister with a look that froze all the words in Valentina's mouth. He was being serious. The boy couldn't be convinced, or trapped by Social Services. And she really couldn't blame him. The foster homes were a nightmare. To have a semblance of a family that treats you badly and gets paid for it is worse than not having anyone. She knew that for herself.

"Okay, *cabroncito*, you can stay here, but nobody is going to touch you ever again."

Valentina took care of him while he was recuperating. She made him give up the street, and she worked double to pay for medicine, bandages, food. She prepared chicken broth, rice, mashed potatoes, and small pieces of stewed veal to settle her protégé's stomach, which was still freshly scarred and upset by the antibiotics. The impact of the misadventure and the unpleasant discussion with his sister had a bad effect on Sirenito. He had a relapse that sent him into a silent melancholy and made him cry at times. Valentina, nervous, tried to do things to distract him, without success. Then she'd repeat, obsessively, "Promise me you won't let this ever happen to you ever again," and Sirena, feeling like the unhappiest being on the face of the earth, threw himself into the cotton-filled breasts and the muscular arms of his *hermana*—she was more family to him than his own. Between sobs and tears he stammered, "I promise you, Valentina, I promise you," and no other sound came from his mouth. With his silent crying he could tell his sister everything, better than with words—the pain of abandonment by his mother, the death of his grandmother, the sleepless nights looking for a place to rest, the anxiety of living with the constant danger of a run-in with the police, being fifteen years old and already living like that, fed up with everything, mistrusting even his own shadow, accustomed to being unloved, used to the filthy lust that thrives in the street, *esa calle*, that was his home and his grave.

When he began to feel better, Sirenito started to help with makeup sessions, to run errands, to take care of pieces of Valentina's wardrobe, to choose bases that obscured more effectively the shadow of her beard. Alert to any need of his *hermana*'s, he spent the whole day cleaning the apartment. During a session of sweeping and mopping, Sirenito found a box under the rattan sofa in the living room. It was a kit complete with syringe, spoon, lighter, and rubber band. Valentina Frenesí shot up. Sirenito carefully put the box back in the same exact spot. He knew what it cost to maintain a habit. He had learned that in the street; he himself had had a *coca* habit during the prosperous times of the partnership, and a good portion of the money he earned he lost up his nose. She had a double load now—the expense of the medicines, the full rent, and his meals—and Sirena understood the sacrifice his sister was making for him. The favors she must be doing in the street for drugs, exposing herself like that. He decided to confront her when she returned. But his *protectora* continued to insist that he not return to work.

"I pulled you out of the garbage and I saved you from dying, which is the same as giving birth to you, so don't argue with me."

"I'm not arguing, but where are you going to get the money for your stuff?"

"For what stuff?"

"For your bases and your heels and your *manteca*."

"And my what?"

"Valentina, I wasn't born yesterday. What about the drugs?"

"That's my business."

"And mine."

"You aren't going back out to work the street."

"Then I'll collect cans or watch cars for people or rob tourists. But I have to do something."

"When you get a little stronger."

When he got a little stronger he collected cans for a while, but the money he earned wasn't even enough to help buy food. To rob tourists he had to go with them to their hotel rooms and Valentina made a big fuss as soon as Sirenito proposed it. There wasn't any other choice. He had to return to work the streets now and then.

Those nights Valentina watched him like a hawk. She waited on the corner with a hit of *coca* in her hand, ready to alleviate the fear of death that came over Sirenito as soon as he climbed into a client's car. Valentina made all the arrangements herself; out of the corner of her eye she memorized the license number of the car in question, just in case. And she made him renew his promise never to let anyone stick it in him again, not even for all the money in the world.

"With your pants at half mast you're at a distinct disadvantage, *papito*. And I would die if something happened to you again."

But, despite Valentina's vigilance and the *coca*, el sirenito couldn't rid himself of the fear that had entered his body the night he was attacked. He couldn't find a way to recapture his former spirit, to forget the risk he ran each time he got into a client's car. When the car doors closed, he didn't even see faces, he didn't want to know when the *señores* finished their business. He was far away, as if buried in a fog on the other side of something that had happened somewhere off in the distance. He stopped being interested in the *clientes*. The only thing that mattered was getting their money, surviving that night, those hands, those lips, just getting everything over already. Just for the *clientes* to drop him off on his corner, safe and sound.

One night, as a very circumspect gentleman was sucking between his legs, Sirenito, blushing, remembered one of his *abuela*'s boleros. Before, when he was overcome with melancholy, he would hum tunes or sing bits of the chorus, but the bolero itself escaped him, as if he suffered from an illness that made him forget the words as soon as he remembered the melody. However, that night, for some inexplicable reason, he remembered an entire bolero, and then another, and another: "Distancia," "Miseria," "Dime, Capitán," then, suddenly, "Bajo un Palmar," "Silencio," "Teatro," and it wasn't that he liked any of those songs, he simply heard them sung in his head by his *abuela*. His *abuela*, her trembling voice, her inert body carried off in the ambulance, she was bringing all the boleros to his breast, word for word, the perfect memory of their melodies. Each song made his face hot, made him feel things that he had dispatched as useless. He sang, first in murmurs, with his eyes closed, then more aware of the sound of his voice. The client stopped moving for a moment, but then went on sucking, numbed by the adolescent's song. El sirenito continued with the boleros, one after another, and the deeper within

69

he pulled from, the slower the man sucked, the more tender the corners of his mouth were and the softer the pressure of his hand against the base of Sirenito's penis, the more his tongue felt like velvet. His excited saliva smelled sweet, like milk and honey. The circumspect gentleman seemed like a young girl in love, scared to death and overcome with desire, stung by his own pleasure, his soft hand on the boy's naked thighs to feel the warm, taut skin, ready to swallow all his juices, any that the boy was willing to offer him. It was a miracle, that feeling was a miracle that reminded him of other times. Sirena sang for twenty-five minutes without stopping. Nor did the *señor* stop caressing the boy with his mouth and tongue, anxious and melancholy and lonely. Suddenly, at the end of the song "Tentación," Sirenito signaled, with a thick stream, the eagerly awaited end of his litany of memories. The very circumspect *señor* swallowed the whole thing, anointed, feeling himself part of a strange communion. He licked every drop remaining between his fingers, on the boy's thighs, even the ones that ran down his own chin, and the ones that dissolved into the cloth of the boy's pants. He held the boy's face in his hand and murmured, "*Angelito*. My little angel," and his eyes became a deep well.

Sirenito regained his sight. He closed his mouth. He waited for the client to release his face and start the ignition and drive him back to his corner. Without looking at him during the return trip, he took the money in payment for his services and got out of the car. He didn't even count the bills to make sure the amount was correct. His *abuela*'s boleros were all the wealth he needed to protect himself from nights on the street forever.

uest list for the dinner party. Solange fretted. The essential people, only those, I don't want it to be too crowded. *A ver . . .* Ingeniero Licariac and his wife, that old harpy Angélica, such bad taste she has in clothing, always wearing gaudy colors, *modelitos* she buys in Bal Harbor so later she can throw it in our faces in the middle of every conversation. She might as well buy them in Calle Duarte. The belly that poor woman has grown. She never regained her shape after the *ingeniero*'s last child. At the gala dinner for the National Library last month she wore a Pucci outfit that made her look like a merengue dancer. So many brightly colored ruffles, she looked like a clown. But what is one to do? Angélica has to come if I invite her husband. I must make sure that there is whisky at the bar, that's all the *ingeniero* drinks. After I killed myself looking for the best wines. *Una botella cada tres invitados,* one bottle for every three guests, I can't forget that. I hope twenty cases of Château Lafitte are enough.

He must be an alcoholic, you can already see the signs of his addiction in that nose he has, the web of broken capillaries. And that stench that comes out of his mouth every time he says hello. How he grabs one all the time, like an octopus. He just won't leave one alone. "Ay, *mi querida* Solange, how lucky Hugo was to have married you. He doesn't know how fortunate he is. . . ." And handling my rear end while I have to laugh and pretend not to notice. If he weren't a colleague of my husband's, I would have him kicked out of the house.

Imelda Nacidit and her husband, I have to invite them. What *is* that Italian's name? Marinni, Marcini . . . There's no escape from her. The patience one must have to put up with the stories about her latest trip to New York and the ton of money she spent on Pratesi linens for their bed. I can hear her already: "You don't know how hard it was to find them in a shade of mint green that would match the décor of our bedroom. But Pratesi is the best in the world, you simply never recover from the expense, because you want one of everything, that store is a dream. . . ." Such torture to bear her. *Una pesada*, a bore and a vulgar woman. Describing her spending habits at full volume so that everyone at the gathering can hear. And the worst is when she starts to finish her sentences in Italian, just in case anybody forgets she's *almost* European, what with all those years she spent in Italy, where she snagged that lout who passes for a husband. Marcini, Mardini . . . He seems to have a touch or two of mental retardation. All the time he's spent living here, and he still doesn't understand Spanish very well. Not that it's even so different from his own language. He spends the time looking all around with empty eyes and nodding his head as if he really understood what people are saying to him. He thinks no one notices.

Brooks, Hannover, Chiddale, and their wives. The representatives of the pharmaceutical companies here on business. I have to concentrate on them. "Very charming wives, very elegant gentlemen, please make yourselves at home." The fans won't be enough. These Americans are always complaining about the heat. I'd better have the staff turn on the central air a few hours before the party starts, so the living room will be cool enough. Have they finished waxing the floors yet? And the tablecloths, are they back from the cleaners'? If I find a single stain, I am going to eat them alive, those slowpokes.

The packages from À la Vieille Russie came yesterday. Five tins of beluga, five of classic gray, three of imperial. If some is left over, wonderful, I'll save it for another occasion. *Oof*, when Hugo sees that bill! Well, he told me not to scrimp. The guests must be impressed. I'm not sure whether the gravlax I asked the hotel chef to prepare will be ready in time. Check to see that the Scandinavian salmon has arrived, I mustn't forget that. And the escargots and the cheeses. Jarlsberg, blue, Brie, smoked Gouda . . . I will have to go off my diet, because I want to eat all of these things, even if I get as big as a cow. *Ay, señor,* I've gotten rather broad in the middle lately. It's just that having three babies one after another has its effects, the beautician told me. At least my belly isn't covered with stretch marks like Rosita Perdomo's. I don't know where she gets the nerve to go the pool at the club in a two-piece bathing suit. Such poor taste. *Ay,* Rosita Perdomo, I have to include her on the list.

I really must lose some weight. Maybe I have time to call Yadia to give me a massage with algae on my thighs, and a wrap. Yes, because really, the Galliano I'm going to wear at the party is just a little tight in the hips. Make a note, call Yadia. Everything must be perfect. Hugo will be happy, the guests pleased, the food exquisite. Everyone falling over themselves with praise for me, that I took care of the most intricate details. Then Hugo will realize what he has at his side.

Every last detail. Add the Thompsons to the list, and Don Manolo Aybar and his wife, and the Dessalines. I almost forgot the centerpiece for the table, and the fruit platter! No grapes—I saw that at the benefit lunch for the children's hospital that Diana Puig organized. It should have melons, pieces of apple, and fresh strawberries. Those Americans always go around complaining of the heat. Let them refresh themselves with fruit until dinner is served. Adding a few tropical fruits will give an exotic and very elegant touch to the tray, a few pieces of pineapple, some mangoes . . . The flowers must be impeccable. The florist better not show up with those ugly birds-of-paradise or anything else so ridiculously common. Lilies, orchids, irises, a big arrangement for the corner table and the dining room table.

Not a single detail can escape me, not a single detail. Instead of the Galliano it would be better to wear the Kenzo dress that Hugo likes so much. Besides, it will soften my figure a little, with those layers of transparent blue veils. It was so big on me when Hugo bought it. It's been so long since I've worn it. *Espera,* Solange, wait a second. . . . Which of the guests has already seen you in that dress? Go over the list: Imelda, no, Angélica, Matilde, Jessica Thompson, Señora Licariac, no, no. I think I'm safe. With perfect makeup and the Hidalgo necklace-and-earrings set I bought a while ago, I'll look stunning. Just a touch of Joy de Patou behind each ear. The living image of elegance. Careful not to overdo the perfume, it's so concentrated, it can be nauseating. But that's what everyone is wearing these days.

Maybe the party will get Hugo out of the bad mood he's been in for months now. What is going on with him? Nothing seems to suit him lately. Who knows, maybe he'll be impressed with how careful and efficient I've been in making a splash for his guests. And, finally, he'll be happy. Who knows, maybe, after the guests leave, he'll want to . . . Where did I put my Alfaro lingerie? I should take it out and leave it on the bed, just in case. . . .

16

*A*long a little path on the patio, birds singing, clouds making shadows on the ground. I watch them, a caterpillar, I move closer, the shadow hovers over me. Who is that looking at me as if I am a bird, a caterpillar, the clouds, the earth, they all look at me and I want to run but I can't, I want to touch, but my fingers are holding a hairy, wriggling caterpillar. The caterpillar's legs are yellow.

"That caterpillar is a nuisance, Leocadio, but it's pretty. It eats the leaves of the rosebush." He takes my hand and takes me to the rose-bushes. "It eats the leaves of the ficus."

"What is a ficus?"

"That tree." He points. His hand is a caterpillar with many legs, a fat, hairy caterpillar, with soft, beautiful legs twisting among the fingers of my other hand. "That one is called dwarf bamboo, and those are desert roses. You plant them like this." He takes my hands and helps me make a little mound of earth.

Along the path on the patio, caterpillar-bird-cloud-earth, he tells me, "You have to trim the roses," and hands me the clippers, the wooden handle among his red caterpillars with chocolate veins. Alfonso is big, a *niño* like me, but big.

"When you grow up you could do this; you have a good hand, everything grows well for you."

Mamá is cleaning the *patrona*'s house.

"Look how the seeds you helped me plant last week are sprouting."

I catch another yellow caterpillar. I don't want to kill it, but it will eat my plants if I let it live.

"I'll be there in a minute, Alfonso. I want to throw it in the bushes."

"I'll come with you."

"No, I can go by myself." A tickling weakens my knees, I don't know why.

And all day, caterpillar-bird-cloud-stone, I help sweep leaves off the patio, I help cut the grass, fertilize the gardenias and the bougainvillea that twines through the balustrades on the balcony. Three branches have to be cut so they don't damage the balustrades. Alfonso surprises me, putting a flower behind my ear. Caterpillar, he looks at me, a storm rises, the trembling that weakened my legs in the morning. Bird-cloud-rock, I look at the ground, timid, at the path. He is *un hombre*, but a *niño* like me, Mamá has told me.

"You are still too young. You can't start to work," she said.

"What about Alfonso?"

"He's four years older than you, his voice has already changed. He's on his way to becoming a man."

"What do you mean, he's becoming a man?"

"Don't distract me anymore, *muchachito*, with all this work I've got to do."

"What do you do to become a man?"

"You use this," Alfonso tells me, and he grabs me between the legs playfully. The trembling returns, I move behind him, I taunt him, showing him my fists. There's a storm in my eyes, yellow and gray. He laughs at me. I want to hit him, make him bleed, for grabbing me down there.

"Where, here?" And he does it again. No, don't even dare. Don't touch me again, and don't laugh like that. And don't show me how to make mounds of earth to plant seeds.

"The lilies you planted have bloomed. I picked this one for you to give to your mother."

He looks at me, caterpillar-bird-cloud-stone.

"I have a woman, Leocadio, she works near here. We've broken up, but I'm going to win her back."

"What's her name?"

"Coralia."

"What's she like?"

"Like you. She looks like a lion."

"Don't compare me with women."

"Even your names are similar. Leocadio . . . Coralia."

A cloud forms in my eyes. It's always the same, the water collects in my eyes, betraying me. Now I really want to hit him. Force him to beg forgiveness for comparing me to a woman. I throw myself on him and punch him. He laughs, I pinch him, bite him. His flesh tastes like salt and earth. He escapes from me.

"Don't run away from me, coward."

"Leocoralia . . ."

He laughs, running into the brush. I follow him. He turns suddenly and traps me, holding my arms behind me. He's so big, a *niño* like me, but gigantic. I can't move, the way he's holding me. I try to twist free, like a caterpillar, try to escape, but I grow limp, then get upset. Then I feel the warmth of his embrace, his body on my back. Path-clouds-bird-caterpillar, the shadows fall on the hill and the hill behind, then on me. I open my mouth and what comes out is a birdcall. But in my eyes a gray and yellow storm gathers. I look at his thick chocolate hands that hold my yellow ones. He moves both lower, down to what he had grabbed before.

I must refuse. I am growing hard like a rock, hard like an animal hunting for birds, the *patrona*'s cat eating lizards and caterpillars. I hear the steps of someone approaching.

"Mamá, the *patrona*'s cat ate a lizard."

"Alfonso, I need you to help me unload some azaleas that I brought from the nursery."

"*Sí, señora.*"

"Who is that with you?"

"We were worried about your cat, *patrona*. . . ." I murmur with my heart pounding in my throat.

The *señora* turns and hurries back to the house, from which my *mamá* emerges and runs to where I am. Alfonso lets go of my arms, crouches down, looks at the ground. A storm gathers in my *mamá*'s eyes. She grabs my hand and pulls me toward the house.

17

*T*here were rumors that Chino had received some new material from Miami. Valentina wanted to sample the quality. The night before, she had scoldingly told Sirena to take care of herself when he went to see a supplier to score. She was in an infernal mood. It had been a week and a half since she herself had scored. And on top of everything, Valentina felt ashamed that Selena had discovered her habit. She didn't want to set a bad example; she couldn't keep spending money on smack, that *chamaquito* was her responsibility. Besides, she was clearly out of control if her habit was so obvious that even a fifteen-year-old hustler had noticed it. But she couldn't stop cold turkey. Who was going to cover their household expenses if she disappeared from the street for weeks, returning skinny and with bloodshot eyes, while she took care of the demons that lived inside her veins? Maybe with the new stuff she could buy less and still get high, that way cutting down little by little until she could get out of the whole trap once and for all. Money was scarce, and she knew that Chino had always liked her, that in return for spending a night with him she could get enough drugs to last for months. Sacrifices must be made; two mouths to feed are not the same as one without an appetite, used to taking in other kinds of food. Valentina Frenesí left instructions for Selena not to go out on the street. A client who was also an undercover policeman had told Samantha that there were plans for a raid in the next few nights, so it was better not to go out. She left him three dollars to rent a movie or to go to Burger King or something. And he should go to bed early, she didn't have time for any more trouble.

Sirenito wasn't in the best of moods either. His intuition told him why his sister had left in such a hurry. Not going out to work, if she was expecting a raid. She was going to trade her body for *teca*, he was sure that was what she was up to. Even he knew that drugs and tricks should never be mixed. Working the street is a game of sheer control and straight accounts. It's risky enough, leaving yourself vulnerable to a client. Really dangerous if that client has the syringe of your dreams in his hand. There is no hope for negotiation in that situation.

"Tina, don't go. Why don't I go borrow twenty dollars from someone—from Imperia, she got paid for her show yesterday at the new disco they opened in El Condado. You stay here. I'll go out and get the cash and then come right back. Why don't you just stay home and hang out with me? We'll have a ball watching a couple of old movies on cable tonight, one has Marilyn Monroe."

Valentina Frenesí's sole reply was to look at Sirenito from head to toe, pick up her purse and keys, and leave the house, slamming the door behind her. Sirenito just stood there with his mouth hanging open. Anger showing in his face, he turned on the television, thinking what an imbecile his mentor was, she took such care of him only to throw herself away like this. "I would never do something like that. They'll never find me depending on some idiot for peace or happiness," thought Sirenito, trying to distract himself from these unpleasant circumstances with the color screen spewing luxury cars and pure satisfaction.

He should have done something that night; he should have argued at least, or followed Valentina downstairs and forced her to see reason. But how was he to know that the stuff was going to be purer than usual? How was he to know that a haughty look would be his last gift from Valentina, that later her blank eyes would be staring out of her naked body, half made-up, grotesquely photographed by the forensics people and carried out in a plastic bag from some disgusting house in the projects? When he arrived with Balushka at Station Number 15, the police and the journalists were in high gear, interviewing the passersby who had gathered to see the spectacle. A policewoman was searching Valentina Frenesí's purse, looking for I.D. Annoyed, the officers were asking questions so they could at least identify the deceased, notify the family. Other policemen joked about the cadaver: "Hey, Castillo, isn't this your uncle's wife?" Someone else suggested that it was the wife of one of the ambulance drivers. "Your mother, you mean," retorted the driver.

Sirenito arrived with a pierced heart. A path opened among the curious, and when he saw that it really was Valentina, he ran toward the body, brushing off the policemen and forensic photographers who grabbed at him to ask questions, questions he couldn't answer. "What was your relationship to the victim? What do you know about what happened?" Tossed into a sea of pain, Sirenito choked on his own breath, held Valentina's head, and kissed her face and her hands, beautiful hands now lifeless and without a single farewell caress for her *hermanito*. The forensics men pulled him away from her body, to carry her to who knows what morgue, where they would never let him see Tina again.

"Do you know the name of the deceased, the real name?"

And Sirenito responded, wiping away tears, "Valentina, Valentina Frenesí."

18

*H*ugo Graubel alone in his beach house at Juan Dolio, smoking and drinking rum by the balustrade of the terrace. Hugo Graubel watching his children play on the beach at the Hotel Talanquera, deep in thought. Hugo Graubel, rinsing the salt from his body, the hair standing on end when he touched himself. Hugo remembering how he mounted his sighing wife, young like Selena, dark-haired and pale like Selena, but without her angular fifteen-year-old body, without her diminutive rear end swaying along the dirty sand on the beach where excrement floats. Hugo Graubel ruminates on the fact that he's never given it to a man.

I will love Sirena like I've always wanted to love a woman.

His employees found him on the terrace and told him they had done their work, the business was settled. *El muchachito* lingered in the vestibule, waiting for his host as he glanced around the living room. The boy said his artistic name was Sirena Selena. And would need a pianist and at least two afternoons to rehearse. She (he referred to himself in the feminine) hadn't come here to steal money or to be made a fool of. She was a professional and would stake her reputation on that.

The host walked inside to greet his guest.

Sirena Selena was standing next to the sofa. . . .

"Señor Graubel, when you see me descend these steps in the dimmed light and stand beside the grand piano, when you see me open my mouth and hear me sing, I promise that you will leave this world, its troubles, its worries, to ride away on the sound of your Selena's voice."

"My Selena?"

"For three hundred and seventy-five dollars a night, I am all yours. By the way, how many nights will it be?"

"As many as it takes to dazzle my guests. Not me; you have already dazzled me."

"I see that, Señor Graubel. But for the others, two nights will be more than enough."

Sirena walked deliberately, leaving her host speechless before this immaculate performance. Not for a second had she stepped out of character. And she wasn't even wearing makeup. In Hugo Graubel she awakened more than desire; there was the curiosity to know more about this *muchachito* who knew exactly how to convert himself into the living image of desire, into the woman of his dreams, into the impossible. Who was this boy who called attention to himself and hid behind masks in his attempt to seduce Hugo (that was for certain) and to seduce away from his wallet more than $375 a night, to seduce away his entire fortune if possible, everything he had accumulated through blood and struggle. Sirena Selena was a magic well in which he could see things in the future and the past. But the reflections were hazy, confused. Graubel was going to need time, more afternoons of rehearsals, unexpected meetings in corridors, conversations beneath a palm tree. Wooing was needed, and subtle distraction of his wife and children; he needed to buy time to be able to immerse himself in the well (glorious or ordinary) that was Selena.

While the host hatched strategies for his approach, Sirena strolled through the estate's reception room. Calculatingly, she leaned against a table with a mirror above it, to better watch the magnate's reaction. One look between them was enough for her to realize that the show was a pretext, a delicate smokescreen. Hugo Graubel had other plans for her. If she was not careful, this game of seduction could turn against her, set back her plans, and leave her trapped in the wrong situation. But Selena always bet on the best horse, and she was the best horse on this track. Although she had to admit that the competition was tough, not because of the racer, but because of his material resources. She was impressed by the elegance of the mansion. And she couldn't block out the image that sprang to her mind—of being set up in an apartment, having a checking account in the magnate's name, enjoying the beautiful life. It would be difficult to fight all the glamour with which her host could tempt her. Very difficult. "Watch out, this is a trap," she told herself, and proceeded to focus on her routine in order to ward off the spell of the house and its furnishings.

The meeting in the magnate's house helped her to visualize her performance. Glamour always made Sirena feel good. She hadn't known that there were millionaires like this in the Dominican Republic. On the news they only talked about Dominicans fleeing in boats—encrusted with salt, or gnawed at by sharks and floating belly up in the Mona Passage. She didn't know about the acres and acres of sugarcane that had paid for her host's estate. She didn't know about the Haitians toiling over pots to ensure that the sugarcane syrup achieved the perfect consistency; she didn't know about the peasant leaders chopped up by sugarcane plantation owners in San Pedro de Macorís, fertilizing the red earth stolen from the sea, nor about the succulent *cocolos* always served as a snack to hungry children in the Graubel household. All the members of the family were friends of army generals, advisers to the Ministry of Commerce, intimates of the vice president of the republic, who worked for them for many years. At home, the little coiffed wife was planning her debut as a poet at the National Library.

Selena wasn't aware of all this. She only knew that glamour always made her feel good. The gorgeous blocks of pink marble would accentuate the rosy sparkle of her skin; the white Philippine rattan furniture and the velvety light on the interior patios would highlight her melancholy-sylph silhouette. Her pale olive complexion, the complexion of a *criolla* from the forties, would glow against the pastel wallpaper. Her jet-black wig would glisten silkily against the satin curtains covering the walls in the Graubel residence. The furniture made of old mahogany and hand-carved *guayacán*, the Italian tiles on the patio, the immense Expressionist paintings, and the chandelier of cut-crystal teardrops in the reception hall would offer, finally, the perfect stage on which Sirena Selena could present her image. Her favorite flowers were calla lilies. By chance, and almost as if expecting her, there was a vase filled with them in the vestibule of the house.

"So when do we start?"

"Whenever you are ready."

"I was born ready."

Bienvenidos, my dear audience, how are you tonight? How is everybody doing, isn't everything too fabulous, just too much? Well, I want to welcome you to the Martha Divine Show, on behalf of the whole management of Club Bocaccio, this den of iniquity for *locas*, local and international, tourist and native, and for the undecided and openminded boys, *buchas*, and biological women who like to sit and watch men cackling—the poor things. I want to dedicate the show tonight to *los indecisos*, the undecided, those men who when they're asked, '*Oye*, are you gay?' twist their mouths in surprise, act cool, putting on an air of being about to say something profound, and answer, '*Ay, mi amor*, I don't believe in classifications. Maybe I'm bisexual. You know, one has to be free to explore bodies, passion, desire.' 'Explore fresh meat' is what they mean! Well, honeys, they can all come up to my dressing room after the show for an in-depth look at the Discovery Channel!

"But still, I want to dedicate this show to them, to those men who still don't know what they are, but with any luck will find out tonight. Who here is an *indeciso*? Let's see, raise your hands. Nobody. And closet cases? Who here is still in the closet? Let's see, girls, risk it a little, *Mamí* and *Papí* are either at home watching television or walking to the parking lot after church and nobody's going to go gossiping to *them*, because it would make them look a little ridiculous, too. Imagine how silly they would look saying, '*Ay, mire*, Doña Margot, you know at Martha Divine's show the other night at Bocaccio's I saw your son raise his hand when they were counting the closet cases. Martha is such a divine stand-up comedian. She was fabulous, with a long-sleeved silver pantsuit and a wig with big curls that fell halfway down her back. I don't know how that *cabrona* can dance whole routines when she's up on those too-stunning stilettos she wore the other night. They weren't from here. I didn't dare ask her where they were from, but Joito told me that surely she had bought them from a catalog in New York. With the flippers that woman has for feet! Doña Margot, you'd better watch out, that son of yours, when he comes out of the closet, he's going to cause *un escándalo*, with that cute little behind that he has. . . . He could get himself into some trouble.' See what I mean? We are gossips, but suckers we'll never be. Don't worry, your secrets are safe with us. . . .

"And who do we have here? Papito, and those shaved pectorals? *Ay, que rico! Ay, mira,* the hair is already starting to grow out. Doesn't it itch? The same thing happens to me when I shave here by *las verijas,* you know, so the hair doesn't show when I put on my bikini and do splits in my routine. It's for the show, so don't go thinking that it's because I have crabs or anything like that. Allow me to clarify for you and the rest of this the select audience here tonight—Martha Divine doesn't have crabs, or gonorrhea, or psoriasis, or AIDS, or dandruff. One has to speak plainly, because these *locas* who work here with me are so evil-minded and envious, and such gossips, that it wouldn't surprise me if one of them went up there to the owners, making up a story about me. '*Mira, loca,* didn't you know? Divine has crabs. I am not going to step into that hot, cramped dressing room to share even a wig with that *cabrona.* What if I get them, *ah?* What is my husband going to say? That I'm whoring around at work. We are going through a very delicate moment, I'm not leaving myself open to that. So, now you know, go see if you can resolve it, and when you have just let me know. Martha is burned out anyway, always repeating the same old tired jokes. If I were you . . .' *Ay sí, nene,* let me tell you, we *locas* are backstabbing traitors, that's why the community is like it is, they steal husbands, they steal from their jobs, they spread AIDS, they fight on street corners. But I am not like that. I am gentle as a cat. Purrrrrrr . . . meeeeoooooo . . .

"What town are you from? From Cataño? Oh, my God! Such a divine man from such a pitiful town. And you, are you straight or gay? *Indeciso?* You know how much I like *indecisos*. Look how understanding and supportive I am, Papito. I even dedicated my show to you. Are there many *indecisos* in Cataño? *Sí!* Dulce, I hereby renounce this life of glamour and wantonness and I'm moving to Cataño to look for one of those aggressive husbands, to fry him pork chops and set up a beauty salon there, to support him. Don't you worry about me, I know what I'm doing. I will come visit you every week, because I am sure the show would fall apart without me. But before I assume this municipal duty I should ask a question: how do you get from Cataño to here? Did you take a boat to get here? A boat and bus Number One, I'm sure. You drove? You have a car? What luck, a motorized hustler! Dulce, Amelia, I found a husband, darlings. So you know how it is, don't call me, I'll call you. . . . And wipe the *coca* off your nose, there's still a little bit there, no, *chicas*, under your nose, that's it, say hello to the audience. Very good . . . *Ay negro*, I don't know if I can go to Cataño with you, because these people don't know how to do anything without me and the business will collapse. We'll talk about it after the show. Okay, Papi?

"*Pues sí, público selecto.* My next song is by Diana Ross, and deals with impossible loves, like the one I have with my new husband, from the town of Cataño. One more *indeciso*, like all the others here tonight. But who doesn't suffer moments of indecision in this life . . . ?

20

The whole day wasted, just killing time in the city. All dressed up like a rich *señora* out for a walk in the capital of this dirty island, which is well below her level of taste, a little below the level of her own island, and with more armed guards standing watch over useless monuments.

In the middle of the plaza, a cathedral serves as a backdrop for Martha's stroll, blocks of limestone sparkle beneath a sun that would make any woman's hormones heat up. On each corner, big mulatto men in tight uniforms smoke. Doubly armed, they shift their weapons from shoulder to shoulder, from pant leg to pant leg. Every muscle is clearly visible beneath their shirts. Hungrily, they look at her, but they are beneath her class. She entertains herself by teasing them—a little, nothing more, like when she was young and worked the streets and she used to see police cars pass by with their headlights off. She remembers how it smelled inside those cars, of violent officers yearning to try out their clubs. One had to temper nerves, test the challenge. Between clients she entertained herself by teasing the officers. Like now. With a little difference. Now she is a stylish *señora* shopping in the capital city of an island that can't compare in sophistication with her boredom. And she is a stylish lady because she dresses stylishly and gets bored trying not to get bored. Now she has the power and she flaunts it with a disdainful air.

Martha Divine turned the corner of the plaza, had a lunch of *moro de gandules* with stewed goat and a salad on the Paseo del Conde, bought genuine amber necklaces in the jewelry shops of the Hostal Nicolás de Ovando, drank a beer in a pub in the port. She killed time. She spent the entire day going from store to store. She bought souvenirs for her girls in the Mercado Modelo, masks, scented candles, two *damajuanas,* and snake oil for her kidneys. She had to distract herself somehow. She couldn't wait at the hotel any longer, counting the minutes by the pool, asking every four hours if there was a message from Señor Contreras. And Selena was still missing. She must have found some boyfriend on the beach. Some businessman who would pay for a night of lust and an afternoon of drinks by the sea. Let her spend the night away if she wanted. Let her spend the night and the next day broiling herself in the sun. Martha was not interested in those things, especially considering the damage those ultraviolet rays do to one's skin, not to mention the time it takes to mount a whole beach production. She would have to shave her entire body, protect her implants from the vagaries of the sun, take care not to sweat in her makeup. . . . No one knows how a *loca* suffers on the beach. Let Sirena go by herself. She could still change between bodies without major trauma. Effete boy or fabulous queen, few others could afford the luxury that la Sirena could. Martha knew she could afford it least of all. It had been years since she had dressed as a man, and she laughed aloud thinking about herself decked out in a long-sleeved shirt, silk tie, leather belt with metal buckle, brown polyester pants, and shoes without a heel, like when she was a boy and her parents dressed her to go to church on Saturday night. *"Qué horror, Jehová!* Without heels I couldn't walk from here to the corner, not even if I had a gun to my head." It took so much work to learn the difficult art, mastering the stilettos and the thin straps, at the beginning of her transformation. A whole year it took her to forget the mannerisms of the Pentecostal youth she once was; to learn about glamour, begin collecting dainty poses, the eyelash-batting, the smiles of famous singers, the undulating runway walk, until she found the perfect combination for her new identity. A masculine production would do her no good at this point in her life. She had already forgotten the choreography that gives the gender its true form.

"*La hijadeputa* hasn't called me. . . . Not even a message. Two days away from the hotel! She hasn't lost the bad habits of the streetwalker yet, never mind with all the sweat I've put into advising her. Well, she has to come back. I have her return ticket, safely held in this purse," thought the businesswoman to herself as she walked toward the corner of Calle el Conde.

Anyone who saw her walking *como toda una señora* would never guess that she was one of the pioneers. Miss Martha Divine. The queen of the putdown, the fabulous mistress of ceremonies of the midnight show in a half-dozen bars in good old Boricualand. Vibrations, Cotorrito, Bocaccio's; she even appeared at Arcos Blancos, promoting dozens of *loquitas* trying out routines. She saw the start of it all.

Her talent lay in her tongue, dangerous as it was, and a sense of humor that disarmed the bravest soul. Her training as a preadolescent evangelist had to serve her somehow. And her eye for glamour had no logical explanation; she had an elegance never seen in her environment, especially amazing when people learned that Martha Divine had grown up in a small town, with a Pentecostal mother and father. They were three children, two boys and a girl. The girl became a missionary, one of the boys a drug addict, and he—well, he left home at sixteen, never to return, after his father broke two of his ribs with a bat and burned some dresses that he had made with great sacrifice, he didn't even know why, and which his mother found as she was looking around in her children's closets. When his father, with the face of a vengeful archangel, poured gasoline on his dresses, he knew that the next thing burned would be him. Definitely him, because how could he be sure that it would be possible to control the urge to find rags and to use his mother's sewing machine to transform them into the gowns of his dreams? How could he veer from the destiny that was so naturally unfurling between his fingers, and his toes, driving him toward daring polishes for fingernails, high heels with straps, diamond rings, and fine gold watches? How could he promise not to allow himself to be carried away by temptation, to refrain in order to remain part of that ugly, fat, hairy family who wore guayaberas, flowered rayon shirts, and polyester skirts, their backs turned from

91

any ornament but a Bible beneath the arm? He couldn't, since Martha Divine, before knowing what he was, did what he did to transform himself into pure seduction. And his father was a vengeful archangel. The son had to flee far away, as far away as possible.

Far away were the capital, the clients, the Honduran husband. Far away were the three years spent in New York, eight years after the successes of Stonewall. And there he met the most fabulous drag queens on the planet. Lady Bunny, who later went on to be the organizer of Wigstock, and Joey Arias. The *boricuas* Sylvia Rivera and Holly Woodlawn, who grew up in Miami and was one of the stars of Andy Warhol's Factory. One night as they were leaving Studio 54, Martha's husband invited Holly to the apartment they rented in Chelsea, at Nineteenth Street and Seventh Avenue, to snort cocaine, drink, and listen to Holly talk. At that time Martha was barely an adolescent, blond, very skinny, and with a Honduran husband who cared for Martha, abused him, and fed him in the most imaginative, succulent ways ever dreamed of. That was when Martha started to dress like a *nena*, for the husband and his friends, who were the jet-set of drag, and a few others, rich gay men, most of them Latin Americans, who only on business trips allowed themselves the luxury of letting go, of being free and feeding the desires they kept under lock and key back in their respective republics. At home in their countries they reproduced, inherited, buried grandparents, rode horses on their haciendas, and acted like the future fathers of their countries. But here, in New York, they loosened the ties of their gray suits and dropped their suitcases with the export permits for flowers, minerals, or coffee. Out from among bottles and hallucinogenic pills and powders flew feather boas, lipsticks, and effete boys in skirts magically appeared, rescued from the streets to show the businessmen real pleasure and debauchery.

And look at her now, walking down the street. Martha had shared stages with the best: Barbara Herr, Pantojas, Renny Williams. She was the one who got Rudy Martínez started in his show. Everybody credits Miss Martha with discovering the man who would later turn his house into one of the most stable drag families on the whole island. Rudy Martínez, mother of Samantha Fox, mother of Alex Soto, grandmother of Imperia Montalbán, an institution in her own right with the boys she plucks out of the gutters and the trash and raises as her own. She sends some of them to school, to universities, imposes order and authority, respect for the profession, pride in who they are. Mami Rudy, who has raised so many, who would she be if Miss Martha hadn't given her a break? So Sirena had better not come to *me* with her attitude and her bad manners, who does she think she is? Who does she think she's dealing with? Miss Martha has earned all the wrinkles on her taut implants, she has earned her stripes as a businesswoman and her elegant walk on every street on every island on the planet. She has earned the poise needed to speak to the businessmen who need to be spoken with in all the hotels. She has finally earned the right to rest, free from the weight of so much toiling, so many years of selling herself for crumbs and pretending to love for even less. So don't mess with her; she knows what she is capable of. Just ask her Honduran husband what she is capable of. If Sirena puts on too many airs, Miss Martha can very happily put her back in the trenches, find another talented *loquita*, and start the promotional work all over again. Miss Martha knows better than anyone that the gutters are filled with beautiful *loquitas* desperate for the rest of the world to know how beautiful they are.

Martha hailed a taxi to take her back to the hotel. She couldn't bear to see any more painted ceramics, silver, or boxes of domestic cigars. She wanted a decision about the show, and if one wasn't forthcoming, then it was time to march on. She still had to make a few telephone calls to other hotels. It can't be that the hotel owners on this island are that stuck in the moralist quagmire when it comes to making money. The wealthy tourist's urges must be satisfied. Folkloric dancing and merengue orchestras will never be able to seduce them so deliciously. Variety, gentlemen, variety. That's what the public wants. In their own countries, even drunk, they wouldn't go to a show of *locas*, but once they're lost in the salty *arrumacos* of a Caribbean island, rum in their veins, skin scorched by unfamiliar temperatures, any novel idea would invite them to relax their prejudices. They would applaud la Sirena insanely, buy her drinks, sell out the house every night. In continuous debut your featured star, Sirena Selena, would be the ideal personification of what they came here to find. Lust, mystery, temptation, the whole package wrapped in an amorous bolero and in the sparkling body of an adolescent *travesti*. Let Martha run a hotel. She would teach them what it was like to have a businesswoman's blood running through her veins.

Back at the hotel, Martha made her usual inquiry. "Any message from Señor Contreras?" With the negative response she turned and walked toward the elevator, furious. Grumbling curses, she took out her key, tortured the carpet with her heels until she reached her room. Inside, she went to the dresser to look for her telephone book, ready to arrange other auditions with hotel managers less indecisive than Contreras, who had made her waste time and money with this waiting. He could go to the seven hells, he, his hotel, the mother who gave birth to him! She was not a woman to stand around waiting.

On the nightstand, Sirena's note still lay beneath a bottle of moisturizing cream.

21

*A*t first Doña Adelina had started with three boys, now she had about twenty. But she wasn't going to take another, she promised herself. It had to end with Leocadio, because there was no room in the house for any more. Doña Adelina lived in the house of her aunts. They'd ended up raising her after her mother sent her, as a young girl, to the capital to work as a maid in the new houses they were building in Esperilla. She remembers them well. They always asked her, "How much are you going to send your *mamá* this week?" Yes, of course her mother depended on it. To take care of the babies she kept spitting out. Worse than a rabbit, the woman was. But even sending a little help every month, Doña Adelina managed to save a bit for herself. Even her aunts had no idea how much she had put aside. She never told them, as a precaution, although she loved them and trusted them and took care of them when they began to get old and doddering. Perhaps because of her selflessness, and because they thought she was helpless, her aunts left her their house.

They weren't real aunts, just like she wasn't really related to the *muchachitos* she ended up raising, some of whom she rescued from the street. She never had children of her own, but had developed an inexplicable maternal love, an instinct, for the children. The thing was, it pained her to see them wandering like stray dogs. She started by picking up three, from the street. The first was a little mulatto with yellow eyes. He had run away from home because his father threatened to kill him if he caught him doing filthy things again. He chased the boy to the edge of their property with a machete and, highway to highway, truck driver to truck driver, the kid made it to the capital. Marcelino had found Mulatto in the street and they became close friends. They had the same habits and they watched out for each other when they had to jump through hoops to steal something to eat or while they worked the street. He was older and stronger and he protected Mulatto and Chiquito, who was like a little *señorita*, very thin and pale, from Santiago de la Vega. Doña Adelina took all three of them in.

That was the beginning, when there was still room in the house. Doña Adelina had tried to impose good manners on them, but Mulatto, Marcelino, and Chiquito had become accustomed to wandering the streets, it was natural for them. What could she do? Besides, when she had worked as a servant girl, she had sowed her own wild oats, enjoyed little escapades with her bosses, and her bosses' sons, and lots of boyfriends whom she met in the streets. That was how she had built up her savings. She still did little things every now and then. She still had her charms. Ever since she was a small girl she had been very *machera*. Like the others around her . . . Some people are born that way. What's wrong with following the natural inclination one came into the world with?

The boys who began to fill her house were such loves. But she had to send some back to the street because they took drugs or had the bad habit of going around stealing even when they didn't need to, coming to her with their contrived stories. That she could not tolerate. But the little ones who came to her dressed in rags, beaten, lost, those she took in, clothed, and fed, and some she sent to school or to learn a trade. She started with three, but they multiplied. Marcelino, Chiquito, and Mulatto spread the word to every lost child they found in the street. "Doña Adelina took us in and is very good to us and lets us do this and that." And since the *tigeritos* had their own little businesses in the streets, they were able to give something back to Doña Adelina as a contribution toward the household expenses. They knew that she took care of them out of pure kindness, she had no obligation, and yet she treated them better than they had been treated in their own homes. Some had their clients. She knew that. And she worried. That was at first. Then she learned to live with it.

Doña Adelina's house had a very large living room, with two floors, plus a basement and attic. The exterior was somewhat in need of painting, but inside it was in good condition. There was a pleasant patio in the back, with a stand of lilies and a fountain that was always turned off, because she didn't see the sense in having a stream of water always gurgling. The patio was surrounded by leafy trees—mango, avocado, orange—and had brick planters and pots filled with ferns. At first she thought she would add rooms to the house to better accommodate her charges. But the boys told her that it was better just to buy cots and arrange them in the existing rooms. That worried her. Putting two or three in the same room, as precocious as some of these boys were, could invite dangerous circumstances. "Doña Adelina, there's no other way. Where are we going to get the money to pay for the work?" That's what Marcelino had said, the smartest of the boys and the one who had been in the house the longest. So, still worried, she agreed to the cots.

At first she spent entire nights awake, with her ears open in case some wise boy went after one of the younger ones. But she soon realized that no one there was going to abuse anyone else. What had accidentally formed in her aunts' house was a family—a little strange, yes, but a family nevertheless. It had its older brothers, its rites of initiation, its cliques, and its share of fights. She began to sleep peacefully, even when sometimes she thought she heard, from the crack under the doors, a light sigh and a creaking of springs that didn't seem like the usual sounds of brothers sleeping.

When Marcelino grew older, he went to study carpentry and he built Doña Adelina a terrace of wood and tiles where her charges could sit and talk in the afternoon. He added two rooms to the right of the terrace. He also restored the balustrade on the interior staircase and the balcony on the second floor. Good boy, that Marcelino. He had already made a family and he took them to Doña Adelina so his children could call her *abuela*.

97

There were months when Doña Adelina wasn't able to feed so many mouths. Her meager savings weren't enough. "Here we all eat or no one eats," she said. So they called a meeting. All the boys would gather on the terrace while Doña Adelina explained the situation to them. Among them they organized an emergency plan. She would help cover the household expenses by taking in laundry with the help of the younger boys. The boys doubled their efforts to find "errands" to run, or if they had jobs, would ask for advances. Doña Adelina alerted her former charges and they always pitched in a little something. But as time went on and her savings dwindled, Doña Adelina had to look at the long-term situation. She had to allow the boys to commit little thefts, and the ones who worked the streets began to bring occasional clients to the house. Doña Adelina never felt comfortable with that, but the *señores,* once they had finished their business, left a few dollars on the table in the entry hall, which were sorely needed in the house. And she wasn't about to complain. "If they're going to do it in the street anyway, it's better for them to do it here," she thought to ease her mind. Some of her charges who turned tricks liked the idea, because going out in the streets made them feel vulnerable. They were easy targets for hoodlums, abusers, police officers, and others. Remaining at home protected them from all the traps set out to catch them. Others preferred to keep going out in the streets, feeling it would be shameful for their friends to see them turning tricks. Doña Adelina consoled herself by thinking that the visits only occurred on special occasions. Once they were back on an even keel again, the *señores'* visits would cease. But the visits never diminished. It wasn't so much that the house filled up with clients, rather one or another spent an afternoon there each month.

Little by little the house's fame grew, but in the most peculiar way. It was never just any old house of assignations. It sat very discreetly on a residential street with other homes occupied by established local families, on the way out of the city, near the river. There had never been quarrels, or debris from parties littering the grounds. The neighbors did notice from time to time that some older gentleman, a foreigner, had spent several hours closed up in Doña Adelina's house, doing God knows what. But these visits did nothing to interrupt the normal course of events in the neighborhood.

Still, it had to end with Leocadio. She wasn't going to bring in one more little devil. But the truth was that little angel had touched her heart. He was so soft and fragile. Soft downy hairs covered his perfect oval-shaped face. He was dark, with that deep ruddy tint of polished wood. His eyes were heavy-lidded like Mulatto's, but greener, and his hair was a mass of tight yellow curls, which stayed plastered to his head when he combed it with brillantine. His drowsy but alert gaze, his thin, firm little body, his high rear—a truly beautiful boy who fascinated everyone who looked at him, his mother was right. Adelina, who had had her wild days, knew something about passion; it can't be explained. Creatures like that child Leocadio exist, who without trying to do so stir up people's blood and emotions. "Men are very stupid. They just react to what's in front of them." That was what Doña Adelina had learned from her experiences, and putting that creature in front of men was a provocation in itself. So she agreed to take charge from his mother, who bathed Leocadio in kisses as she bade him farewell, then couldn't seem to find her way back out of the house.

Leocadio sat there on the stairs, crying. Soon two or three of the other boys who had been with Doña Adelina came down and little by little began to console him. Doña Adelina's heart broke to see the boy so downcast. He was a jewel of a child and it was a cruel injustice for him to be surrounded by so much tribulation.

Doña Adelina was determined to drive away Leocadio's sadness. So she began to think about how to bring a little joy to her new charge's life, how to help him swallow the bitter pill of spending his first night among strangers. Suddenly an idea came to her. Smiling, she went to a corner of the kitchen, put her hand in a can and pulled out a little money put aside for daily expenses. Then she put on some perfume, quickly brushed her hair and went out to buy three fresh chickens from the butcher on the corner. She was going to make a welcome dinner for her little *tigerito* that would leave him licking his fingers. Maybe that would help alleviate the bitterness pressing against his chest.

22

"S elena, I've been looking for you," said Hugo as he approached. "I have bad news. The pianist from the Hotel Talanquera can't come practice with you until Friday at two."

"But that's the day of my show," she replied.

"Well, we'll have to postpone it until Saturday, or perhaps until Sunday, won't we?"

"I don't want to cause any inconvenience, if you prefer we'll cancel the show and leave it at that. You can just pay what you owe me and tell me how to get back to the hotel safe and sound."

"It's no inconvenience at all; besides, it's too late to cancel the show. Don't make me beg you, Selena."

"The bill is adding up. . . ."

"Don't you worry about that one bit. About that or any expenses you might have while you're working for me."

"That is very generous of you."

"I can be even more generous, if you'll let me."

"Oh, really?" Sirena holds the magnate's glance for an instant, flirting. She wets her lips, blinking slowly. Then her voice reverts to that of the consummate artist. "For now, I'll practice a little more, it's just a matter of putting together the list of songs for when the pianist arrives. I'll see how I can entertain myself in the meantime."

"If you'd like, I could take you for a drive around the town later."

"*Muchas gracias*, that's very kind of you."

"And tonight, we're preparing dinner for you here in the house. You still haven't met my wife."

"Señor Graubel, don't worry about me. You don't have to entertain me. It would be better if I just ate alone in my room. Besides, all these formalities make me a little uncomfortable. You do understand?"

"How could that be, Sirena? You are my guest. No one here is going to disrespect you, especially my wife. Besides, this way we can take advantage of the opportunity to talk a little about your show. Solange is dying of curiosity."

"Talking about a show beforehand brings bad luck."

"Well then, your presence will be sufficient. Please come, Sirena. I don't want word to get around that Hugo Graubel is a bad host."

"All right. You convinced me."

"*Perfecto*. Dinner will be served at eight."

Selena smiled and lowered her gaze to her work. She was polishing her nails on a chaise lounge beside the pool. Now she was really showing off her unusual boy-girl ambiguity, lying there in shorts, a hand-painted T-shirt (Santo Domingo, a palm tree, a beach, a hammock), her hair in a ponytail, polish on her nails, concentrating on her task. She tried to act indifferent, but at the same time she was watching her host out of the corner of her eye. She suspected what was about to happen. This rich man who had hired her wanted conversation, confessions of her sordid life, mysterious encounters to stimulate the game of seduction. But she wasn't up to those games right now. She had to practice, make sure her performance would be flawless, perfect. She would take care of Graubel, in her own time.

But not today. Today she had to polish her nails, put on a mud mask, pluck her eyebrows, and shave her face. She had to walk around the living room until she knew every corner by heart, examine how the lights fell on the black grand piano, convince the help to order another dozen calla lilies for the night of her debut. Today she had to think about all the old songs her *abuela* had taught her and choose several, the most appropriate for the occasion. She had to go over her repertoire, so that her audience would suddenly think they were in a luxury club, the Tropicana, hearing this Creole bolero singer croon songs of unrequited love, so they wouldn't be able to believe what was before their eyes. She had to create the most perfect de-

102

ception. There was no time today for seducing a rich, perverted man. Graubel would fall, maybe the very day of the show.

Graubel arose from the chair where he had sat to speak with Sirena, and walked slowly toward the house. He thought that she avoided looking at him out of shyness. He could have sworn that for an instant he saw a hint of shame on her face. And then immediately afterward, he saw how Selena's face was transformed, how it changed back into that of a gold-digging *muchachito* trying to be beautiful and elusive in the eyes of his host. And that was how he bewitched Hugo Graubel.

Walking thoughtfully toward his house, Hugo recalled things he thought he had forgotten. Like when he was a boy, walking through his father's sugarcane plantations in San Pedro de Macorís. He remembered the day he escaped from the house and the *finca* . . . so boring. Soon he would go abroad to study. He had just turned sixteen. He was afraid of women, he was afraid of men, he was afraid of everyone, of the staring *cocolos* who glared at him as he passed with all the hate that any person could harbor. He was afraid of the streets in his town, which he hardly knew. He didn't know the streets of San Pedro de Macorís, or even those of the capital. He had gone out thousands of times, to gatherings, birthday parties, museums . . . *nada*. He had spent his whole life behind glass—the rearview mirror of his father's cars, the windows of his house—as if those surfaces were screens upon which scenes from an old movie were being projected. The day he escaped he wanted to see things the way they really were, before he went away. Smell them for real, soil his shoes with their dust and dampen them in puddles. He remembered wandering through that *pueblo* of seven streets, along a path that led to a fly-infested market, where people buzzed about buying pieces of goat meat, cabbages, tomatoes and grains, straw brooms, and onions. He turned to look at the village women carrying water in aluminum containers, cane cutters walking with their machetes under their arms, in pursuit of some broth and a drink of rum. The people looked at him without seeing him, or pretending that they didn't see him, the son of Don Marcial Graubel, that feeble white boy who looked like a girl. There were some who couldn't control themselves and looked at him with a mixture of desire and hate, the way a lot of people looked at him, some of his uncles, teachers, friends of his parents. He was already accustomed to that. It was the same in school. Several years before, a group of older boys had convinced him to go to the bathroom with them and to play with himself while they whispered in his ear the name of some desirable young female classmate. He never felt anything, hands rubbing, words that weren't for him. He had allowed himself to be taken to the bathroom, as he had allowed himself to be taken to the movie theater in his father's car. The others were the chauffeur; he, the passenger.

That day, his father found out that he had escaped out into the streets without permission. "What in the world were you doing wandering the streets in town, you little devil? Who do you think you are, some little street urchin? Where were you going in those streets? huh, where?" Don Marcial had shouted, as soon as he walked in the door. *Maldito pueblo chiquito,* damn tiny village, Graubel remembered thinking that day, as he trembled in anticipation of his punishment. His father didn't punish him; rather, he abruptly walked away and spent the remainder of the afternoon locked in his office. It was already night when he came out. Hugo was in his room, almost asleep. He heard his father's steps in the corridor, heard how his father's strong hand opened the door and how his deep voice unemotionally ordered him, "*Vístete,* we're going out." Then he remembered hearing his father walk quickly to the garage and start the engine of the Jeep in which he made his rounds of the cane fields when he went out to watch the workers during harvest. "He's going to kill me," Hugo thought that night as he got dressed, "he's going to kill me and use my body as fertilizer."

Don Marcial drove in silence that night. And Hugo didn't dare ask where they were going. He limited himself to looking out the window, and to waiting for some sign of action from his father. He saw that they were driving through the streets of their *pueblo* and then they were moving out of its center toward the outskirts, to a green wooden shack with a tin roof. Don Marcial parked in front of the shack and honked the horn. A *mulata* with honey-colored eyes came out. His father got out of the Jeep and said something to her that Hugo couldn't hear. Then he held her by the arm and led her to his son and ordered, "*Mijo*, this is Eulalia. Go with her, I will wait for you here." Hugo saw Eulalia smile shyly, then take his arm. And he let himself be taken (as always) into the house.

Inside, the house didn't look as poor as outside. It was tidy, painted white. There was a good set of pine furniture, straw chairs, two shelves filled with ceramic figurines, and a television blaring a Venezuelan *telenovela*. On the walls were two pictures—one was the Holy Virgin and the other was the Sacred Heart of Jesus—and a current calendar.

Eulalia led him by the hand down the hallway of the little house to a back room that reeked of insecticide. In the room, she sat him on a four-poster bed and, without bothering to turn off the lights, she started to undress. Hugo had never imagined that this was why his father had brought him here. He didn't know what to do, so he didn't do anything. He silently watched as the *mulata* finished taking off her clothing, as she approached him, as she lowered the zipper of his trousers. Hugo allowed her to lick him, as if he weren't involved in the matter. His body responded, but he wasn't there. He was watching what the *mulata* did to him from outside himself. Observing everything through glass, through a haze, like in a movie. There was a movie in which a *mulata* named Eulalia let him see her mound, thick with curly hairs the same dark honey color as her eyes. She opened her inviting vulva. She put her fingers in her mouth and wet them with saliva, then moistened herself between the legs. Everything happened in a haze and he felt he had been sent there as punishment, his flesh throbbing, his hands sweating, but inside, empty and slow like a sandpiper flying just above the water. She pushed him back, climbed on top of him, with her expert hand guided him into her opening, and began the ritual of riding him. It lasted almost half an hour. Wet with sweat, he felt a sudden stirring in his chest and a blast of something liquid hitting his belly. Returning to his body, intrigued, he closed his eyes and took a deep look within, he was now so far from everyone else, from himself, and the terror was so great that he choked in an ocean of fear. Then he let out a desperate howl. His father, who was waiting for him outside, thought the howl was a sign that the pupil had found the path to becoming a man. But it was a howl of fear, the strongest emotion he had ever felt in his life, the one that was closest to him, to his own skin, to his will. Shaken, he watched a thick liquid begin to stream from between the *mulata*'s thighs, running along his stomach, spreading over the sweating hollows of her still-galloping pelvis. That signaled the end of the ritual. It signaled the beginning of something else. Efficient, the mulata climbed off the boy from the hacienda, went to look for something with which to clean up the mess, and along the way told the *señor* that it was over, that the *niño* had had his first *mulata*. "A stud, Don Marcial, it seems like he already knows his business," he heard her lie. Through the room's improvised curtains, he watched his father give the woman more money than was owed and heard him laugh with her. He even remembers hearing her murmur on her way back down the hallway, "The filthy things one has to do to survive."

Hugo entered the house, went up to the second-floor balcony, and watched Sirena walk away from the pool, her nails freshly painted with Sweet Coral 107. He remembered that after Don Marcial took him from the *mulata*'s house, Hugo asked him to take him drinking. Don Marcial bought a bottle of rum in another hovel in San Pedro. The novice drank the whole bottle as a purgative. He wanted to feel once again the sensation of his body distending, doubling. He wanted to go back to seeing things from behind a screen, through a haze, then go through the painful pleasure of quickly returning to his body, of feeling his flesh and his consciousness unite, even if only for the briefest moment of terror.

But he never was able to achieve that state. Not drunk, not sleeping with seven thousand *mulatas*, not in the Turkish baths, bridges, and alleys of foreign countries. Nothing. He was never able to return to the terror of his body. That sixteen-year-old boy was somewhere, on some corner, waiting to be found again, to meet Hugo Graubel, after the night when he became a sugarcane magnate, a businessman, the principal stockholder in pharmaceutical companies and hotels, a health-care professional. But the boy and his pure terror were still his life and he was going to find them somewhere in this world, in some body, they had to be somewhere.

Hugo Graubel followed Selena with his gaze, as if his eyes were those of a robot. He followed her every step, watched her climb the stairs to the patio. He watched her enter the interior rooms. Hugo moved to the windows of the balcony that overlooked the living room. From there he could easily see the entry hall with its marble staircase. He entertained himself for a while watching Sirena plan her entrances and exits, her diva's poses, her turns, and her stroll to the grand piano. He took a cigarette from his pocket, lighted it, moved over to a wicker chair, and sat down. As if in a movie theater, he watched the delicate, wicked boy-woman gracefully setting the stage for her intricate love song.

23

could charge up to fifty in my better days. Four men a night, and that was two hundred pesos in my pocket, tax free." Sirena remembered Balushka's boast "The police used to try to scare us; most of the time they ran us off, beat us up 'to teach us to be men,' or took us to jail. Just to screw with us, because the charges were usually dropped. The idea was to mess up our night. Margot, the tall redhead who used to have a show at the old Cotorrito, said that one night a gorgeous black officer picked her up, just as she was leaving work at the Danube. Funny how life is sometimes. Margot wasn't even working the street full-time, because she was bartending and was getting some dance routines together for a modest little show. Anyway, the stage at the Danube is too small even for midgets and the crowd is so high that I really understand why Margot didn't go to the trouble of coming up with a fabulous production. She was calmly going to see if she could get her last trick of the night when these two officers appeared in their police car, young, probably just out of the Police Academy or wherever it is they graduate from. And they arrested her.

"'Excuse me, Officers, but what's the charge? Walking to the corner?'

"'You know very well why we detained you,' one of the officers answered, the black one who looked like a prince. He said it with such masculine poise that Margot just stood there with her mouth open and a delicious chill running through her entire body. She decided to stay calm—after all, trying to reason with a police officer is like talking to a wall. And she already had something to bribe them with, so there was nothing to worry about. Besides, that little chill running up her spine was so divine.

"The two officers got out of the patrol car and put Margot inside. They were silent as they drove, which was strange. They didn't exactly look like teachers or moral vigilantes. They drove for a long time. Margot was starting to get nervous. The officers weren't heading toward the police station, but were driving around in circles through the city's streets. She thought they were going to beat her senseless, then dump her somewhere. Suddenly, one of the officers got out in front of an apartment building. The other one, the gorgeous black one who had left her woozy with his voice, turned and said to Margot, 'If you give me a freebie, I'll let you go and won't say a word to anyone.'

"That's how the romance between Margot and the policeman began. I was a witness myself one Thursday, when he came by the Danube looking for her. That was the arrangement. Every other Thursday he would go looking for her in an unmarked car, alone. He took her to the highway by the docks. Margot told me how, in the throes of love, the smell of dead fish made them drunk and breathless as they groped each other in the car with the windows closed. Then the policeman would make her get out and he would enter her passionately, but not violently, her back always to him, always with her face against the hood, in complete silence. Margot imagined that he was whispering in her ear that he adored her, that he would move into a room with her, he would leave the police force to live in bliss with her.

"For that one, Margot would have left the street, the business, she would have opened a hair and makeup salon. She was an expert with bases and shadows, a true artist, we all knew that. She could make the most worn-out face look smooth, youthful, full of innocence, as if never exposed to the crueler side of life. She drew out eyes sunken by alcohol and smack, restructured the most sinuous curves on lips destroyed by bites and cigarette burns. She didn't 'do makeup,' she transformed faces, she was *una verdadera artista.* . . .

"The romance with the policeman lasted almost a year. Then that gorgeous black man disappeared, and was never heard from again. To make matters worse, Margot couldn't do anything about it. It had never occurred to her to ask his name.

"*Ay mija,* sometimes the nights in these bars last an eternity. You have to entertain yourself telling stories. What else are you going to do? Go home and heat up dinner for your husband? Make sure the kids do their homework?

"*Oye,* the way some things turn out. I don't know why, but for us love just doesn't seem to work. You kill yourself trying to convince the world that you deserve at least a tiny bit of love. You take care of your mother, send money to your brothers in jail, maintain your husband, and for what? And I tell you one thing: it doesn't matter how many Bibles they read and how many Our Fathers they say, those bastards won't reach even the second step in heaven. They pray all the time and accept our care and gifts, only to scream in our faces that we make them sick. . . . Well, for all I care they can all go straight to hell. Beginning with my mother, who doesn't even deserve to be mentioned.

"Margot doesn't work the corner anymore. It seems like that last bit of trouble took away the spark for her. And without the spark, you can't survive on the street. They tell me she went to Philadelphia, to live with a relative, and that she's out of the gay scene. She works in a beauty shop there. That's what they tell me.

"Girlfriend, pray that you never fall in love. That's the advice of Balushka Bolshoi, this veteran of life. And I'm not saying that because I'm drunk, I'm saying it because it's true. Love is bad in this life. It's bad for anyone, but for a *loca,* it's death."

24

Señor Contreras, honestly, I have spent several days waiting for an answer. Patience is not one of my most prominent virtues. I am a woman of action. And you have me trapped here, walking all over this city, which I now know like the back of my hand. It would be better if you would just tell me now whether or not you want the show; you'd be losing a tremendous opportunity, but you have that right. Speak frankly with me, and I will happily go to some other businessmen with my offer. I won't waste your time, and I hope you won't waste mine."

Contreras begs Miss Martha's forgiveness: it's not in his control, *que sí*, he was very impressed with her artist's performance, but just give him another opportunity to arrange everything he has to arrange before signing the contract. It's only a matter of a couple of days. They would cover all of her hotel expenses.

Wait a couple more days? Not a chance, Señor Contreras, she's going to go crazy. She didn't come here for a vacation, though she certainly deserves one after working as hard as she has in this life. But that's beside the point, she's not here for that and she can't keep wasting time stuck here in the city.

Contreras says don't worry, let him help make her feel more comfortable while she's waiting. If she would let him make a few phone calls, to other people who would surely help Martha later, to talk about future contracts. She wasn't going to spend the day sitting there watching cable television. He would arrange for a dinner with some other hotel owners.

The suggestion of dinner with other hotel owners wasn't bad. But Selena hasn't appeared, not even to pick up more clothes. And she left that sorry note, as if it would fix this mess she's gotten herself into. *"Bendición,* Mami: I got a fabulous offer to do a private show at the residence of the gentleman Contreras introduced us to! We are going to be rich!!!" Just wait for the talking-to she'll give that child when she appears. She better not come here making up stories. Martha wasn't born yesterday and she has no time for this foolishness. *Ya verá,* the little ingrate, she'll see. But now, what is she going to do? Christ Almighty! How is she going to get out of this trap? She'll have to make something up and keep pressuring Contreras. She'll lie to cover the absence of her star. Give them copies of a demo tape of Sirena singing, a promotional photo, and make appointments with them individually to stall for time. Maybe she can pit them against one another to up the offers for the show. Businesswoman's blood pumping.

But everything would fall apart if her lost *ahijada* didn't appear. Everything, everything everything everything. Her plans for the whole year, the opportunity to expand her business, to finally capitalize on all her sacrifices. That little devil had better appear. Where could she be, now when she's needed most?

And Contreras made a fuss in his office: "Get Mr. Graubel on the telephone." Why does he get himself involved in such trouble? He has enough problems at work. That's what he gets for going around playing pimp. But this is the last time. If Graubel doesn't get him out of this mess, he'll just disentangle himself from the whole situation. Maybe he'll even give a little information to that thing drinking free Champagne up in her suite so she can go find her lost treasure; the boss better not dump his shit on him. He still has an ace up his sleeve. Finally they connect him. . . . "Señor Graubel, Martha is getting anxious and I can't keep giving her excuses. Isn't today Sirena's show? When do you plan to return her? Please, see what you can arrange, *patrón,* because I've run out of ideas."

And Hugo replies, "Call Ingeniero Peláez Aybar, and Vargas, the man from the Quinto Centenario. And call Montes de Oca and Vivaldi, the owner of La Strada. Tell them to make plans for a dinner with Miss Martha on Sunday evening. Let them entertain her a little. I'll take care of the rest. *No te preocupes,* Contreras, don't worry." And Contreras: "No, I'm not worried, but you must understand that this takes time away from my job." "Which I got you," says Graubel, a little angrily, and Contreras swallows. "And for which I am very grateful, but I'm going to have problems if I use my time to work as a procurer." "You don't know what a favor you're doing me, Contreras." And Contreras: "No, I really don't know, but I hope it's worth all this trouble, because really . . ." "*Sí, que lo vale,* Contreras, it's worth it."

Contreras calls Martha back. "So we're set for Sunday at five-thirty," she responds, noting the detail in her little book. "Just to make sure I understand correctly: you said they were four hotel owners?" "No, really there are three who work in the hotel business. One is Ingeniero Peláez, who is a good friend and a distinguished businessman." "*Ah, sí,* yes, how wonderful," lies Martha, while in her head she can't stop asking herself whereisSelena, damnthatIlethergotothatnastybeachallbyherselfdamnathousandtimes, "you don't say." Well then, Doña Martha—Oh, don't use the "doña," please, just call me Martha—then, Martha, the company car will pick you up at the hour we agreed upon. They would have a nice dinner and have a few drinks to make their conversation more agreeable. It's settled then, ciao, until Sunday.

And Miss Martha can't stop asking herself, "Where is that ungrateful girl, where is she, where where where where?"

25

*H*ugo hung up. In his chair on the balcony he could feel clearly that his life was going to change at eleven o'clock sharp on Saturday night. Selena would come bouncing, wet, on the waves of her voice to satisfy Hugo's desires, which not even marriage to the daughter of the shipping magnate could satisfy, despite her black hair and milky-white skin like the snowcapped Alps her peasant mother emigrated from to an unknown, verdant island in the Caribbean, the smell of milk still between her legs.

Solange's thighs smelled like milk too, her vulva like milk, a little *lechita* that he delighted in would form between Solange's legs. When they were first married she let him lick her, and she'd low softly; she was barely fifteen, still a sighing teenager. So Solange sighed and let her husband lick her. Her *lechita* distracted him from afternoons on the beach, from the hired hustlers, from his desire for the preadolescent sons of his industry colleagues.

One day, Hugo found Solange sighing more than usual. When he pressed her repeatedly, she confessed to her husband that she felt shamed by so much licking. She asked him why he didn't mount her, which was a man's duty to his wife. Crying, she complained that after a year and a half of marriage she was still technically a virgin, though fingers had entered her. It was as if her husband's tongue had become the natural appendage in her milky vulva. Hugo had come on her stomach so many times, it was a miracle that, through her flooded navel, she hadn't already conceived.

To avoid greater problems, and confident that he was on the verge of curing himself of what was wrong with him, Hugo Graubel let Solange have her way. That night his wife opened beneath him like a sacred mountain soursop and, resigned, Hugo proceeded to mount her. The surprise ended there and the trips to the beach started all over again.

Two, three children in six, seven years. Solange was twenty-three and already old beside Hugo Graubel. The heir had resigned himself to his perversions—until he saw Selena. And now he had her in front of him, down there in his living room, while he followed her with his eyes from the second-floor balcony. He followed her with his eyes and worked the telephone to gain time for his seduction, for getting her into his life, to see if she was the one who could finally satisfy the hunger that gnawed away at him. That damn loneliness. He had just spoken with Contreras. Made arrangements to throw Sirena's *mentora* off track, while he watched his guest rehearse. Now he had to convince Solange to agree to have dinner with the guest. That was going to be a huge battle. Solange had better get used to it. She had better start realizing that she wasn't going to be able to do anything to prevent what was coming.

Downstairs, in the living room, Selena practiced. She climbed the stairs once more to see how she would descend them the day of the show, dressed as a graceful and sensual *bolerista*. At the top of the staircase she closed her eyes. On her skin, she could feel the silence of the room trickling over her. With her eyes still closed, she opened her mouth, closed it again, taking in mouthfuls of dense air, air direct to her lungs and her stomach, silent air that swelled her completely. She was finally ready, falling into a trance. When she opened her eyes she was already someone else. Without releasing a particle of air she opened her mouth as much as she could, relaxing the muscles of her face, her jaw, in preparation for her voice. This time she didn't want to remember anything, she didn't want to imprint any emotion on her singing. This time, just a rehearsal, what she wanted was to measure the range of the sound that inhabited her. She started to descend the stairs and to release that abstract sound she had inside. She glided all the way down the staircase, slowly, carefully to the last step, while she released an uninterrupted stream of song. She knew that from above, on the balcony, Hugo was watching her. Hugo was melting in sighs for her, Hugo melted with desire on each step as she descended barefoot. At the bottom of the staircase, she held the last note for a long time; she let herself be emptied by the sound until she grew dizzy. When she had no more to give, she smiled with her mouth open, teeth glistening, and laughed, dizzy and mischievous. She looked up, toward the terrace. There was Hugo frozen in a gesture, with a cigarette in his hand, no particle of his body revealing any movement, like a statue. Selena lowered her eyes. She grabbed her stomach and bent double, throwing herself coquettishly on the rug of the central hallway, dying of laughter.

26

*B*ut, why did you move, *abuela*, if you liked it so much? asked Sirenito. What are you talking about, *muchacho*? About Campo Alegre—why did you move away from there? *Ay, mijito,* the turns life takes. Hand me that mop. No, not that one, the one with the green strings, *ese mismito.* Tell me, *abuela,* don't be so mysterious. Why are you asking me things when we've got so much left to do? Let's go put these clothes in the washing machine. And you'll finish telling me the story there, right, *abuela*? *Si, nene,* I'll finish telling you when we get there. So why did you move? *Mijo,* the neighborhood changed. Above the butcher shop they opened a house of ill repute and the girls spent all afternoon with their breasts uncovered, taking the fresh air on the balconies and showing off their attributes to anyone who passed by. To create a little competition for that business, some man started building little wooden rooms and he rented them to the girls working *en plena calle* so they'd have a place to take their clients. And the barrio kept changing. They opened about seven bars on Calle Duffaut. Even Diplo had a girlfriend there. Who was Diplo? A very famous television artist from my childhood. He painted his face with shoe polish and did the funniest little bits of comedy. Why did he paint his face, *abuela*? How should I know, maybe because the people at the television station couldn't find a real *artista negro* to give the role to. That's pretty strange. Do you think so, *nene*? Of course, *abuela,* there're plenty of *artistas negros* in this country, musicians, dancers. Now that I think about it, I guess you're right. Maybe they painted Diplo because they didn't want to hire a black actor. The things you notice, child.

And then what happened, *abuela*? You couldn't go down to the plaza in peace, without being mistaken for one of those women. But still, I loved living in Campo Alegre. Especially when some ship came into the port at San Juan and they gave the sailors leave. They all came to visit the bars on Calle Duffaut, and to dance with their lady friends. The barrio filled up with sailors. Dressed in white, they looked like doves in the middle of the street, because the sailors never walked on the sidewalks, God knows why not. If you could have seen them, all dressed up in white, like a bunch of gentlemen. You could spot them right away because of their hats—you know, the ones without a brim, they're like hard berets with colored ribbons on the strap in front. On the right side of the ribbon were the insignias of their boats—*San Sebastián, El Cano, Maradona, SS Seabourne.* . . . As soon as we saw those insignias, they transported us to other lands. As if those hats were the ships themselves. I was so young, and I must say those *marinos* really made an impression on me. Whenever they came into the barrio, I looked for any excuse to go out in the streets, to walk around the plaza. Then I would imagine myself as a movie star, Myrna Loy or Greta Garbo, waiting on a bench for my lost lover to return in his sailor's uniform to pledge his eternal love. I remember that when they came up from the port, the sun was shining so brightly off their shoulders that you could hardly see their faces. You had to lower your eyelids, look at them indirectly, through your eyelashes. I guess that's why sometimes the sailors looked like they were shrouded in a haze, a radiance like the ones that surround virgins when they come down from heaven to work miracles among the mortals. . . . They came from all over the world—Dutch, Panameños, Spaniards, French, Americans. When the sailors arrived, Campo Alegre dressed up for a fiesta.

But Papá spoiled it. He was fed up with them confusing his daughters with loose women. According to him, those sailors thought they were better than everybody else. He cursed and muttered about them, but it was all just talk, until he caught Finín in a bar on the corner of our street, flirting with a Polish sailor. Papá was rabid. He went back to the house to look for his machete and for Geño, my older brother. Papá knew his son loved a fight so he wouldn't have to ask him twice. They grabbed the machete and went back out into the street. While my brother took care of the sailor, Papá grabbed Finín by the hair and pushed her outside. He dragged her from the corner to the house, in the middle of the street, beating her the whole way. All of Campo Alegre found out about it. To me, it seemed that Geño and Papá Marcelo went a little overboard, because after the beating Finín rebelled and turned into *una puta de verdad*.

Mamá almost died of shame. After that, Papá told us that he was going back to Caimito. He was going to buy two acres of land with some assistance the government was offering, and he would sleep under a cardboard box if he had to, but he was leaving the neighborhood. He took Mamá and the youngest boys, Renato and Ramón, who still live out in the country. But Geño, Crucita, Angela, Finín, and I stayed. The city got inside us and there was no way to get it out of our veins.

Are you hungry, *nene*? What, *abuela*? I said, Are you hungry? *Claro que sí*, I could eat a horse. Come on then, let's go to the kitchen to see if we can find something in the refrigerator. Although these people have the strangest tastes in food . . . Then we'll sit and rest awhile, my bones are already aching. *Mi santo, si te digo*, getting old is the worst thing in the world.

I didn't know you had more family, *abuela*. *Si mijo*, there's a whole bunch of us. What happened was that I grew up with the older ones. Every other weekend or so, Angelita, Cruz, Geño, and I visited the old folks. But after they died, we didn't go back anymore. Renato and Ramón kept the *finca*. I only know my nieces and nephews from photographs. But don't you worry, one of these days I'll take you to meet all of them.

Virgen pura, what a mess. We're going to have to scrub this pile of dishes to see if we can find somewhere to eat. *Ave María, abuela*, these people are pigs. Hush, child, if the *señores* come home and hear you, we'll be in a real pickle. *Abuela*, why don't we have family in Santurce? *Pues, mijito, la vida* . . . After Papá Marcelo went back to the country, Angelita got together with a big, caramel-colored dock-worker with kinky hair and sleepy eyes. She started having kids right and left. How that girl loved to give birth! The husband's name was Esteban. A decent fellow. He accepted her other children and raised them like his own. I lived with them for a while, when they lived in Villa Palmeras. Then they went to New York.

Geño started working in construction and bought a house in the Colectora. He had the patio fixed up real pretty. He planted breadfruit trees and soursops. My brother even raised chickens on that patio. He lived there with a girl he brought from Caimito once when he went to visit the old folks. That girl stayed inside the house all day long, like she was scared or something. She didn't speak to anyone, not even me. Geño said it was better that way, because the women in San Juan are very nosy and they'll share confidences with anybody. *Mira, nene,* look, there's ham, cheese, bread, and salad. We'll make some sandwiches and sit in the living room to watch television. Then we'll finish cleaning.

What happened to Finín and Crucita, *abuela? Pues, mijo,* the Lord has them in his glory. No, *abuela,* I mean did they have children? He didn't let those two give birth. After the family went to live in the country, they went off to live together. Finín convinced Crucita to become her business partner. They did pretty well. It didn't take them long to make enough money to rent a little storefront and open a bar. It was called El Pocito Dulce, the Sweet Well. I escaped there every chance I got. At that time I was living with Geño and his wife. At the Pocito Dulce was where I fell in love with your grandfather, a Galician who worked in the merchant marine. He was the one who disgraced me.

Crucita was serious, but you could see the sweetness in her eyes. She turned out to be like Mamá. She took care of all the hard work of the bar: the shopping, the bookkeeping, maintaining respect from the clientele. Meanwhile, Finín made the place pleasant with her presence.

I loved Crucita more than anyone. Finín inherited Papá's temperament and she was very different from Crucita. She loved commotion and parties. Ever since she'd gone to live on her own she was the most sophisticated, with *polvos* Maja in her room and gold earrings and muslin robes to cover her nightgown. She had picked up the bad habit of smoking, drank more rum than a dockworker and one day I found her in the plaza with her hair dyed red. That night she had to open the bar and I stayed to help her. When the clients started to arrive, one of them stared at her in surprise and teased her, "Hey Finín, what did you do to your hair? You look like a Polish woman." He said it with every intention of taunting her, choosing the description to remind her of the public beating she got for flirting with that Polish sailor. But you know what, Finín loved the nickname. After that she only answered if people called her La Polaca.

And Auntie Cruz? Crucita? *Ay mijo,* don't tell anyone, but I think she was kind of a *machorra.* Really, *abuela?* Yes. I even knew her girlfriend. God knows how they hooked up, but one afternoon I went into Crucita's room and found her all curled up with that other woman, gazing into her eyes. Crucita caressed her face as if she were going to kiss her. I quietly closed the door and tiptoed down the staircase. She never knew that I had seen her. And who was the other woman? The wife of a man who had a stall on the plaza, Don Nicolás. Efigenia, yes, that was her name. She was a gorgeous brunette, with wide hips and big eyes like almonds and curly hair that she gathered in a bun at the back of her head. I don't blame her for falling in love with Crucita, because her husband treated her like a Pentecostal tambourine. All he did was beat on her and make her life miserable. When she became a widow, Crucita bought her a house in Calle Las Delicias and moved in with her. They stayed together for a long time, until Crucita had that stroke, you remember. *Si, abuela,* you took me to see her in the hospital. Efigenia took care of my sister until God took her away. She behaved like a saint.

Crucita was so good. Her heart was so big, it wouldn't fit in her chest. She helped me a lot with your mother, when I started having trouble with her. I can't fault her a bit, even if she never wanted to marry a man, like the Bible says she should. But if that would have made her unhappy, like I was, then it was better for her to have a woman in her house. I don't care what people say. You don't have to be a certain way to be decent. Decency comes in all colors and all flavors. *Así mismito es.*

Virgen de las Mercedes, let me shut my mouth and get to work. And don't you get me talking anymore, it's almost four o'clock. The *señores* will be home any minute now and we're still mopping the floor. *A ver, nene.* Pour some more water in that corner, it's still a little soapy.

*D*on Homero, we're going to stop rehearsing now," said Sirena. "I can't go on. I'll get hoarse if we keep going like this."

"When should I come tomorrow?"

"Don't worry, I'll let you know in time. Let me speak with Grau-bel. You know he's the one in charge around here. I'm just a foot soldier. You'll be at the hotel tomorrow, won't you?"

"Yes, I start work at three."

"Don't worry then, I'll send you a message at the hotel. *Hasta mañana*, Don Homero."

"Hasta mañana."

Sirena had been singing for two hours. Two hours, plus the whole afternoon preparing for the show. The previous day she had painted her nails beside the swimming pool, choosing the appropriate polish for her wardrobe. She had gone into the house and studied every corner. She had prepared a subtle choreography for descending the staircase, standing beside the piano, and singing. And today, punctually, she had rehearsed with Don Homero, the pianist. They went over the accompaniment for a song that Sirena had added to the repertoire. But they'd had to stop. Her throat was hurting, her feet ached. And she was tense. The night of the show was approaching and she still didn't know which song to open with. She had to rest, but not in her room. She wanted to stay in the living room, let the space enter her body, so it wouldn't feel so foreign to her.

Truthfully, Sirena felt a little lost among such luxury. The marble staircase, the waxed floors, the mahogany tables, the mirrors—everything went too perfectly together. And she didn't want to be dissonant with anything, not with the guests, not with the décor. This task was more difficult than she had thought at first. And it seemed that the magnate's wife was going to make it even more difficult, if Sirena gave her the opportunity.

Sirena doesn't even want to remember dinner the night before. Her hair stood on end just thinking of it. Such a disagreeable woman, that Solange. After two rehearsed questions about the songs she was going to sing, the *señora* didn't speak a word to her for the rest of the evening. Every chance she got, she looked at Sirena as if she smelled like rotten garbage. Then she went on talking to Hugo about the menu for the party, the linens, the wine, the guest list. You could have cut the tension in that dining room with a knife. Sirena excused herself and went out onto the balcony for a moment. She felt as if she were choking, as if her throat were closing up. That woman made her feel so uncomfortable, so out of place. As soon as she returned to her room she gargled with warm salt water and put a little Vicks on her neck. She said a prayer to la Virgen de la Caridad del Cobre and lay down to sleep. When she awoke the next morning she remembered having dreamed about her *abuela*.

Sirena went to her room to look for some fashion magazines and returned to read them in the living room, sitting quietly on the sofa. Maybe that would calm her, clear her mind. She knew she was a true professional. They were not going to make her doubt her status now. Whether Señora Solange liked it or not, she was Sirena Selena, the brightest star in the troupe of *dragas* at the Blue Danube and for miles around.

Whether they wanted to admit it or not, these rich Dominicans were hiring a real professional. And she would prove it on the night of her debut.

28

*L*eocadio looks just like a little lion dreaming, mused Doña Adelina, with his yellow head on his front paws, a honey-colored mane, the face of a sleeping angel. He is a love, it's no wonder his mother didn't know what to do with him. And look where she left him. I don't even want to imagine the place where she lives, that *señora* watching over him as he dreamed, as I do now—anxious about protecting him, guarding him so they don't crush him alive. It is for the best. When he opens his eyes I feel my heart leap. Those almond eyes filled with clouds, a small storm in each one, rain approaching. A face that looks as if he's searching for something he lost and only you know where to find it. He could stir anyone up, with that fine down on his body that becomes translucent in the light. That's what he looks like, *un leoncito dormido*. Look how he sleeps. What could he be dreaming about?

The others aren't like him, not even Migueles, who most resembles him. And it's not that they're ugly, it's just that they don't have what Leocadio has. That which has no name. As hard as I rack my brain, I can't find the name for it. He doesn't talk to the others much, or play rough games like other growing boys. He sits quietly on the patio, looking at the flowers, making small mounds of earth where he plants seeds that always sprout. And even with dirty hands he looks like he's playing with gold. How will his face change when he becomes a man? How strange, Leocadio becoming a man, I can't imagine it.

What could he be dreaming about? His mother, probably. His mother, who came to see him last week. It wouldn't be a bad idea to take him to visit her there, at the *patrona*'s house. Poor little boy, as attached as he is to his mother. Yes, I should take him to visit her.

It's not so far away. It's been a while since I took some time out for a little trip. How badly I need it, with all the fuss the boys cause. Leocadio and I will take an afternoon and go there, just the two of us, him holding my hand and naming the streets he knows. It will be a nice afternoon, a little rest from all these problems and agitation.

But when, Virgen Santa? These boys don't give me a minute to breathe. They eat you alive. They break everything. There are no more bedsheets and I have to buy Chago a shirt, he can't wear his usual rags to that new job at the cabinetmaker's. A job—finally. That one has me worn out. The trouble that *tigerito* gets into. But he seems to be settling down a little now. Migueles helps as much as he can and earns good money at the hotel. To tell the truth, I don't really know what he does there. I'm going to ask him, but without sticking my nose in too much, he's not a baby anymore. That boy is so responsible. If it weren't for what he brings me and what Marcelo sends every now and then, we would have been in a pickle a long time ago. They cause their share of headaches, but, really, *mis nenes son una bendición.*

When was it that Migueles asked my permission to try to find Leocadio a job at the hotel? I hope they give him one, but something light. Better to take advantage of the time now that school's out, because I'm going to enroll him in the public school when classes start again. Leocadio has potential—he's so quiet and attentive, I'll bet he learns everything they teach him right off. Meanwhile, Migueles can take him to the hotel. He can't stay cooped up in the house all day. And Migueles better watch out for the boy or Leocadio will have to stay here, even if he's bored to death.

Gently, gently. Let me close the door so the street noise doesn't bother him. I'll use this chance to go down to the *señora* on the corner to pick up her laundry. The monthly supplies are almost gone. Flour, *arencas,* plantains. Holy Virgin Mary, where does the money go? I'll go down the street right now to pick up that laundry. With that and what they will pay Leo at the hotel when he gets a job, we'll be all right. God squeezes but he doesn't choke. . . .

29

C arajo, Hugo, how could you consider bringing a *travesti* into our house?" Solange screamed, slamming their bedroom door.

"You're as stubborn as a mule! Solange, I've already explained a thousand times that I hired Sirena to sing a few songs. What is the problem?"

"What do you mean, what is the problem? You brought a freak into the house. You brought it here without consulting me. And let me congratulate you on the dinner. A nice touch. It was beautiful. To force me to sit at the same table *con esa porquería.*"

"And who do you think you are, Solange? *Quién?*"

"*Mira,* Hugo, don't make me talk, because I can drag out a lot of dirty laundry, too."

"*Está bien.* Enough is enough. But remember that you are not the only one who decides who comes and who goes here. Besides, this is a dinner that I am having for my guests, in my house, with my money."

"And all the work I'm doing to help you? Doesn't that count for anything?"

"Don't try to make me feel guilty, it's not going to work."

"And what do I have to do to make you see reason?"

"Just don't get so worked up, don't be so melodramatic. I mean, really, what's the problem? I hired an artist to complement the dinner. After a few songs, the artist leaves. Then it's over."

"*Si, señor,* whatever you say. The subject is closed."

"The subject and the discussion are closed."

"No, Hugo, it's not over yet."

"Look, Solange, do whatever you want to. Argue with yourself if you want to. I'm going to the bar at the hotel."

"I hope you're struck by lightning."

"*Gracias, mi amor.*"

Bring a *travesti* into the house. That's how it always is. That's how he always is, with his plans and her behind him, following them. Speaking to her husband was a waste of time.

As always, Hugo did what he wanted. Well, he'd better not come to her for support. She remembered well the days of cropped hair and shapeless clothing. The days of lounging in bed with him stuck to her groin, licking her like a dog day and night. She remembered his childlike face between her legs and the shame that it caused her to see him come. The look of near agony on his face. Then he would fall into a sad silence; later, he would wrinkle his brow and start over again.

I will love you, Solange, as I've always wanted to love a woman. . . .

When she married Hugo, she wasn't yet a woman, but she decided to become one for this sad man who wanted to love her. That *señor* was going to pull her out of the asphyxiating decadence of her family once and for all. She had to repay the favor somehow.

"Astrid, make sure you put everything back in its place as soon as the rehearsal is over," she roared from the end of the corridor to one of her maids.

"*Sí, señora.*"

But playing the role had changed her. She had become a *señora.* And it fitted her marvelously, she couldn't deny it. Habit had converted her into Solange Graubel, wife of the millionaire businessman Hugo Graubel, mother of his two heirs, member of the board of directors of the National Library, patron of the arts. She really was *una dama.* She had already forgotten the image of the woman she had once wanted to be for Hugo, that strange thing with *leche* between her legs and a husband like a nursing dog—licking, licking; that ambiguousness of hair and girlish hips and flowering nipples. Yes, she had already forgotten how her flesh laughed and sighed as she silently joined the game of the millionaire, the man to whom her father married her off when she was fifteen. Now she was a different woman. Her waist was thicker, she had given birth, she had learned to speak, to walk, to differentiate between the salad fork and the meat fork, to host soirées for stockholders, to dress like a lady of style, so decent. She had left Hugo behind, lost in his illusions, incapable of getting rid of her. She made herself socially indispensable.

One two three turns she made as she closed the door to her suite, now far from everything and everyone. In her mansion, Solange was more of a *señora* than all her sisters and her mother combined, her mother who had hidden her away in a convent school, only to pull her out because there wasn't any more money. "Solange, your father drank everything, he gambled it all away." And the child Solange never learned which was the salad fork. She decided to grow up slowly, to keep up appearances with her mother, who began little by little to sell the furniture and took her youngest daughter out of the exclusive girls' school where she was studying. Solange was deathly afraid of her *alcóholico* father, who presented her so cordially to people to whom he owed money, to his business associates. Solange felt as if he were trying to sell her. She could still see those business associates looking at them disdainfully—at her, at her father. They turned their backs, they invented any excuse to leave or to remove her drunken father and her by the back door. She grew slowly because of the shame.

But now Solange has her mansion and she is staying put. Now she is a *señora* for real. Now she has a house and forks and calla lilies and heirs. She has property in her name, has invested in jewels that she doesn't wear. She has paid tuition for her boys in advance, five years. She has bought stock in American pharmaceutical companies and in resorts for Italians in the northeastern part of the country. She knows what she is doing. She knows very well where she is going. She is going to the top and no one can move her from there. You need status at the top, and Hugo gives her status.

"Give me your *leche*, Solange." Solange opens her legs without blinking.

"You don't have *leche* anymore, Solange."

"I have given it to my children."

Hugo gets up and goes, poor devil, destroyed. This woman is no longer the woman that he was looking for. Solange knows it, she knows very well what she is doing.

"Come, *hija*, I want to present you to a business associate."

"For the love of God, Papá."

"Obey, and don't be discourteous."

She does as she is told, endures the shame, and sees her father's humbled face as he tries to turn her into a delicacy for gentlemen.

"*Hija*, this is Hugo Graubel."

Hugo Graubel doesn't turn his back. He is younger than the others. He has the face of a frightened child. He smiles when he sees her, he looks at her shyly, and she is so young and growing slowly. He smiles again. He invites her to the movies. Her father insists that she go. She thinks that this is the one who's going to eat her like a little bird. But just the opposite. He treats her decorously, he takes her to the movies and then back home for one, two, six, nine weeks. He asks for the hand of the *niña* Solange. Solange does as she is told. She has a plan.

"Do you accept this man as your lawful husband, in sickness and in health, for richer for poorer, until death do you part?" Solange says yes, knowing what she is doing. Not a cent more than is necessary for her father to buy a debt-free death. A grateful kiss for this stranger whom she married, whom she distrusts. What is this man's game? When will he give me a disgusted look? It doesn't matter now, anyway. She only needs him now so she can be a *señora*, know about forks, have her place assured for all eternity.

*A*n arrangement of calla lilies near the double doors, and another by the piano. The glass goes on this table, in front of the mirror." Sirena was giving the servants final instructions. There was barely any time left. It was just a question of a few hours, and then she would finally be ready for her debut. She had every detail prepared, the order of songs, her wardrobe, the choreography, the pianist was rehearsed . . . everything was ready. Only a few last details needed to be taken care of in the living room, to give it a special touch. Then she could do her final rehearsal, testing the song that she was thinking of using to open her show.

Luckily, she hadn't run into the *señora de la casa* since dinner the previous evening. She had seen her from a distance, receiving packages, and arriving at the house carrying packages. Sirena hadn't even approached to say hello. She had decided to keep a low profile, to avoid any potential confrontation. And it seemed that the *señora* had made the same decision.

But her luck is about to run out. At the precise moment when Sirena is busiest with her preparations, Solange walks through the living room. She is coming from the beach, where she has been watching the children play. She sees how the living room of her home has been changed, how Sirena orders her servants to change the lighting in the room, asks for an arrangement of flowers to be set on a table, turns her décor completely upside-down. Solange interrupts Sirena.

"Calla lilies?" she asks, perturbed.

"Yes, calla lilies and half a glass of brandy, to warm up my voice and to create a little atmosphere," Sirena responds haughtily. No one is going to question her authority.

"Atmosphere of what?"

"Of glamour, of luxury."

"You think this house doesn't have a luxurious enough atmosphere as it is?"

"Señora Graubel, don't worry. I'll only be here for a short time, and before you know it I will put the glass of brandy and the calla lilies back where they were."

Solange turns abruptly on her heel and heads for her bedroom without a word. She approaches her bedroom door, turns the knob to go in, and waits for the maid to appear. There is no doubt. She is Señora Solange Graubel, celebrated lady of high society, who smiles, turns on her heel, and closes the door after giving her order. That door is hers, and the maids too, and the boys playing on the beach, and her whole destiny is hers and is in her hands. No one can take that from her.

She suffers—she is a *señora*, but she suffers, Sirena thinks. A rich woman, but she suffers. She has furs, breakfasts each morning with fresh fruit shakes and croissants, but (insert a tear) how she suffers, because of a problem she cannot solve. Selena thinks that she is perfect for the role of Solange. She drinks in Solange furiously ascending the stairs, drinks in her face, the aggression of her high heels. She warms up her voice and her emotions, to get into her role. Sirena Selena will dramatize Solange as she imagines her; their frustration will be united. She remembers how much she has suffered in this life, and her throat becomes hoarse. She is going to need all her pain to play the *señora*. That is how she will move her *público* of businessmen and their wives in that luxury mansion. She is going to remind them that even with all the wealth in the world, there are troubles that have no solution, absolutely no resolution; troubles that no glamour, money, or fur can compensate for. She keeps warming up her voice. Her throat is growing more hoarse. She opens her chest wide.

I walked with my arms open, without finding love or a single friend, and you have given me only lies, only sadness, misery . . .

Misery, I've had you in my life for so long, like a tragedy hidden in suffering. Solange, because you suffer, there comes a moment when you grow tired and nothing matters anymore, not fashion or designers or boleros. And you have to put up with *crumbs of kisses,* you're always *begging for love,* that's all you get, *like a wretch, like a criminal.* You can never be what you want to be, not even with your elegant hairdos, or with the croissants you eat in the morning. Just like me. But don't believe it. Even singing, I am not who I want to be, but I am closer to a level of perfection, to a sad lady, very sad, but beautiful. Solange, see how I suffer for your guests.

Misery that fills me with fear because you don't love me. Misery that is hate and fear because I know what you are. Oh, yes, Solange, I know. You're a climber like me, a young girl dressed like a woman, who believes in reaching the top. And you suffer, you are rich but you suffer, there are memories embedded in your soul that you can't shake. They come to you in your dreams, with your morning shakes and croissants. How unstable it is at the top, ah, Solange, so much depends on the one who puts you there, on his whim!

Sirena Selena, *la dama triste,* the vigorous woman full of glamour and hate, descended the final steps of the curved pink marble staircase. Strong, rich, she knows she's a star. But she doesn't forget. She is a star who suffers from the irremediable. Slow and mellow, the timbre of her voice suffers and waits. Who knows how long it will keep waiting *for her luck to change or for death to come, like a blessing?*

On the steps, Sirena held the last note as long as she could. The pianist, completely absorbed, was unable to add a coda of arpeggios to the bolero. The servants helping move furniture and flower arrangements couldn't move. Sirena had stirred up old hatreds within them, terrible urges to cry over lost causes. Some of the cleaning women began to applaud, weeping. Everyone applauded. The pianist was stupefied, his hands resting silently on the keyboard.

Sirena Selena took a breath and continued organizing her show. She was the hired star. They were paying her to astound the guests. And this time, she really wanted to astound them. This was her opportunity to astound even herself and to believe that she was a *señora* descending the curved marble staircase from her luxurious rooms. Below would be the hostess of a society party, which she would make more agreeable with her melodious voice, just like a Hollywood star welcoming her special guests. Yes, she was going to astonish them, because the sparkle in the eyes of those around her had to astound her, at least for the course of the evening, even if it is only that night and nothing more.

Sirena Selena ascends the staircase once again. As she does so, she hears orders:

"Astrid."

"Señora?"

"Bring the children in from the beach, I don't want them to catch a chill."

"Sí, señora."

Selena immediately recognized Solange in that *"Señora,"* Solange as a ventriloquist wanting to put her in her place. Let her know who was who, so there was no confusion; clarify for everyone that she, Solange Graubel, was no fool. For her, Sirena Selena was no invited star, but a miserable child with the airs of a diva. That maid's *"Señora"* was in reality a "Don't fool yourself," escaping obliquely from Solange's mouth. "Here, you are a diversion, a clown, a tool to throw in the trash once the party I organized for my husband's colleagues is over."

And at the top, Sirena turns on her heel (behind the locked door, Solange also turns). She clears her throat and smiles maliciously (and in her room Solange gives a faint smile of satisfaction). She opens her mouth but doesn't let out a single sound (Solange reflexively puts her hand on her chest). And she sings.

Solange hears the monster. The animal's powerful voice slips under the door. She begins to fear. What if her husband doesn't care about appearances now? What if that animal bewitches him against his will? She knows that since her *leche* dried up, Hugo has gone out to the street to look for someone to carry on his game at regular intervals. But he always did it discreetly, on the other side of the *malecón*, in another town. Not right under her nose.

Ese monstruo, that cursed monster, she cannot get close to Hugo even for an instant. Just thinking about it makes Solange's soul slide out of her chest. She grabs it with her hands. She needs Hugo to maintain her position.

"And if he's not mine, I'll never share him."

Sirena is the devil's servant. Her voice continues to filter under the door. Solange hears, not wanting to. She hears how *el engendro* sings, she hears how it opens the corners of its mouth, she hears clearly how, note by note, the voice emerges. She struggles, covering her ears, clutching at her chest; she doesn't want to fall under the spell of that voice. Her eyes close and she sees how Sirena passes her tongue over her lips to moisten them, how Sirena swallows saliva to cleanse her throat, how she takes in air to fill her chest again. She tries not to fall under the spell, but it's too late. Sirena's voice holds her in its passionate arms with kisses of death and carries her to the very abyss of loneliness. That *monstruo* is dangerous. Its voice is not of this world.

She returns to the closed doors of her suite to double-lock them. A scandal now would kill them. She would still be rich, a business-woman, but not a lady. A scandal now, after so much work, would be the death of her prestige. It would turn her into the misfit she was before; into the milky child held captive for the highest bidder, trans-formed into a lady only in her dreams, returned to earth again like an ordinary victim—and because of a freak. Better to stay on the sidelines. Better not to even want to know anything. And if Hugo got himself into deep water with the monster on the stairs, she'd better be prepared for the worst. Let the scandal sink him, not her. Let the scandal find her on an airplane, on the way to Miami. Leave this cursed island and go there with money, jewels, stocks that will buy her appropriate status. No one knows her there, no one knows her father, or her mother, or her strange husband always looking for *leche* and not caring about anyone else. Yes, she would leave the island. And in the meantime, she'd just stay out of the way, play innocent, and wait and see what happened if her idiot of a husband decided to fall, to fall into the clutches *de aquella mujer de fantasía.*

31

*H*ugo watched Sirena's voice come out of his own chest. He was
outside, beside the pool at the Hotel Talanquera with a beer in
his hand. He felt it. That voice had come out of his own chest. He
felt it resonate against his ribs and become tangled in his lungs, mixing
up each beat of his heart. He swallowed hard. He couldn't help but
fall under her spell; he had to close his eyes. He saw Selena's tongue
wetting her lips, Selena's saliva loosening her throat, Selena's chest
filling with air. He saw Selena descending the curved pink staircase,
dressed in her anger and her pain, just as he was dressed in his, and
in his vast loneliness. He took a drink of his beer to shake off the
spell. But the spell still held him, like a broken mirror. He counted
the hours, the minutes, until the show. "Five hours and thirty
minutes," he murmured.

Hugo Graubel took his eyes off his watch and walked toward the
house. The rehearsal would be over now and he would have to pay
the pianist. Solange would be up in her room, selecting her outfit for
the evening. Selena would be free, alone. He hurries, clenching his
fists. He's nearly there. Selena comes out onto the balcony, with liner
and gloss on her lips, but only halfway through the process of her
illusion. Hugo applauds from a slight distance.

"Sirena, you sing like the angels. I was listening from out here."

"You heard me from out here? Well then you must have heard
the pianist who kept getting lost in his accompaniment. I had to extend
the rehearsal by an hour. You don't mind, do you? Or do you, my
gracious host?" And she takes him by the arm, perfect in her flirtation.

"*Por favor*, Sirena, how could I mind? I will take care of the pianist."

Sirena clutches his arm tighter. That Solange will see who she's messing with. This is the moment for revenge. Sirena looks at Hugo through languid eyes. Her glance slides to his mouth. She parts her lips and extends the tip of her tongue for an instant and then smiles.

"I assure you, my dear host, that tonight you will be fully satisfied."

"I am sure I will be."

"Well, that's what you're paying me for."

And if there had not been a single cent between us, or luxury, or a marble staircase, Sirena? The question sticks in Señor Hugo Graubel's throat, and he only smiles, a look of exhaustion from enduring silent boleros in someone else's eyes, he retreats toward the living room of his house in Juan Dolio. Equally stuck in him is the desire to take in his hands the face of that insolent boy, press those cheeks hard, so that they hurt, and plant a deep kiss, full on his mouth. Leave him wet with saliva as a warning . . . but no. Not yet. There are still five hours and thirty minutes to pass before the kiss. Then the gracious host will drop his role and abandon himself to his will and to the pleasures of Sirena's mouth.

"Another thing, my gracious host. I think that tonight it would be better for me to have a room at the hotel, so that I can fully dedicate myself to the preparations. There are many things I need to take care of in order for the performance to be perfect. And afterward, I will need somewhere to escape and relax, far from the commotion that follows a performance. I would look pretty silly closed up in the little room off the pool, in the middle of all your guests. One has to maintain the magic, you do understand. . . . Now I will accept your offer to stay in the hotel. And who knows why else I might need my own room after the show?"

Sirena, mischievous, smiles as she walks toward the house. Hugo Graubel follows her with his gaze. The pact is settled.

"I'll call the hotel right now," he answers from a distance, "to make the reservation."

32

*T*he Cold War is over, *mis niñas!* Listen to Miss Martha! We won't have to travel to New York to compete with blond drag queens who've been speaking English since they were babies. We won't have to worry about trying to convince our audiences that we're not all incarnations of Carmen Miranda. I am moving to Moscow . . . and I'm already dreaming of a full-length fox coat with a matching ermine muff. Like Dietrich in *Catherine the Great.* How divine I will look! I am sure to become the newest sensation over there. With this nice color given to me by God, the sun, and the mixed-up breeding that all Puerto Rican women carry in their blood. As the saying goes, '*Aquí el que no tiene dinga, tiene mandinga.*' Everybody here knows that we've all got some African blood running in our veins. Even the girls who are ashamed of being black. But I am not like them. Look how proudly I carry this nose, these full lips and these sweet, shapely hips. *Mis amores,* we will surely steal the show. My guess is that a *caribeña* will cause a scandal over there. Exotic, sensual, a sought-after jewel. Like Josephine Baker when she moved to Paris and wore that fabulous little banana skirt. The ex-czar himself is going to want to collect me. But he better bring an interpreter to speak with me, *eso sí*, because the only things I know how to say in Russian are 'vodka,' 'Gorbachev,' and 'perestroika'. . . .

"Can you all imagine if instead of the United States it had been Russia who had colonized us? Villa Caimito would be called the Kremlin, Crash would be Prosit, Bocaccio's would be . . . oh, I don't know, Pushkin. Like the bars that are opening now in Miami and New York: Red Square and the Warsaw Ballroom. But ours would really be Russian and not silly Epcot Center copies. And don't try to tell me that our bars wouldn't be more chic if they had European names. So divine!

"That's why I want to dedicate my show tonight to the fabulous country that will soon be my home. Where, in the not so distant future, free trade and unbridled degeneracy will reign. To Russia! *A ver, chicas,* raise your glasses, we're going to offer a toast. I propose a toast in honor of the ex–Red Threat, to that beautiful country where snow, fur, and multicolored domes rule. . . .

"Wait, wait, wait, hold on a minute. *Nena,* where's your glass? Why don't you have a glass? We are in the middle of a solemn moment and the *loca* doesn't have a glass! You see, dear friends. That is why we will never be well received in Russia. We have to present a united front, full of harmony, communion, good manners. Cuqui, *papito,* tell the bartender to send a glass over to this *loca,* even if it's plastic and full of cola Champagne, we're not going to give out free alcohol. That's it, *mi amor, gracias.* Now are you ready for the toast, *mamita?* Yes? You better be.

"Okay, let's get back to where we were before we were so rudely interrupted. Raise your glasses. A toast to Russia, to our sisters across the seas, anxious for the iron curtain to finish rising. A toast to their being able to import those indispensable depilatory creams and high heels in large sizes. A toast for the Russians to be compassionate and to understand us for what we are, the best of two worlds, and to the proposition that when the Drag Brigade in Defense of Glamour, Puerto Rico chapter, lands they accept us as their mentors and spiritual guides. Because the poor things are going to need some coaching. So many years doing without everything, without Hollywood movies, without *Vogue,* without *Elle* translated into Russian so they can understand it, without designers or famous models. They're going to need us, so we'll toast them. And, finally, we'll toast Gorbachev, for his bald head and that little red mark on his forehead. Without him my dream of being a real-life czarina would never have been possible. To Gorbachev and his perestroika—*salud!*

"Cuqui, this isn't Champagne. It tastes like 7-Up without bubbles.

Nene, so nasty! That's why I'm going to Russia. This bar is about to be closed by the Department of Health and the Consumer Affairs Office. The times they've tried! But we've kept up the battle. We have spies everywhere who keep us informed about their operations. Like the Russians. That's why I identify so much with them, with how hard they have fought to better themselves, all those years of doing without, that's not easy, *mis hermanas.* To be *loca,* Russian, and communist must be hell! But when you think about it, being a drag queen and a Puerto Rican is no piece of cake, either.

"That's why I have formed the Drag Brigade in Defense of Glamour, the DBDG. We fighters love political organizations. If you want to be an exclusive members of the DBDG, I'll warn you right now to start learning about Russia, its geography, topography, natural resources. Don't you go and embarrass me. With all the dumb *locas* we have in this country!

"You don't believe me? Well, it's true. This country is full of dumb *locas.* Do you want me to prove it? Listen to what happened to me the other day. I had just finished my show, which was to die for. I changed my clothes and came down to the bar to visit my admirers, my friends, the crowd. . . . Beside me was a group of *jevos,* around thirtyish all of them. Two people in the group started talking about politics. Neoliberalism and the consumer society. . . . I pricked up my ears, because a girl never knows what she might learn. Just then a young boy approached the group, dressed just so, very trendy with his wide trousers, his tight shirt, his cork-soled shoes, and two earrings in each ear. I had never seen him in the club before. That seemed strange to me, because I know all the girls in the *ambiente.* 'Fresh meat,' I thought, and moved closer to the group, to see if I could catch the new arrival's attention.

"But the little bonbon didn't even notice me. He was sort of anxious, with an agitation somewhere between his skin and his soul that wouldn't let him be still. He was probably just coming from the bathroom after a quick hit. He didn't stop moving, as if he was waiting for one of those intellectuals to ask him to dance. Suddenly he decided to change strategy and participate in the conversation to see if he could pick up someone in the group that way. He turned sideways, changed his air, arched an eyebrow, then listened. At that moment the others were discussing perestroika. And do you know what that *loquita* asked them? You can't imagine what he asked them. The *jevito* opened his mouth and said,

" 'Perestroika? And who is the *loca* with such a divine name?'

"Am I right, or what? You see, you have to educate yourselves. You can't just go around in a daze. So read magazines, listen to the news, and pack your suitcases, we're all moving to Russia. The Cold War is over, *mis amores*! The world is ours from East to West. . . .

"A little quiz now. *A ver, niñas*: point. Which way is east? Dear God, how stupid can you be? No, morons. That's *south*."

33

*P*erfect. The company car was there, just as Contreras had promised. With a driver and everything, a black luxury sedan, its spacious interior upholstered in gray leather and air-conditioned to keep out the heat. And there was Contreras, all smiles, a little nervous to be sure. Was she too done up, were her seams showing? Of course not, she had looked at herself carefully in the mirror before leaving. Martha Divine had made sure that she looked like a real *señora* for the dinner. She was wearing a Nina Ricci dress, purchased at a discount store in New York on her last trip there. She accented the outfit with a black bag, closed-toe, square-heeled pumps, dark glasses, and a watch with a braided gold band. She had even gathered her hair into a chignon so as not to look out of place. If Contreras was nervous, it wasn't because of her. But, just in case, Miss Martha Divine took out a vanity mirror to check her makeup as Contreras walked toward her from the circular drive where the hotel car waited.

"I'm impressed, Señor Contreras—you are so punctual. I appreciate it with all my heart, because in this heat, I would be in very poor shape to meet your business associates."

"Greetings, Doña Martha. Shall we go?"

"And the other guests?"

"They will be waiting for us at La Strada, the restaurant I took the liberty of selecting for our meeting. It has a very pleasant ambiance. Do you like Italian food?"

"I love it."

Contreras reminded himself. He couldn't forget to ask Martha about the singer. "And Sirena, she's not coming with us?"

"She's not feeling well. Something she ate didn't agree with her," lied Martha.

"Food from the hotel?"

"No, no, from outside. Yesterday we took a walk in the colonial district and she wanted a fruit shake in a café. I told her to be careful, to wait until we got back to the hotel. One spends one's life advising her, but you know how the young are. They have to learn from experience."

Contreras leads Miss Martha to the car and opens the door for her. She settles in comfortably on her side of the seat, smiling lightly at the driver, who is wearing a two-piece uniform and white gloves. Martha has never been in a similar situation. She is going to have to watch her manners carefully so as not to stand out.

"You're going to love La Strada, Doña Martha. Excuse the use of Doña, it's a habit."

"Don't worry, I appreciate the gesture. You were saying?"

"La Strada is an exquisite restaurant, you'll love it."

"Tell me a little more about the other guests."

"Well, Ingeniero Peláez is the principal owner of the Hotel del Quinto Centenario, which opened this year to commemorate the fifth centennial. He's a very good friend of the president. I think he invited his business manager this evening. Augusto Montes de Oca. A good businessman."

"And Vivaldi?"

"Vivaldi is the owner of La Strada. He has another restaurant in the Hotel Talanquera"—*Cuidado*, Contreras said to himself, don't say too much—"which is just outside the city."

"Are there hotels in Santo Domingo outside the tourist zone?"

"About forty-five minutes away. Since we don't have beaches in the capital . . ."

"Yes, I noticed."

"Many tourists prefer to vacation in other areas. The majority of our vacation complexes are outside Santo Domingo."

"If I had only known before . . . Señor Contreras, perhaps you could put me in touch with some of those hotels, to sell them the show—after we fulfill our commitment to you, of course."

"You can call me Antonio, if you prefer."

"Antonio. I was beginning to think your parents hadn't given you a first name."

"Look, Martha, I want to apologize for the delay that I have caused you. It is not my intention to complicate your plans, but the decision to hire Sirena is not entirely my own."

"I understand, Antonio. But you must give me a yes or no."

"By Monday at the latest you will have a clear answer. I have already communicated with the hotel's budget management office, who are the ones holding up the negotiations. But let's not talk about it anymore now. To the right here, Gastón. Park near the entrance. Come, Martha. The other guests must be inside waiting for us."

This is a four-star restaurant, thought Martha as the driver parked. I'll have to keep an eye on Vivaldi, he seems to have a good thing here. And I can't forget what I told Contreras about Selena. Wouldn't do to cause any confusion.

Inside, the restaurant was softly lit. The maître d', dressed in a black linen suit and white shirt, received them courteously in the vestibule. Martha Divine felt as if she were in the middle of a foreign film. She was Sophia Loren, walking along the central aisle of a luxury restaurant. Marcello Mastroianni would play the lead, in the role of a very influential man who would fall madly in love with her at first sight. Martha expected him to appear at any moment.

The restaurant's décor was impeccable. On each table there was a simple centerpiece consisting of a candle surrounded by an arrangement of dried flowers. The tablecloths and napkins were white linen. The tables were carved mahogany. In the dining room there was a semicircular wooden balustrade painted to match the wainscoting. Several tables were occupied. La Strada was obviously a good business.

Martha walked slowly over the wine-colored carpet. She felt imbued with the elegance that enveloped everything, the walls of the restaurant, the waiters, the subtle music playing for the diners' enjoyment. La Strada was a dream. And Sirena is missing it, wandering around out there in the streets, she said to herself.

And soon, among the candles and the tables and the white linen, Marcello Mastroianni appears. Yes, there he is at the table, smoking a cigarette, waiting for her with a glass in his hand. She and Contreras approach. Marcello waves to them. He stands up, as a signal for his companions to rise also and welcome the new arrivals.

"*Buenas tardes,* good evening, gentlemen."

"Don Antonio Contreras, it's so good to see you. Welcome to La Strada," says Marcello Mastroianni. It seems that tonight he will also play the role of host.

"Vivaldi, Vargas, gentlemen, I want to introduce you to . . ."

"Martha Fiol Adamés."

"I didn't know your full name, Doña Martha."

"You know only my artistic name. But now that we are moving to another level, I feel comfortable divulging one of my secrets."

"And do you have many secrets, Doña Martha?" asks one of the other guests, teasingly.

"Many," responds Martha, completely ignoring the man who asked the question. She directs her response to the Marcello Mastroianni of her movie, while she holds his eyes, for no more than a second.

Marcello's character is that of the owner of the restaurant, Lucchino Vivaldi, who offers a seat to Miss Martha Fiol, right beside his own. Meanwhile, Contreras, Peláez, Vargas, and Montes de Oca accommodate themselves as well as they can around the table for five, having to ask for an additional chair. Vivaldi helps to resolve the problem with the chairs, from time to time bestowing a smile upon Martha, and with a knowing look begs her forgiveness for the delay. Martha watches everything with a distracted air. She smiles inside. She is beginning to plot subtle seductions in her script.

In reality, there wasn't much to distract Martha from her pursuit of Vivaldi. Peláez, the owner of the Quinto Centenario, was a gentleman with a large belly who bore a certain resemblance to her former husband the *hondureño*. Montes de Oca, Vargas, and Contreras all seemed to have been cast from the same mold. Olive complexion, mustache, receding hairline; each neck was imprisoned by a tie that made its wearer look uncomfortable, as if his aorta would rupture if they were to find themselves in an unpleasant situation. Vivaldi stood out from the others. Not that he was the image of beauty. But he breathed a certain distinction. You could see his worldliness in every gesture. He and only he was the protagonist of the film *A Dinner at La Strada,* the perfect vehicle for Martha Divine to show how elegant and seductive a lady she was. The setting suited her to the last detail. The restaurant's half-light brought out the brilliance of her large black eyes. The tenuous flicker of candlelight accentuated the luster of her midnight-auburn hair. The temperature of the room would keep her fresh for the entire evening. Even the outfit she wore perfectly matched the ambiance and the host.

The plot she was hatching was also perfect. The sidelong glances from her leading man proved it. Vivaldi: "Allow me to order the best wine in the house for you . . . Rivas, two bottles of Château Margaux." Then he began to ask her about Puerto Rico, the economic situation, the purpose of her trip. Martha found herself adorning the truth with her businesswoman's language. She explained to her companions that she was the owner of a piano bar (and whorehouse) on the outskirts of El Condado (near the shooting galleries), in an area where some of the best discotheques in the country are found. Recently she had decided to expand her business to the production of shows. She came to the Dominican Republic after setting up an appointment with Mr. Contreras, whom she called at the suggestion of a mutual acquaintance. According to the script that Martha had carefully prepared, this was the most opportune moment to take her leather purse, open the clasp, and take out a studio portrait she had taken of Sirena for business purposes. Slowly she puts her manicured hands on her bag. She opens the clasp. She takes out the photograph. It is passed to Vargas; to Montes de Oca; to Vivaldi, who looks at it somewhat interestedly. But the leading man quickly turns his eyes back to Miss Martha, as if for him no one else existed. Nice detail, thinks the businesswoman. Vivaldi really knows how to treat his guests.

The others can't stop looking at the photo. They are enraptured by it, a full-length shot of Sirena with her hair loose, a little disheveled by the artificial wind in the studio. In the photograph she appears perfectly made up, wearing a black beaded dress, like Lucy Favery, with a faraway look in her eyes. But her face, the wind playing with her hair, and the way her arms fall evoke something else. This isn't a photograph of a simple cabaret singer, but the very image of a damsel in distress. The figure on a ship's prow; a mythological goddess; a fallen virgin: that is what Sirena seems, with her parted lips, her provocatively absent gaze. The photograph reveals her innocent profile, the image of pure desire created anew for each eye that gazes at her. "And you haven't even heard her sing yet," Contreras says to the others, stirring up their curiosity and admiration which only enhance the artist's uncommon beauty. The dinner companions' faces hide the first hint of a suspicion. And of a consummate seduction.

Miss Martha Fiol courteously takes back the photograph. She opens the clasp of her purse and puts it away. She looks smilingly at her potential clients. "You can't imagine how much work it took for me to transform him"—emphasizing the word "him"—"into a diva. Training the voice was the easiest part. He came to me with talent to spare. It was the other part that was so difficult, the choreography, the wardrobe, developing a sense of elegance. Difficult material to teach, *muchachos, muy difícil*. But I managed, and Señor Contreras can tell you about the result." And with that she finished her sales pitch. She wouldn't speak another word on the subject. She would leave them hanging, imagining the sort of show that she could produce.

Then it was time for dinner. The waiter brought the menus. There was so much to choose from. As an appetizer, prosciutto *di Parma* with melon for the *señora, pomodori al Gorgonzola*, pancetta, and *zucchine ripiene. Minestra di verdura, zuppa di pesce,* and two orders of *crema di funghi* for the gentlemen. Spaghetti *al succo de carne,* linguine *alla Diavola*, and gnocchi. *Primi piatti, ossobucco, cotoletta di manso alla fiorentina, vitello tonnato,* and *trota farsita* for three. Then they ordered salad and cheese. Miss Martha Fiol was so full she could barely breathe. But when they brought the dessert cart, she capitulated. It was delirious. Zabaglione, *zuppa inglese, torta di fragole,* crème caramel. Martha selected the strawberry cake with coffee, then breathed deep and surreptitiously undid the waist button on her skirt, simulating an itch on her back. She couldn't help thinking about Sirena. She had told her protégée many times: staying with Miss Martha Fiol was the surest path to success. *El que no oye consejos, no llega a viejo,* she said to herself. The old saying about not reaching a ripe old age unless you're willing to listen to advice was one of her favorites. Then Martha picked up her fork, ready to put a piece of the delicious cake in her mouth.

Throughout the conversation over dinner, Peláez and Montes de Oca showed considerable interest in the artist she represented. Vargas asked her to call him directly at his office. They couldn't assure her of anything at the moment, but they would have dinner again, in order to be able to speak more at length about the matter. They would discuss every detail, schedules, fees, lodging. . . . But Miss Martha didn't believe a word. They looked at the photograph with an interest different from that of businessmen. And the experience with Contreras had already shown her that on this island, hiring a *travesti* meant that one had to negotiate long and hard. *"Pero, negra,* you never know," Miss Martha said to herself and took their business cards, just in case.

Lucchino Vivaldi offered after-dinner drinks. The guests looked at their watches, some realizing that it was time to leave. Vargas and Montes de Oca were the first to depart. But Peláez and Contreras joined Miss Martha and Vivaldi and ordered Sambuca. While they sipped from the cut-crystal glasses, Vivaldi came up with a brilliant idea. With his most seductive smile, he interrupted the conversation to propose, "Why don't we continue the evening at the Hotel Colón? It's a very interesting place, Martha. I would like you to see it."

34

*A*part from the fact that it doesn't have a pool, this is a very nice hotel. Perfect for our kind of tourism, and our kind of entertainment, if you know what I mean." In the murmur of voices in the bar at the Hotel Colón, one was a bit louder than the others. "It's so difficult for us to travel abroad, especially to the Caribbean. I don't want to criticize, you know—with all the problems these islands have, it's understandable that they're less evolved than we are. I mean, we had Stonewall, we had ACT-UP, we have a history of political activism in our countries. For instance, in Canada, with all our liberal tradition and social programs, there are totally out scenes in Toronto and Montréal. Nowadays, it's easy for us to be what we are. Well, easy enough if you aren't one of those chip-on-the-shoulder AIDS activists, a full-time drag queen, or a street boy. If you're sort of 'normal,' that is.

"Yeah, yeah, the eternal question, 'What is normal, anyway?' But you have to agree, we don't have it as tough as they do here. You can't compare our problems to the atrocities a gay man has to face in these countries. I mean, where do they go? How do they meet? It's all hanky-panky in the dark, like in the fifties in Canada. Of course, you're not going to find discos and bars that are easily identifiable. And you don't have time to break any secret codes, anyway. You're here on vacation. For a week or two. You don't have time to play hide-and-seek with the local queens. If they even know what they are! No honey, I did not come here to play the spy or to give free psychiatric counseling to my Caribbean sisters in distress. Been there, done that, without having to pay airfare. That's no way to spend a vacation. As if there aren't enough emotional complications waiting back home. I came here to have my moment in the sun! And to play with the boys . . .

"And then again, traveling to Europe has gotten so expensive lately. Ibiza? You can't go to Ibiza these days. Who wants to go there? It's so overrated, like a first-world gay convention. You don't meet the locals. It's just not a surprise anymore. Now, Australia, everybody tells me that's the place to go, but not for a week. Maybe for a month or so, to get your money's worth. The plane ticket alone can cost over a thousand dollars. And I'm not talking Canadian dollars. That's not an easy trip. The Canadian economy is good, but you pay so much more in taxes. You see, I'm from Canada, and like most of these fairies, I live in Toronto. That place is almost in the freaking Arctic Circle. The winters are eternal. You can ski, downhill and cross-country, but sometimes you want to be half naked, running around a beach full of pretty boys.

"And where can you get that at a reasonable price? Only in the Caribbean! The beaches, the sun, the laid-back atmosphere . . . The only problem is the infrastructure. It's a drag when the electricity fails. You can't take a bath, the air-conditioning goes off. And most of these little hotels don't have their own electric generators. Except this one. Stan, the owner, I met him the other night. He's from Sweden or some other Scandinavian country . . . I wonder how he ended up here. But he's a real businessman. Puts ads for the Hotel Colón in the *Village Voice*, lists with gay-oriented travel agencies, all the right places. The hotel is very neat, very well kept, and the boys he finds! Let me tell you, they are unbelievable! Pretty chocolate skin, incredible bodies, even though they've never lifted a barbell in their entire lives. And let me tell you, there's no problem with *their* infrastructure! Sorry to get so excited. I am *such* a size queen.

"Some of them play hard to get. Especially the new ones. You have to shower them with gifts to convince them to come upstairs with you. They come right out of the countryside, young, inexperienced, what have you. Most of them don't even know they're gay yet. They go to bed with you, enjoy the whole thing, but as soon as it's over, they revert to that whole Latin-lover-macho role they grew up with. It's kind of sexy watching them do that. So cute. Anyway, as soon as they figure out that they can make more money spending a single night with you than working at the hotel for a whole month, the roles change. They're on you like flies on honey. Most really need the money, and I'm happy to oblige. It must be so tough to be gay in this country.

"But it's true, they don't have a pool. Thank God Stan worked out a deal with the Nicolás de Ovando. That's where you're staying, isn't it? It's still an inconvenience, though, having to walk two blocks just to take a dip in the pool. So hot here in the city. But next time you and your lover come to the Dominican Republic, stay at the Colón. Nobody bothers you here, or looks funny at you. And best of all, there are no ugly tourist families on vacation with the screaming kids and the hairy dad with the beer belly watching them by the pool. Just a laid-back, sexy party atmosphere. This is my second time here and I haven't regretted it."

35

*L*eocadio awoke from his siesta and looked at the cot next to his. It was empty. Migueles had already gone to work. Or maybe hadn't come back yet. He had the strangest schedule. Sometimes, Migueles had to work the night shift. He had explained that to his friend. Because they were friends, had been from the beginning, when Leocadio arrived at Doña Adelina's house and sat on the stairs crying. Poor Doña Adelina spent a pretty penny on making him a chicken stew and some red beans with pumpkin to cheer him up. But Leocadio couldn't get over finding himself without his *mamá* in a big house with so many strangers.

After the feast, which he barely touched, Leocadio returned to his perch on the stairs, to look out onto the street. He wanted to hold in his memory the image of his mother walking away with her back to him, turning to look every now and then to assure him that she would come to see him the following week. He didn't want to forget a single detail of her clothing, of the way she walked. The afternoon she left him at Doña Adelina's house, she was wearing a yellow blouse with little red flowers that had buttons down the front, a long cotton skirt, down to her ankles, and her black low-heeled street shoes. She had done up her hair, pulling her long curls back with a clasp. She smelled like flower water and talcum powder. Leocadio went over every detail in his mind. He would commit them to memory and wait. The moment would come to throw them in his mother's face, one by one, when he was grown. That way she would know that maybe she had forgotten about him, but he had never forgotten her. One day, when he was a man, he would take the *motoconcho* all by himself, and he would go to the *patrona*'s house. There, he would ask to see his mother, who would be old and broken down from working so hard. They would meet in the living room. She would embrace him and cry, and when she least expected it he would say to her, "Do you remember the day you took me to Doña Adelina's house? You were wearing this and that and you walked like this." He would pull each detail from his memory. He would make her feel ashamed. He would take revenge on her for leaving him alone.

Leocadio felt the door to the house open behind him. He didn't turn to see who had come in. Whoever it was should just let him be, alone in his corner of the staircase. Probably just Doña Adelina, with more tidbits to try and console him.

But no, it was Migueles. He found out when he had to turn around, because a body wider and taller than Doña Adelina's cast a shadow over him. Migueles sat down next to him. He was one of the older boys in the house and was already working. A little mustache had started to sprout on his copper-colored face. Migueles offered the younger boy a cigarette and lit one for himself. After a long silence during which they both contemplated the night, he said, "It's hard to find yourself alone, isn't it? But that's how you become *un hombre*. Facing life on your own. And you are already *un hombre* even though you are not old enough, because you have to take care of yourself. As soon as you earn a little money, you'll get your mother back and you'll take care of her. Then no *patrona* can separate you. No one will be able to keep you apart, because you will be *el hombre de la casa*. Don't worry, *hermanito*, it's just a matter of time." It was true that they looked like brothers, the two of them sitting there on the stairs, cigarettes in hand, watching the night pass.

Leocadio wanted to talk to Migueles. He told him where he came from, told him he would love to work as a gardener. "That doesn't pay well, *bacán*. You have to do something more lucrative, like me—I work in the hotels. Just from the tips my clients give me I can live a life of luxury. Drink, smoke, go out with women . . . *Pero yo no soy pendejo*; I'm not going to throw away my money whoring around. I'm saving up so I can leave Santo Domingo. A person can't live here anymore. You have to do the same—look for a good job that pays good money, save, and then go out and try your luck."

Leocadio choked on the cigarette smoke and Migueles looked at him with a mixture of amusement and warmth. "You don't smoke? Then put that out, I don't want you choking on me. Don't do it just to impress me. We *hombres* don't have to impress anybody. Just the women, and then you take them for rides in your car. But you do that with money, not cigarettes, or drinking too much, or shouting. With a hundred pesos in your pocket, and a great car."

Leocadio had never been treated like a man before. He was always his *mamá*'s boy, overprotected because of what happened to him once, and then again, and again, in the *patrona*'s house or in the barrio where they rented a room. His mother warned him to be careful; she said he was different, fragile, vulnerable, and Leocadio believed her. He walked around full of fear, trying not to provoke anyone in the neighborhood. He never succeeded. Someone always appeared who would take him away to some distant corner, who wanted to touch him. That night on the stairs was the first time he realized that he could become a real man, with responsibilities in life, like taking care of his *mamá*. "You have to take care of women," he heard Migueles say. "Mothers especially, because they are sacred." From then on he was Migueles's friend. Migueles treated Leocadio with respect, and gave the boy advice as if Leocadio were his younger brother.

Leocadio loved to wait for him in the room they shared, to listen to his stories about his job. Sometimes he arrived a little drunk, smelling of tobacco and rum. They would sit on Migueles's bed, which was a little bigger, to talk. They kept their voices low so they wouldn't wake anyone, or so that no one would hear the secrets that Migueles shared with Leocadio. Only with him. Migueles had told him he didn't want anyone else to know the details of his work in the hotel. Not even Doña Adelina, although he knew that she wouldn't mind. "All work is honorable, as long as it doesn't hurt anybody," they had heard her say on more than one occasion. But he was *un hombre* now, and a man keeps his secrets. He doesn't go around telling everybody what he thinks and what he's doing. *Los hombres* are reserved and they don't like gossip. And Migueles insisted that he was a real, honest *hombre*, without a doubt.

But he liked talking to Leocadio. "You have to unburden yourself with someone," he had said during their third or fourth conversation. The older boy confided in him because he saw that Leocadio was quiet and solitary. And Migueles wasn't like the other boys in the house, who were always running around and squabbling; he wanted to avoid trouble, especially where he might have to use his fists to be respected. Because he would have to use his fists if someone made a fuss about his job. Many times Migueles has gotten Doña Adelina out of scrapes. And he helps out with part of his paycheck for the household expenses; what is left over he sends back to his *pueblo*. But he keeps all the tips from his clients, which are significant. They are all saved in a brown paper bag hidden under the boards of the balcony on the second floor; nobody knows that. Only Leocadio.

"As soon as I save up enough for my ticket, I'm heading for Puerto Rico. That's where the real money is, man. I have a cousin who went over there four years ago. He already has a house and his own business, doing tile work. He started working for a Puerto Rican, but those *boricuas* are all lazy. They don't like to work. He told me last Christmas that the boss was a *boricua* who charged the doctors and lawyers he worked for a ton of money. He had three or four *dominicanos* and made them work from sunup to sundown, paid them next to nothing, and went around in his big car visiting his girlfriends and drinking. That's what he did all day long. And my cousin and the others sweating like dogs in those big mansions. The big boss would come when all the work was done. He'd wet himself down a little, making it look like he had worked, and when the owner came back, he gave him the bill. Puerto Ricans don't know what real work is, they just fake it, the lazy asses. Seeing the situation, my cousin saved, he bought the machines, the materials, a truck, and he printed up some business cards and started competing with his boss, charging less for the same work. And who was going to say no? He bought a brand new car, a luxury Cutlass Supreme, and has a plot of land in his town. There's a lot of room for progress on that island. It's just that the *boricuas* don't know how to take advantage of it."

"Why not, Migueles?" Leocadio asked him, dumbstruck by the story.

"Because they are used to being gringos. Don't you know that Puerto Rico is part of the United States? Over there they don't have the corruption or the poverty that we have here. But what they do have is a lot of crime and tons of drugs. Most Puerto Ricans are drug addicts. That's why they don't work. Because they have so many privileges, so much free time, because the government provides for them so they won't rebel. But that's in our favor, because we can get there and start working right away. And my cousin tells me there's no trouble finding a Puerto Rican woman to marry you for money, so you can arrange your residency papers."

"There's no poverty over there? Then why do the women marry for money?"

"For drugs, Leocadio, they're expensive."

"The women over there do drugs too?"

"In Puerto Rico everybody does drugs. You'll see it with your own eyes when you come work with me."

Those were the things they talked about. Sometimes until dawn. Most of the time Leocadio listened attentively and asked a million questions. There was so much that Migueles knew. Often he'd mix in phrases in English, or German, or Italian into the middle of a conversation. He had learned the languages at work, dealing with his clients. When he came home from work, he described them, the brands of clothing they wore, the drinks he served them in the bar, how they treated him.

Leocadio thought Migueles was very privileged to be dealing with different kinds of people and getting paid for it. He himself had never spoken with anyone who wasn't Dominican. Maybe he'd spoken with a Haitian, but they didn't count. How could they count, if sometimes even in the poor barrio where he lived nobody wanted to rent them rooms. Haitians lived like stray dogs. They weren't like other foreigners, elegant and with a lot of money in their pockets. And Migueles knew those foreigners. He spoke with them: Americans, Italians, people who came from rich countries far away. It must be fascinating. But Migueles always made a face when Leocadio spoke enthusiastically about the subject. "Don't believe it, Leocadio, those tourists can be like the devil himself sometimes," he said. "They can make you crazy with all the money they have."

Ironically, that was the only thing that Migueles hated about his work: waiting on the clients. Sometimes because of them he would get home angry. On those nights he didn't want to talk to Leocadio. In his bed, he would turn his back to the younger boy, growling, "Leave it for another day, *mamón*, and don't bother me anymore, I'm tired." Soon he was snoring, leaving the boy yearning to know what had happened at work. But other times, he came home happy and talkative. Then he would show Leocadio the gifts his clients had given him. Expensive shirts, fine leather belts, gold bracelets. One day, Migueles gave Leocadio a man's gold bracelet, because he already had one like it.

"Those tourists are so crazy, they buy everything they see." An Italian who lived in New York and was passing through the capital had bought it for him. "I liked the man, I don't know why," he said. "When I finished my shift, he invited me for a few drinks in the hotel bar. I got so drunk, *bacán*. I didn't even know what time it was. I had to stay in his room. That was the day before yesterday, remember when I didn't come home? The next day I was off. But today, when I went back to work, there was the Italian. He gives me this little box and says, 'Here, this is for all your trouble.' At first I didn't want to take it. I gave it back to him, but he insisted and I accepted the gift, so he wouldn't take any more of my time while I was supposed to be working. I didn't want the boss to catch me goofing off. When I opened the box, this bracelet was inside. And fifty dollars, folded in half. It looked like wrapping paper. I couldn't believe my eyes. I closed the case, put it in my pocket, and kept on working. The bracelet made me laugh, because another client had given me one just like it the month before. The other guy was German. He was really nice to me—he even rented a car so we could drive over to the beach when I got off work. He took me to an expensive restaurant and didn't try anything strange with me. Sometimes what they want is just to spend time with someone, to have some company. . . . The Europeans are better than the gringos. They know how to respect *hombres* and they don't try stuff, like kissing you on the mouth, or holding your hand in public. They do their thing and that's it. But in the end, they're all the same. They love *dominicanos* and that's why they come here. They even give the same silly gifts.

"*Toma*, Leocadio, I want to give you the bracelet. One day we'll go for a walk along the *malecón*. You with yours and me with mine. Jewelry looks better on you than on me. You look sharper. Besides, what do I want two bracelets for? I'm no *maricón*."

When Migueles offered to find him a job at the hotel, Leocadio couldn't believe it. He was so excited, he tried to run upstairs to ask Doña Adelina to take him to tell his *mamá*. Migueles stopped him and advised him to calm down. First he had to convince Doña Adelina and ask her permission properly. "As much as she spoils you, she could get upset if you don't do it right. She might not let you work, out of spite. That's how women are sometimes, spiteful. Even mothers. When they think you're going to leave them, they hold you tighter. Let me take care of it. You'll see, everything will work out just fine." Migueles explained his plan to Leocadio. First, he had to go to Doña Adelina with the story that maybe he could find a little part-time job for Leocadio. Then he would have to assure her that the work would be light, during the day, just until Leocadio started school. And to push her over the top, he would tell her that this way, Leocadio would learn a trade, which certainly couldn't hurt. "I'm sure that'll convince her. You know how Doña Adelina hates laziness."

Since Leocadio was still a young boy, Migueles could only get him a job in the kitchen washing dishes, or one changing sheets in the rooms. But he didn't care. The idea was to be close to that world, so new, so magic. Finally he could belong to the secret society of those who hang around with tourists. He would learn the foreigners' languages; he would accept their gifts and their grateful looks. And their money, lots of money. Who knows, maybe one of them could help him resolve his situation. Maybe, with the money he earned in the hotel, he could be reunited with his mother, set her up in a house so she could rest, buy a little piece of land in the country, or even go with her and Migueles to Puerto Rico to open their own business. And, once he was earning his keep, he would really become *un hombre*. Like Migueles. And for that, he needed a lot of money.

36

*B*athed in sky and sweat

      Sirena

            descends from the height of her dream

   step

      by

        step

She leaves her shimmering tail by the sea

there on the shore

her foot enveloped in gauze and tenuous light. Step. Thickly strapped high heels, silvery wrapping from the beginning of her days. Toenails polished, in coral-mauve. One by one the painted toenails of the very first foot, Adam's foot in high heels, the foot of the genesis and the dream.

Step. Smoke from dry ice glides over that perfection of flesh. Dry smoke. Step. Gasps from the audience. On the guests' tongues, a stunning foot glides in foam, on the dry words that surround her. The thin, smooth legs of a sylph emerging from the deepest waters. The soft knees without childhood marks to give her away. Soft, smooth as they had never been . . . as if in her life a scarlet line had drawn them, only kneeling to pray on such softness. Dry smoke swirling around her legs,

Selena

    descends

        a

            step

                then another

                  and another

                      until the witnesses can no longer breathe, the dry air encircling her delicate waist, slender enough to hold in one arm, in one embrace. And flames pour from Selena's eyes, dry blue flames, flowing from the fragile face of a cornered gazelle, already leaping in those heels. Her waist undulating like a shimmering sea in front, and behind, from her naked back, hurricanes, cataclysms . . . and the sea foam covers her, quietly shielding her little dove's chest, her narrow chest with two shallow protuberances there, breasts of syrup, waxy fruit, the softest imitation of a peach, with the soft down of a fifteen-year-old girl.

Flame at her toe, flame at the dry ice that is the foam that navigates toward the neckline of her white sequined dress, swimming, lost, like a fallen girl but immaculate, a marvel of purity, and only her thick wrists and the starved thinness of a ballerina give her away. Selena

    open like the moon of the poor

        and so, more closed than an abyss

is she, oh yes, the door to every desire.

She stops in the middle of the staircase. The witnesses remember having heard a piano in the background, behind her footsteps. They remember the piano and the time lost since she placed the first white, flaming foot on its marble tray, in its rightful place—dry smoke and a painful memory. They remember a few introductory notes to a bolero, like a cascade of tiny sharp stones trying to stop but unable to, they remember a hand that grabbed their throats, and down below, some fingers—whose?—touching them. And their breathless amazement pushes the memory back, to the same place as the breath and the burning flesh shrouded in dry smoke.

In the middle of the staircase Sirena stops,

cold.

Then everyone remembers the piano but fixes their eyes on her face, exquisitely made up. The almost perceptible lines drawn by hand, perfumed in shades of precise scent, the hazy powder clinging to her skin, alighting on each dancing pore, the touch of blush on each cheek, just a hint, the agile brushes outlining the fine lines of the round mouth of this carnivorous butterfly, lips wholly for kissing and ballads. Rose-mauve and tones of coral, parted like a smiling clam. The colors that define her nose, that very thin nose with its closed pores, the siren's compass. And the black eyes, as black as the jewels in the windows of department stores, with the same solitude as rhinestones. Lost somewhere deep inside, they only look at the reflection of her image. The wide forehead lost in thought, beautifully colored in mauve around the edges. And as a frame, some of her black curls fall onto her shoulders. Others are piled high on her head, daringly revealing her neck, as murmuring and smooth as the rest of her. Not a drop of shrillness—

not a drop. Not a drop in her expression, that of a doll startled by her own beauty,

by her own image.

The witnesses remember hearing the tossing sea behind the notes of the piano. The women anxiously put their hands to their hearts and relive desires they once had at the edge of the sea. Desires that some of them drove away long ago and that others have secretly fulfilled, right there on the beach by the Hotel Talanquera, far from their husbands, far from their own eyes, so they wouldn't confuse them with those salt-covered bodies that gently licked the shadowy absence of someone who gave them pleasure and added the murmuring of water to that brief touch. The men couldn't help grabbing their bellies, they were pained by Sirena's presence, by the presence of this angel, translucent beneath her vestments of fire and smoke. And she was the beautiful son, the nubile niece who one day sat on their laps and made them crash, made them run to the saddest bar, made them fill shrill jukeboxes with coins, made them implore the burning malefactor to leave their flesh in peace. They remember how they escaped, spent years running as fugitives through the streets and the houses of ill repute on Calle Duarte. And all for what? Only to fall in Sirena's trap.

She lowers the mask of her desire
(and they murmur softly: I will love you . . .)

She opens her mouth. Now, half open, she draws all the air out of the room. The calla lilies wither and, nearly dead, they faint before Selena's hungry chest. Her moon approaches the balcony, full. The apocalypse is about to occur. Sirena, standing still in the center of the staircase, sings, *An invasion of tenderness in your steps, and your old dreams burn. I feel in your steps the fear of looking for other steps that walk away with the same rhythm . . .*

But everything stopped, everything. The audience anchored in its uncertainty, in its double betrayal by time. Not a single heart beat, not a single drop of sweat formed on skin. Not a single cell multiplied while Sirena sang. Time obeyed her voice, her voice was the only proof that life was unfolding. Her throat delicately muttered

as yours . . .

and then

(step) *such subtle magic in your steps* (step) *they left a halo in your wake* (step) *I still feel your hands on my face* (step) *and I feel in mine* (step)

El aire, air, was escaping. A banker's wife felt elevated by the ethe-realness; she grabbed her husband's arm—wanting to murmur to him not to let her go like that, flying over the heads of all those illustrious guests, over the black hair of this adolescent *travesti*, the pure incarnation of the impossible.

(step)

(step)

But she couldn't whisper anything. Time hung from Sirena's chest as she searched for the final note of her ballad. And completely open, completely *loca* with her own incarnation, she gives herself completely

your lips . . .

There was still a quarter of the staircase to go; crushed memories flooded the entire living room of the house in Juan Dolio. The ex-hausted audience struggled to grasp the life preserver of thunderous applause, thunderous so as to dispel the illusion. Sirena lowered her eyes without smiling. She leaned slightly forward with her arms crossed against her chest. She finished descending the stairs diagonally, toward the table with the calla lilies. She took one, took the cut-crystal glass filled with brandy that she had placed next to the vase of flowers. Glass in hand, she walked toward the piano. Then she leaned against it like a ship just before it sinks.

> *My heart*
> *is a ship in the turbulent ocean*
> *defying the raging storm*
> *that they call love . . .*

37

*H*ugo is holding a cigarette in his hand, and he almost burns himself. It doesn't matter. How could it matter if his finger is consumed in ashes like a tobacco leaf? He would keep on holding the cigarette in his hand like a dagger. It was his only weapon, his smoke signal. "Here I am, Sirena!" he calls out with the cigarette. But Sirena doesn't hear him. She is singing, lost in her own voice.

She'll hear me soon enough, thinks Hugo, feeling her voice come from the deepest part of his chest. But, curiously, the murmuring vibration in his chest doesn't serve as a bridge to reach Selena. It is a route to other places, faraway places that leave Sirena stranded on the rocks like a shipwreck, while he is the one who sinks, softly, deliciously, thinking perhaps that he needs air, that he can't breathe, but it's already too late to despair. The voice has dredged up its mate. There is nothing to do but yield himself completely.

Hugo wants to yield completely, to finally finish it all. He wishes he hadn't invited anyone. His guests are a barrier separating him from his ecstasy. He is ashamed to feel like this, to be so vulnerable in the midst of so many people. The witnesses are uncomfortable, each one nearly fainting, clutching their chests, their stomachs. Their poses distract him, won't allow him to close his eyes in peace, remain without air, touch bottom, finally confront what calls him from far away. Hugo holds the cigarette that consumes him, burning his fingers, letting the ashes fall onto the floor. He holds the burned filter and he doesn't care; he will show Sirena the wound of his love. Like the others, he needs a rest, needs to explode in thundering applause to shake that heavy weight off his body.

But he is choking, dying of love right there, and the anticipated terror is death, the body pulled between a sound and a burning, point-blank love, a finger in the flame and the voice of his misery near. Hugo passes his tongue over his lips and feels again the taste, the smell of insecticide in a faraway room, the lingering taste of rum after a date with the untouchable flesh. He lets himself go, closing his eyes and releasing everything, opening his fingers and letting the cigarette fall slowly to the marble floor of the elegant residence in Juan Dolio. He stops fighting; he yields completely.

Two songs later the applause explodes. The audience's chests explode, just like the bubble of illusion that Selena had created, that made her look perfect to everyone who drank in her passion. Their reddened hands continued clapping until those applauding arrived at the surface of their fear, of those exterminating boleros sung by Sirena. The audience asked for a recess of half an hour, half a lifetime, before the rest of the spellbinding show. They all went over to Hugo to look at him up close, wanting to ask him questions that wouldn't come out of their mouths, that remained lodged halfway down their throats. They approached Sirena to touch her, but when they reached out their hands, the caresses remained in midair, incomplete; the guests were convinced it was better not to touch that creature, not to take the liberty of feeling her, a privilege for them that eventually became a condemnation. The audience spoke to her, congratulated her with arms extended; the most adventurous rested a finger on her dress and looked in awe at her, trying to discover something that would give her away.

Sirena turned on her heels convinced of her complete success. Just to show off she gave her audience looks worthy of a diva and glanced sidelong at her host, who was still holding his hands in a position of interrupted applause. She smiled a little nostalgically, a little maliciously.

"You're fabulous," she heard someone say. "*Dios mio*, how did Hugo Graubel ever find you?"

"Beneath a palm tree," answered Sirena and, blinking, she looked again at her host who was sighing with relief and eagerness at the same time,

with relief and eagerness ...

Hugo caught his breath while, with his gaze lowered, he contemplated his burned finger. It was red; the skin was dry and rough from the burning filter. The first sign of his proximity to her. That wounded skin was a symbol of his destiny. It confirmed, in a strange way, that among all the guests who wanted to possess her, only he, Hugo Graubel III, would have her near him. Only he would have the privilege of touching her, terrified that he would die afterward with his hand in the air, like a perfect suicide.

38

Solange runs upstairs in disbelief, tears about to form. But no. She won't cry. Though there is more than enough reason, she will not cry. Leaving the guests in her living room astonished by that farce—"and I, I who killed myself to give them the best imported wine, the most exquisite caviar . . . they throw me their crumbs. . . . Not a single compliment, not a single 'Solange, you are an artist, you have such good taste, thank you for all your trouble,' no 'Solange, gracias, amor mío, for helping me entertain my business associates.' Let them stay down there and rot admiring the glitter of that trashy diva." They didn't bother to say so much as a word to their hostess. She can't believe it. Solange holds back a tear on the brink of emerging, but she doesn't cry. Her indignation is worth more than a flood of tears.

Up in her room, she rips off her earrings, throws them on the dresser. She takes off the necklace that is choking her. "I should wear a dog collar, I'm just a dog in their eyes, a piece of furniture." Her teary eyes land on the negligée that she had left on the edge of her bed that very afternoon. "How naive I was, so foolish, thinking about receiving something in return from Hugo for all the work I did. I am a fool and an idiot. . . ." She would throw the negligée into the furthest corner of the drawer and never take it out again.

"Cálmate, Solange, take a deep breath, don't be ridiculous. What are the guests going to think if they don't see you at the party; and the help, what if they go looking for you with some question and they can't find you?" Solange breathes deeply and calms down. No, she won't play that role. She won't give them the satisfaction of seeing her humiliated, not Imelda Nacidit or Angélica de Menéndez or any of the other harpies who are still down there, scrutinizing every detail of the evening. She knows that every minute she spends locked in her room is another minute they'll use to skin her alive. The things they must be gossiping about already! They're probably down there criticizing the wine, her dress, the *travesti* who sang in her living room, whatever. And that she can't bear. She won't give them the chance, especially since they probably still haven't noticed her absence, in their delirium over that *engendro* that just finished singing in front of *her* grand piano.

And Hugo, damn Hugo, damn the hour when I met him, damn the minute when I let down my guard and let him bring that monster into my house, but he's going to pay for it, I don't know how, but Hugo is going to pay for everything. How dare he humiliate me like this? He's the last one who'll ever see me cry. Solange approaches the mirror to dry the tears already running down her cheeks. She walks into her bathroom to look for her eye drops. She will have to touch up her makeup. Unsuccessfully, Solange tries to avoid thinking about what has just happened in her living room. She tries hopelessly to erase the image of Sirena Selena descending the staircase, submerging herself in the denseness of the bolero that flowed slowly from her mouth. Doesn't want to remember, but can't help feeling again how that voice caressed her soul, hypnotizing her too, transporting her to a timeless place where only her dreams existed. She has to admit it: Sirena's voice quickened her pulse, suspended her breath. Suddenly Solange too found herself astonished. Each sound seemed like a tunnel opening before her, inviting her to travel, to leave behind the stares, the looks of disdain, the comments, the reputation, and to give in to the weight of her own desires. As hard as she tried, she couldn't stop asking herself where that voice had come from, from what dark corner, from what evil and bewitching conduit, the hypnotic sound that refused to expose the charlatan for what she really was, a gold-digger, a tramp. What power did that voice use in transforming a wretch into a nymph? A voice suspended in the air, heavier than a spell. Nothing worked against it. How could Sirena have borne it from her chest? Who in the world taught her to sing like that?

... as if she were dying, bleeding to death from the throat, baring her soul—when she wasn't, when in reality she was lying to everyone. She was stealing their sense of peace, stealing the safety her guests had come to the party with. To Solange's party, the one that she had planned with such enthusiasm, taking care of every minute detail, she knows how to spell "minute," she knows what brand of salmon to choose, where to order the best flower arrangements, how to haggle with the laundress so that she dry-cleans and presses the imported Irish linen tablecloths. What does the impostor in her living room know of that, what does she know about the work it takes to memorize all the details that reveal social status, class, pedigree? *She doesn't have to worry. She has her voice.*

And what does Solange have? A husband. That helps, but it doesn't assure anything. It gives her an opening, but it doesn't grant the key with which Solange herself can open the doors to acceptance. How many times has she had to labor over some bit of artfulness to win friendship with a *dama* of society? To how many evenings has she had to drag her tired, unwilling feet to study the subtle choreography of gestures, greetings, and table manners? Her husband's money is an important ingredient, but what really demonstrates class is the meticulous, studied, and constant display of elegance. That is her only protection. Her elegance saves her from invidious questions about the actual condition of her family, her professional training. And now this tramp comes to throw all her work to the ground. With Hugo's help. She can't believe it. *The idiot, the ingrate, how could he allow something like this?*

Sitting at her dressing table, Solange applies a little translucent powder with her makeup brush, puts on some lip pencil, then mascara's her lashes. She searches for the earrings she took off. She can't find them. She applies two drops of Joy de Patou and finally decides to wear some other earrings, the Bulgari. She checks her face in the mirror. The Bulgari earrings really match her dress better. After briefly replacing it, she decides to unfasten the Hidalgo necklace, which was choking her. It has left marks on her neck.

She breathes deeply and walks toward the staircase (step) all smiles (step) but inside a giant wave of bile washes through her.

(step)

Back in the living room, she decides to join the American businessmen, to see if they have enjoyed the show. They are delighted. Solange, struggling to maintain her smile, gives credit to Hugo, who is a little eccentric (step) and likes to bring new things to the country. She tells them that Hugo convinced her, arguing that in New York and Miami they have this kind of entertainment at business dinners in private houses. While the businessmen continue talking, Solange (step) looks for her husband. She doesn't see him. All smiles, she air-kisses a couple of guests who arrived just before the performance. They didn't want to interrupt, so they had waited to say hello. But they assure Solange that they heard everything—that fabulous singer, Solange, she really seems to be from another world. Solange walks from one side to the other of her living room, looking for her husband. She finally sees him, with a stupid expression on his face, approaching a group of guests who orbit Selena. She watches him interrupt, take the singer's arm to accompany her to the bar, leave Solange abandoned, not knowing where to go.

39

After dinner the guests gradually leave the Graubel residence in Juan Dolio. Sirena has been in her hotel room for some time, resting. She left her hosts immersed in the rituals of socializing and saying good-byes. She must keep her distance, to avoid breaking the spell of her illusion. She didn't even eat at the table with the other guests, but went to her hotel and ordered from room service. Later, she escaped a moment to walk along the edge of the sea and enjoy the serene night. She had to take her walk, according to her plan.

As she had expected, Hugo goes to look for her in the hotel gardens. He walks over to where she has stopped to contemplate the sea, and takes a gold cigarette case from his pocket. The case sparkles in the light from the garden lamps. Selena's face is illuminated by Hugo's lighter as it slowly approaches his face. Hugo lights his cigarette and inhales. Selena looks at him quietly.

"What are you thinking?" Hugo whispers into Sirena's ear.

"About which song would go well with a moment like this."

"And if I asked you to think about me?"

"Well, then I would think about a song about a singer who thinks about her man who asks her to think about him."

Hugo decides that Sirena's answer requires a change in strategy. "You were fabulous with the guests. You didn't lose your footing for a second."

"I never do."

"Not even now, when I am so close and my chest is about to explode?"

Sirena remains mute, just as rehearsed.

"They say that he who is quiet surrenders."

"Is that what they say?"

Hugo doesn't let her finish; he takes her in his arms and kisses her with his tongue, long and flowing and tasting of Marlboros, almost entering her throat. He kisses her and Selena lets herself be kissed, she receives her host's warm mollusk in her mouth. Selena lets him continue to kiss her, thinking about the bolero that would be appropriate at a moment like this, the host with her in the moonlight, walking along the gardens in a luxurious residence by the sea. There must be a bolero to sing at a moment like this. Boleros were made for moments like this. Hugo pulls her closer, pulls her closer to him, and then starts putting his fingers in the neck of her dress, bringing his skin closer to her little nipple, the lost siren. Hugo is being swallowed by his hunger, choking, he repeats these words . . .

"I will love you, Sirena, as I have always wanted to love a woman, as I have always wanted to love a woman. . . ."

Hugo's words prevent Sirena from remembering the bolero correctly. They are too close. They twist around in her mouth, in her mind. Selena keeps trying to remember the bolero. Hugo's pulse is quickening. He's already losing himself in the murmuring phantasmal voice that transports him to who knows where. With his lips he sucks the fifteen-year-old's mouth, wanting to drink her words. Sirena is still thinking about the bolero, thinking that, once she recalls it, the song will complete the picture of how beautiful they must look in the moonlight.

Hugo takes Sirena to a more secluded spot. He lowers the zipper of the siren's dress, slides a hand along her back, letting it glide, silky, seditious, finds the beginning of a wrapping, a band of cloth, and Sirena is still transported by her mission. He starts to remove her dress, letting it fall to the grass in the garden. Sirena stands there transformed; her skin, the skin of a nostalgic *niño*, the bones in the tiny chest, the bones of the delicate ribs, the bones of the groin protruding somewhat, the bones of the neck and face, the collar bones showing him the way back to the mouth full of boleros that keeps singing his destiny.

Below the waist, a large band appears, an artifice of cloth covering the spot from which Hugo suspects come all of Sirena's mysteries. He inserts a finger, another, two more, pushing down the binding that separates him from what makes Selena a woman. He lets the cloth fall to her feet. But then a long piece of gauze is revealed, rolled around the nymph's waist. Filled with love, Hugo Graubel begins to unravel it, little by little, layer by layer, unaware of anything that exists beyond his diligent hands, beyond the minuscule, bony body of his bewitching lover. Layer by layer, the only sound that is heard comes precisely from the region submerged beneath the cloth; it is growing under his touch. Heat is rising through his arms, his legs, his entire chest, which expands and contracts rapidly, already preparing for what he sees.

Suddenly everything is still and a profound silence is the witness to what Hugo sees. Sirenita, the fifteen-year-old *bolerosa*, is completely naked in the hands of her host, her pearl-colored nylons around her ankles, her feet still framed in the silver high heels, her clothing lying on the grass, twisted around her feet like foam from the sea. The perfumed curls and the face perfectly made-up in tones of mauve-coral, the delicate body of skin and bones, the tanned, creamy skin, the tiny chest, the little shoulders, the narrow hips, and in the middle of that smallness a succulent *verga*, wide as a water snake, wide and thick, in the very middle of all that fragility.

40

*F*our times a week Leocadio worked at the Hotel Colón. He went in at ten-thirty in the morning and left at three in the afternoon, except Fridays and Saturdays, when he worked until six. He arrived at home tired, after hurrying to catch a *motoconcho* that left him on a corner in his barrio.

The work was easy. It was just a matter of paying attention so that the soapy dishes he was supposed to wash didn't slip out of his hands and calculating the right amount of pressure to pull the sheets tight on the mattresses without stretching the elastic too much. The worst part was that he spent hours doing the same thing, after which came the two or three minutes of the day in which there was absolutely nothing to do. It was in those moments that he escaped from the little maintenance room or the kitchen and wandered around the hotel.

He loved this world. Leocadio ventured through all the hidden corners—the back rooms, the storerooms where provisions were kept, the rooms where piles of freshly ironed white towels waited, along with boxes of detergent and cleaning implements. He also loved to walk around the hallways, and even to enter the rooms he knew were empty, to open and close the cabinets in the bathrooms, the dresser drawers, to breathe that delicious aroma of a clean hotel room ready to receive the next guest. This aroma was different. It smelled like bubbles, like a new kind of plant, wrapped in plastic. It smelled like humidity, like fresh wind off the river. When he had free time, Leocadio climbed up to the balconies on the roof, where sometimes the waiters would escape to smoke, and from there he would look at the capital's colonial district.

The people looked tiny, walking along the street. Leocadio saw their little tourist heads wearing hats, or local heads trying to ward off the midday sun, carrying envelopes and purses, boxes of food or papers along the narrow streets where, from time to time, a car buzzed by. From the roof of the Hotel Colón you could see the Casa de Francia and the facades of the stores across the street. From the roof of the hotel, Leocadio had for the first time a grand view of the city. He was no longer seeing the barrios, Doña Adelina's house, and the alleyways of his neighborhood, from ground level. Now, from the roof, he could see the city, breathing, alive, and complete, and then he would descend into its intestines, the service areas of the Hotel Colón, full of detergent and white sheets.

But there was an area that was forbidden to Leocadio: the hotel's bar. That was off-limits to him and for the other *muchachos* who moved boxes, chopped vegetables, and cleaned the guest rooms. The world of the bar was exclusive to the waiters. That select clan comprised young men like Migueles, strong and broad-shouldered, young men who already knew the streets and the world, knew how to smoke, get drunk, buy their own clothes, and even drive. The second floor was only for them. Mr. Stan, the owner of the hotel, who went down to the kitchen the day they hired Leocadio, had clearly explained that to him. "Don't even stick your head around the edge of the stairs to the bar. Understand?" Leocadio nodded, mute, a little startled to see a man who was so tall and white speak so strongly.

Migueles saved him. "*No se preocupe*, Don Stan, don't worry, I will make sure he follows all the instructions carefully. Leocadio is a good worker, and someone you can trust. You won't regret this." Leocadio saw how Stan looked at Migueles as if studying him under a microscope, and how Migueles held his gaze, with self-assurance. Although Stan was very tall, Migueles seemed to grow several meters during those moments. "*Bueno*," replied Stan, and he went back upstairs. The *jefe*'s body became a shadow that bounced off the walls and the ceiling, it was so big. He looked like a gigantic spider. And Migueles was a tireless intergalactic fighter, battling monsters to save his *hermanito*.

Even so, Leocadio couldn't contain his curiosity. He saw that the bar was where all the hotel guests went, especially on Friday and Saturday when he got off work later. At six the bar at the Hotel Colón was starting to get busy. He didn't dare break his promise to Migueles or his *jefe*. He contented himself with staying in the lobby and listening to the music and the laughter, the murmurs of jovial conversation that sometimes echoed into the reception area. The bar had become an obsession for him. Leocadio suspected that up there lay a special world. He didn't know how or why, but deep inside he felt that there was something for him up there, something he had to learn about. Nothing had ever awakened such anxiety in him before. He had always valued being an obedient boy, quiet, respectful. But his obedience ended where the stairs to the bar began.

41

*T*his was the place. *Definitivamente.* How could it not have occurred to her before? Martha knew very well that every country
had its underworld, its secret locations, which seem to be one thing
but are something else entirely. Why did she think this island would
be different from her own? Why hadn't she investigated further, asked
if there were establishments like this, like the Hotel Colón?

Since arriving, she had studied the place up and down. The hotel,
outside, appeared to be a modest *posada,* enchanting because of attributes other than luxury. It was situated in the colonial zone, near
the Alcázar del Almirante. The structure of the building seemed to
be well cared for, but the restoration wasn't like that of Viejo San
Juan, which had breathed new life into the mortar, bricks, and wood
used to replace ceiling beams and door frames. This building gave a
clear indication of being old, not because it was decrepit, but because
it was somber.

Inside, there was a lobby like that of any other small hotel. A
forged-steel chandelier with flame-shaped lightbulbs swayed gently in
a sudden breeze. The walls, painted bone white, and the dark wood
paneling framed a staircase that seemed to lead to the second floor
and the guest rooms. That was how it appeared from the ground
floor. Once you climbed the stairs, the panorama changed. The second
floor was in reality the hotel bar. The doors to the balconies were
covered over. Not much light entered the room, even from between the
cracks in the planks that concealed the arches facing the sea, because
over the planks hung wine-colored wool curtains with gold tassels that
gave the place the feeling of an abandoned theater. On the wall as you
entered, at the top of the stairs, was a mural, a landscape, depicting a

Caribbean afternoon with palm trees, a branch of green coconuts lying at the foot of a brown trunk, and a cobalt-blue ocean with white foam that glowed in the light because of the glitter that had been sprinkled on it before the paint dried. At each corner of the bar stood an enormous clay pot in which palm trees, which almost looked real, had been planted.

The bar was made of wood. It was long and rounded at the edges, as if to avoid accidents, in case some drunken client forgot how dangerous a sharp corner could be and suddenly found himself on top of one, bruising his pink skin or cracking a rib. A huge mirror covered the rear wall, where an extensive assortment of liquor was arranged along a counter. The mirror was framed in palm fronds. The ceiling of the bar was lined with strings of white lights, simulating a star-filled sky.

On top of the bar were ashtrays with the hotel's logo and a few dishes of appetizers with pieces of pineapple, ham, and miniature *quipes*. Carpet the same wine color as the curtains covered the floor from wall to wall, with the exception of one fairly large rectangle, the dance floor. In a corner of the dance floor was a small illuminated stage. Tables and chairs occupied the rest of the floor space, some filled with people, others empty. Two or three couples were dancing to the rhythm of a Donna Summers remix. The place was very modest and sort of campy, but it looked clean, well staffed, decent.

Martha, Contreras, Peláez, and Vivaldi sat at a table near the bar. Vivaldi was watching Miss Martha very closely, studying her face to make sure that he had brought her to an appropriate establishment. Martha wore a neutral expression, but she made a mental note to remember the lesson. Every country has its underworld, its secret spots; it was just a question of discovering them. She suspected the reason why Contreras was taking so long to hire Sirena. The truth was, things for *locas* weren't as advanced here as in Puerto Rico. There gay men were even on television. Johnny Rey—didn't he even have his own program? Pantojas—doesn't he sell out the house wherever he performs? Maybe not masculine homosexuals, but the *locas* are always given their place in the spotlight, for the comic relief, the laughs, the jokes, *quien sabe*. Even if it is just to laugh at them, they have their chance. But in this country it's a completely different story, like Puerto Rico a couple of decades ago. It's a good thing Martha has been around the block. Her age, her life as a married woman with her Honduran husband, had helped her develop the sixth sense she needed to read the codes of this secret world. But why had she thought until now that she wouldn't need those abilities on this island?

And to think that she, an old fox, had believed that Contreras could really buy her show. Contreras is just a front man; he's obviously working for someone else. I'll advise Billy when I get back. "That *dominicano* you hooked me up with pulled a fast one on you, *mamita*. He's just a rank-and-file soldier with dreams of being a captain." No way would he propose a *travesti* show for the sacrosanct hotel he manages. That would send up flares in his place of work. But she didn't really blame him. If you had to hide so much just to dance with another man in this city, giving signs of being a *maricón* at work must be terrible.

Besides, it was indisputable that Contreras did have some influence. Covering the hotel stay, scheduling the audition—to achieve even that much he must have some power. And on top of all that, he had gone to the trouble of organizing this dinner for her, to introduce her to other businessmen, most likely closeted local homosexuals. No wonder one of them reminded her of her former husband. They had started her along the winding path toward the gay world of Santo Domingo. The thought was almost touching. Well, it was the least Contreras could have done, after leaving her waiting so long at the hotel going crazy with anxiety, and to make matters worse not knowing where Sirena was.

Where is that alley cat, that ungrateful fool? I hope nothing bad has happened to her. She deserves it if I wish her ill, thought Martha, but the truth is she was really worried. It had been three days without a word. Three days and three nights and not a single call. She hadn't admitted it to anyone, not even to herself, but she hadn't slept well. Miss Martha Divine was suffering sleepless nights in her hotel room, hearing steps, bolting awake, then going back to sleep worried. She lied, trying to convince herself that it was waiting for the contract from Contreras that did this. But deep down she knew it was because of Sirena. Where could she be? Who could have whisked her away? The worst part was she couldn't report Sirena's absence to the police. And she couldn't let the people from the hotel find out, either. So the only thing she could do was sit and wait. Blessed Jesus, don't let it be, but if they find her dead, they'd better not come looking for Martha. Her eyes would fall out from crying, her heart would stop beating, but she wouldn't go collect the body for a million pesos. Sirena could just be buried here. I can't say a peep, they would skin me alive.

But now she was at the Hotel Colón. There must be other bars like this one, other hotels with a good sound system and a stage. She had mounted fabulous productions with less. She had built a devoted clientele of admirers of exclusive debutantes, had built a reputation. If she had a hotel like this one, she'd be a millionaire by now. With the potential for development that this place has . . .

While Miss Martha Divine was making business calculations in her head, Stan, the Colón's owner, made his appearance. The man looked like a Viking, he was so tall, easily six feet and several inches. His hair was nearly white, and his skin pink—he looked like an extra-terrestrial. But he arrived with a bottle in his hand and a waiter with a tray of glasses behind him. Obviously he came in peace.

As soon as he approached, Vivaldi hugged him and kissed him on both cheeks. Stan greeted the others as if they were old friends. Miss Martha had not been wrong, they were all local *locas*. It was obvious that this was their element and they felt comfortable about finally dropping their masks, finally showing their true selves. Martha's Marcello Mastroianni, always so attentive, introduced her to Stan.

"This one you don't know, she's a new friend visiting us from Puerto Rico. Be careful of Miss Martha—she's a dangerous woman. . . ."

After pouring glasses of white wine for them himself, Stan invited her to dance.

He spoke perfect Caribbean Spanish. He chopped off his final "s"s, exchanged his "l"s for "r"s, and spiced it all with a good dose of "*ahi vamos*," "*para que tu veas, mi amor*," "*la ida por la venida*," and similar phrases. But his Spanish came out uniform, as if spoken by a reporter for Univisión, and the idiomatic turns he took didn't suggest any definitive provenance. Very mysterious. But Miss Martha was sure of one thing, this red Viking wasn't a gringo. She would ask him where he was from when the opportunity presented itself; meanwhile, as they danced, what she wanted was to gain a little ground. Blondie's "Heart of Glass" was playing on the sound system.

She and Stan danced, then Stan and Contreras, she and Lucchino (she started to call him Marcello, just to flirt), Lucchino and Stan. It was already four in the morning and the tourists had packed up and, alone or accompanied, withdrawn to their rooms. Miss Martha now felt completely comfortable; she flirted openly with Vivaldi, who responded in like manner. She kept smiling knowingly, looking at him out of the corner of her eyes. She looked like a geisha every time Vivaldi looked at her. The seduction of her leading man no longer had anything to do with business plans, or marketing strategies. It was the old game of seduction of the flesh, but for pleasure, not commerce. She surprised herself by licking her lips and imagining Vivaldi in his underwear, Vivaldi stealing a kiss in the elevator, Vivaldi falling on her with his full weight. That was a pleasure Miss Martha had not allowed herself for a long time. *Qué carajos*, I'm on vacation. Besides, how many times in one's life does one run into a Marcello Mastroianni on a neighboring island? I could just bite him. I could just eat him up. And now I have a room all to myself, unless Sirena appears.

But first Miss Martha had to free herself from the churning of another kind of blood, which wouldn't let her rest until she took care of it. Her cursed businesswoman's blood. It was the first time in years her desire had interfered with business plans. Why? Who knows? thought Martha. Maybe if Vivaldi's olive skin weren't so seductive, if she weren't so advanced in age, if she didn't feel so vulnerable with Sirena missing, maybe (she dares to suggest) she would spend her time trying to seduce Stan the Viking. She would overlook the albino hair, the pink, piglike skin, the wide jaw, and the sunken salamander eyes to flatter him and nibble on his ego.

But she could see from a mile away that Stan was hooked by a different kind of bait. Around Martha, the Viking acted like a little boy with a new toy. He didn't miss an opportunity to run his fingers along the seams of her dress or to toss Martha compliments about her purse, her accessories, her makeup. He loved dancing with her, although he looked like a frog electrocuting itself every time he went out onto the dance floor. "What could that Neanderthal be looking for?" Martha asked herself, confused. Then she activated her sixth sense. She added, subtracted, and multiplied. It wasn't difficult to come up with the answer. Definitely, Stan was easy prey, but not for the reason she had suspected at first. That crazy albino, sole owner of the Hotel Colón, was fascinated with Miss Martha because she was the manifestation of his desires. She had no doubt that if the Viking cornered her, he would start asking her about large-size-shoe catalogs and where he could shop for an outfit. It was obvious that Stan was a repressed *draga*, dying to dress up. That was why his eyes sparkled when he looked at Miss Martha Divine. Beloved Father, what a thing seduction is. You just never know where it will turn up, thought Martha, and, smiling, began to plot her next move.

"Stan, you have such divine facial features. . . ."

"What?"

"I said, you have divine facial features; you should accentuate them with a little makeup, but not too much."

"Wait, I'm going to ask them to turn down the music a little," and he signaled to the bartender, who immediately lowered the volume. "What were you saying?"

"That you have beautiful features, you remind me of Marlene."

"Marlene Dietrich? Don't make fun of me—she's my favorite."

"Well, you'd make a fabulous Marlene."

"*Qué va a ser*, Martha! You really think so?"

"*Sí, niña*. With that skin and those cheekbones, that imposing height. Can't you just imagine yourself in high heels? *Un escándalo*, Stan."

"I'm not going to deny it, I've wondered sometimes about putting on some makeup, and a wig, *mi amor*, halfway down my back. Can you imagine it?"

"Of course I can imagine it."

"I would look so ridiculous, with this whaler's face I've got."

"*Qué va cielo!* Don't be silly! You should meet some of my *artistas*. Lizzy Starr, for example, she's a horse she's so tall, and muscular and feisty, like you."

"What do you mean, your performers?"

"Didn't Vivaldi tell you? I am a promoter of *travesti* shows."

"You're not!"

"*Pero, amor*, how else is a *travesti* going to earn a living on this planet? It's not gonna be by giving swimming lessons. I don't know about here or the country where you're from, but on the Isla del Encanto we feed ourselves by putting on shows in bars or doing it in the street, and I'm a little too old for the latter. You see, Stan, I'm a woman with experience in these things, so trust me when I say that you would be *una draga de escándalo*."

"Really, Martha?"

"I swear on my children's health. You should get dressed up one of these days. But you have to do it carefully, with professional help. Why don't you ask one of your *amigas* to help you?"

"I don't have a friend who could do that."

"*Ay, Divina Pastora!* The owner of a gay bar with no *travesti* custmers? And why not?"

"Because this is a tourist bar. The locals don't come here much."

"So you don't have drag shows here, *cariño*?"

"No."

"Not a single one?"

"No, Martha, and it's not because I don't want to."

"*Ay, nene, esto no puede ser,* this can't be. Do you know how much money you're losing? A drag show in this bar is a must!"

"I think so, too."

"Well, Stan, this is your lucky day, because I am going to help you with your business."

And Miss Martha Fiol, never one to miss an opportunity, crossed the dance floor. She returned to the table, opened her purse, and took out her notebook, her calendar, and her gold pen. She took a second to verify that Lucchino Vivaldi was still playing the role of *bombón mediterráneo,* fanning the flames of her desire. She would fall on him later, like a tropical storm. But first, the little matter with her new *amiga* and future business partner. All business, Miss Martha Fiol turned and walked back to where Stan waited for her. With her best smile framing her face, she opened her calendar self-confidently and said to the Viking,

"So tell me, *corazón,* when would you like to discuss this further?"

42

Sirena is walking along the edge of the ocean in front of the hotel, wearing a white dress Hugo bought for her at a boutique in the Hotel Talanquera, and low-heeled leather sandals. Sirena is playing with a pearl bracelet as she walks slowly into the sunset. Musing . . .

Why couldn't she remember that bolero the first night Hugo kissed her? Why couldn't she lose herself, as she'd always been able to do before, in the humming of songs, distancing herself from what was happening to her body as she lost herself somewhere else? Sirena felt uncomfortable. Although the next night she had regained her ability to sing as she was being kissed, she didn't feel as self-assured as before. Now she couldn't avoid feeling moved by Hugo's caresses. Sometimes they even made her cry. This client had changed the outline of her customary plan, and it was more and more difficult to remain wrapped in the illusion of love and surrender that until now had always protected her. Something about Hugo made her vulnerable to reality.

Two days had passed since the show and Sirena couldn't make herself return to the capital. At first she told herself it was because she was tired. Then, it was because of her businesswoman's blood. Hugo promised to get her a contract to perform at the piano bar at the Hotel Talanquera. Meanwhile, he would cover all her hotel expenses. He promised to help her with her career, shower her with kisses, satisfy each of her hungers, love her as he had always wanted to love a woman. . . . Sirena wants to convince herself that she's still in control. I can get all the money I want out of this rich guy, she tells herself as she walks along the beach. Enough to finance my own career without needing a phony agent. He has influence and contacts.

And he gives them to me without asking for anything in return; all I have to do is let him touch me again. So much for so little . . . I know he wants me to fall in love with him. But how am I going to fall in love with him if I don't even know him? I love the luxury that surrounds him, his wallet that is always full of *billetes*, I love their smell, and the path they open for me, with me sitting in the driver's seat and the *billetes* taking me to the very heights of paradise.

But Sirena's no fool. She knows that something strange is happening, that sometimes, at night, she lies awake remembering things that she had pushed to the back of her consciousness. In the midst of her sleeplessness she had hugged Hugo. Pure reflex, she tries to convince herself. But in that embrace she had felt protected and, without really trying, had fallen asleep again.

Last night she had nightmares. She can only remember flashes. Valentina, her face bluish and swollen, forcing Sirena to promise that she would never let any man get close to her. Then her own hands appeared, slapping desperately at the man who had raped her so long ago; she still remembered it clearly. There before her again were the mustache, the thin lips, the red, dilated eyes, the intent to destroy her from head to toe, to put himself inside her and erase her from the face of the earth once and for all. Sirena hears herself moan, but she can't wake herself, not until the man presses her throat with his forearm and, with the other, waves something shiny in front of her eyes. Startled, she bolts awake. Next to her, Hugo is sleeping peacefully, still embracing her.

Sirena walks along the edge of the sea, lost in thought. She thinks about what Martha would have done at a time like this, but she finds no solace in that, either. She runs right into her own guilt. In her mind, she talks to her manager, justifying herself, You would have done the same, Martha Divine, exactly the same as me. Given an opportunity like this, what did you want me to do? Go back to Santo Domingo right away, call you, try to explain why I had disappeared? You would have made a big fuss. You would have insulted me and reminded me how much you've sacrificed for me. I never asked you to sacrifice for me! Besides, you know that the only ones who have sacrificed for me are already dead. You *invested*, which is something else. Anyone could see the ambition in your eyes, your desire to profit by me for the money to finance your final days as a *matrona retirada*. You know full well that in my place you would have done the same. You would have been proud of me if the loser was someone else. You would have applauded my feat, poured me a glass of wine, and laughed with me, saying, "What a witch you are, *niña*, *ángel celestial*! So young and so capable of scratching your own mother's eyes out! That's how it's done, *nena*, businesswoman's blood running through your veins!"

Sirena tried to feel angry. Maybe if she fought with Martha it would alleviate the pain that was inundating her. But she knew better. She suspected the existence of something that was pushing her in a much more profound direction. When that force won, neither her grandmother's boleros nor the fiercest anger would be able to save her from the storm. Then, what was she going to do with her body, which had already become accustomed to luxury, to the protection of a thousand loving caresses? How was she going to escape a destiny like Valentina's or Martha Divine's? For years her predecessors had been stuck in situations that promised to save their lives, calm their souls. Valentina had trusted Chino and the drugs that he provided her. And how did she end up? Dead. Miss Divine gave in to that businessman, whom she turned into an angry, jealous lover. And what did she wind up with? A fake pearl bracelet. Even the apartment he set her up in wasn't hers. And if she hadn't been such a witch, she wouldn't even have gotten enough out of that merchant of hers to open that dump the Blue Danube on that sewer of a street.

No, that couldn't happen. Sirena couldn't allow herself to depend on this host. She shouldn't trust the hand that throws scraps to stray dogs. Yet, as Sirena gazed at the setting sun, she realized it was easy to fall in the same trap as her mentors. It was easy to let yourself be lulled by words, to be impressed by adoration. To open herself to Hugo with his Cartier watch lying on the nightstand and his expensive socks abandoned on the floor, his checkbook out in the open. It would be so easy to take the gift of his confidence in her hands, the gift of his love, which she knew was a lie. But what did it matter? By default she got the caresses, the luxuries, the attention—by default and without his expecting anything in return. Hugo offered to pay for her stay in the hotel. He didn't care if people saw him there with her, but he always insisted that she dress as a woman. And she was delighted to, wearing the gifts he brought her. He bought them in the boutique in the hotel, dresses, Pablo Rubio shoes. Yesterday he gave her a bracelet of genuine pearls, only one strand, *pero genuinas*. She already had more than Miss Martha Divine's husband gave her.

Lost in her thoughts, Sirena walked along contemplating the setting sun. Killing time while she waited for Hugo to come visit her. That evening they would go to dinner, then up to her room. He would want to kiss her. He would repeat his promise, and she would feel like crying. She had to find a way to hold off that moment. Somehow she had to protect herself from that promise of love.

43

With a handkerchief, the host cleans off the liquid running down his chin and staining the collar of his shirt. He collects the juices and puts them in his back pocket. Sirena looks at him from above like an angel and, for a moment, the host thinks he can see her real face. The host rises from his knees, attaining his full height, and looks into Selena's face, which he gazes at as if she has just finished a song. Once more the face of the scared child vanishes, once more she assumes her character. Hugo becomes disillusioned.

"Why don't we go down to the bar?"

Downstairs, Don Homero and the manager of the Hotel Talanquera waited for them. Hugo had asked the pianist to keep his muse's special gifts a secret. Now he begged Sirena to sing a song for them. When the manager (an indebted friend of the Graubel family) heard the singer's voice, he was just like all the others: at Selena's feet. He immediately made her an offer. Sirena could sing all she wanted, sing and let people forget about everything, let them find something in that voice that carried them away to their most distant memory of pain.

"Why the hell doesn't *esa bestia* return to her own damn country?"

"Selena was offered a contract to sing for a weekend in the hotel."

"I believe it. And you're the one who got her the contract."

"Don't start, Solange, don't start with the same old thing."

Solange hid her anger and her shame. For two days she hadn't done anything but stalk around her house like a caged beast, terrorizing the help. In the afternoons she went out to watch her children swim in the ocean and to take pictures of them. What she was really trying to do was trap Hugo, catch him in the act. Then she would have the proof she needed to destroy him. She didn't know how, but she would destroy him. She wasn't going to be the only loser.

Because, even with anger choking her, Solange had to admit it: that monster had won the battle. Very likely Hugo and the "singer" had already been intimate. But that wasn't the worst of it. What infuriated her most was that her husband kept seeing Sirena behind her back, and he didn't care if everyone else found out, the workers in the hotel, the service staff, the bellboys, and the performers in the lounge. She knew that, even though no one said a word, everyone could tell Sirena wasn't exactly a woman, as Solange wasn't exactly a woman when she married the magnate. Sirena's skin had those traces of adolescence, the incipient Adam's apple on her throat, the feet, the hands that were too big for her height. . . . The only one who was deceived was Hugo. The only one . . . All the others knew, they had to know. And they laughed at her behind her back, and at her children and at the family name.

Pero nada, for all her craning of her neck, Solange wasn't able to catch her husband in the act. And now she learned that Hugo got Sirena a contract at the hotel. She started to pack like a crazy woman. She was going back to the capital.

"Astrid, pack the children's clothes."

She stirred up the servants as if a disaster had struck, and Hugo, sitting in the chaise lounge on the patio, didn't even notice his wife running back and forth, abandoning him, rabid with shame. He didn't question her when he saw her practically shoving their progeny into the chauffeured car. He didn't stop her to ask why she was leaving or where she was going. He didn't get up to respond to his children's waving good-bye at him from the car.

Once the car had disappeared down the driveway, Hugo picked up the phone and called his accountant.

"Manuel, I need you to take care of something for me, as a precaution. Transfer half of the balance in my personal account to my corporate account. I smell trouble with my wife. In case she decides to ask for a divorce. You know how melodramatic women get sometimes."

44

Yes, the front desk please . . . Hello, I am checking out today. Martha Divine, room 1105. All the charges are prepaid by the management. That's what I was told by Señor Contreras. No problem? Perfect. And I am going to need help with my bags and would like you to call a taxi to take me to the airport. . . . Let's say in half an hour. *Muchísimas gracias, muy amable, que pase buenas tardes.*"

Done. There was nothing else to do. Contreras, very apologetic, had confirmed by telephone what Martha had already suspected: the hotel administration had come up with a thousand excuses and Sirena's show was simply not possible. But they weren't going to back her into a corner. She already had an alternative plan.

The business with Stan was going marvelously. That morning she had gone downtown to the Hotel Colón. Thinking ahead, she brought her makeup case along. She noticed a few things were missing—some shadows, a lip pencil. It must have been that disgraceful Sirena. What else has she stolen, *la cabrona?* Martha wondered. But she didn't have time to get angry. She had an appointment with Stan.

She met with him mid-morning to have coffee in his office. Martha played her cards well, and at first she didn't say one word about business. She looked at Stan very coolly and said, "*Mi amor,* I brought my makeup kit and I'm going to make you *regia* right this minute. We'll need a bathroom with good lighting. When I'm finished with you, you won't recognize yourself."

They spent more than two hours on the basic assemblage of hair and makeup. Clear base, liner, gray and green shadows, a raspberry rosé lip pencil, and a platinum fall that Martha had brought rolled up in the bottom of her purse. They laughed like little girls. And actually,

Stan made a beautiful woman. As a man, he looked like an aberration. Because he was blond. Platinum blond. And a mature, blond man is the ugliest thing in the world. Martha had always thought that blond hair, pink skin, and light-colored eyes were appropriate for youngsters, or runway models. Being blond is appropriate only in the world of glamour. That was why Martha had decided to become a blonde. With her dyed mane, her paleness created with a little help from clarifying creams, her broad-brimmed hats, and staying indoors, anyone would bet everything was natural. Martha saw her features as a mark of distinction among the mulatto, olive-skinned, and black bodies abounding on these Caribbean shores. Anyone could be a beautiful black woman, but a stunning blonde in the middle of these islands . . . that was another story.

And Stan really could become one. As soon as he saw himself with earrings and liner and fleshy lips he acquired a lightness of gesture that completely transformed him. Even at his height, he became graceful; his movements were no longer clumsy. And Martha thought, *Just as I suspected, this Swede is a natural drag queen.*

Stan breathed deeply, put his hand to his chest, contemplated himself at length in the mirror. He turned his eyes toward Martha, to look at her coquettishly and sensually, pleased with his new image. Then Miss Martha Fiol saw her opportunity. And she decided to seize it.

"*Mira*, Stan, as *regia* as you look now, that's how stunning the girls are in my establishment. I could subcontract them out to you, two or three of them, to see how they do over here. It wouldn't be for long periods, maybe three months total."

"This is really intriguing. . . . The only thing that worries me is the clientele. Most of the guests here are *turistas*. If your girls perform only in Spanish, there will be problems."

"And who said my *muchachas* aren't bilingual? Honey, *tú sabes*, Puerto Rico is something else. We are almost a state of the U.S.A. . . . One girl who works for me, Lizzy Starr, lived many years in Nueva York. The same with Balushka—she was born in Miami, raised in

Levittown. Those drag queens are incredible! It's just as easy for them to do a show for you in English as in Spanish."

"How much would you charge me?"

"In Puerto Rico it's two hundred dollars a show. Of course, that depends on the production, whether it's with dancers and choreography, special lighting, or just lip-synching. They do one show a weekend. I charge the artist a percentage, of course, for my work as agent. They cover their own wardrobe costs. You cover salary, sound, lights, and promotion."

"Promotion? So the police can close me down?"

"I forgot, we're not in Puerto Rico. Better for you. A few photos on the bulletin board in the hotel lobby and that's it. The locals will find out by word of mouth. And they *will* find out, you can be sure of it."

"And what will we do about visas?"

"What visas, Stan? You hire my *muchachas*, they arrive with their birth certificates and their American passports. They stay a month, do four shows, collect their money, and go back home. You aren't going to offer them a retirement plan or medical insurance, are you? And they aren't going to ask for it. So why bother with those problems?"

"I know—if they stay in the hotel they can come with tourist visas. That way they don't have to declare a domicile. What are the names of your bilingual girls?"

"Lizzy and Balushka."

"Well then, we'll start with them."

And they shook hands on it. Now, reinvigorated, Martha had to go back to her island, convince the two *locas* to commit themselves to spending a month on Santo Domingo, send them to get professional photos made, and arrange the details of the show. The money was good. Forty percent for her; they'd better not complain. She had gone through enough hard times to get them this gig. The worst was having lost Sirena.

There was nothing she could do about it. Miss Martha Divine

resigned herself to not knowing where her *ahijada* was, whether she lay disemboweled in some ditch or sat drinking expensive wine in some restaurant or fanning herself beside a pool. She wasn't going to stir up that hornet's nest. Maybe this whole ordeal was her final payment for what she'd done to her husband. Martha hoped Sirena was okay, but she'd better not get it into her head to show up at the Blue Danube, because Martha couldn't be responsible for what would happen then. She was likely to give *la niña* a whack for the hard times and the sleepless nights she had caused. But Sirena wasn't a fool. Martha knew that she would never see her again.

At least she wasn't going back empty-handed. She was arriving with a firm deal, a new business partner. It wasn't what she had expected; the Hotel Colón could never compete in luxury and plenty with the other hotels in Santo Domingo's tourist zone. But what could she do? So maybe it would take a little longer to retire and raise the money for her operation. But she was sure she would manage. She could feel it in her businesswoman's blood.

The bell rang. Miss Martha opened the door for the bellboy who had come to take her luggage. She went down to the reception area with him, passing at the desk to leave her key. She stepped out onto the front walk. Before getting in the taxi she took one last look at the hotel grounds, with her brow furrowed.

"*Espéreme un momentito, señor conductor.*"

Martha returned to reception, asked the girl behind the desk for an envelope, and rummaged around in her purse for a moment. She asked for a pen (she couldn't find hers) and scribbled a few lines on a piece of paper. Then she took out an airplane ticket and put it in the envelope, with the note she had written. Resuming her great-lady air, Miss Martha Divine said to the receptionist:

"*Señorita.* If by chance anyone inquires about me at the hotel and identifies herself as the person whose name I wrote on the envelope, please do me the favor of giving it to her. I would very much appreciate it."

45

A new custom had been established in Doña Adelina's house. The other boys would gather around Leocadio during dinner, asking him how his day had gone, and he'd tell them what had happened at the hotel. Leocadio understood better what Migueles had said to him that night when they sat smoking on the stairs. That stuff about becoming *un hombre* and making a life for yourself. He was learning that little by little you earned the respect of others. His new status as a salaried man had won him the friendship of other boys in the house, and now he could even allow himself a few luxuries, like going to the movies or buying ice cream and walking along the *malecón* with his new friends. Having money in your pockets makes people treat you differently.

Sometimes days passed when Leocadio didn't see Migueles, even though they worked at the same place. As if they belonged to different clans, Leocadio had to stay most of the time in the service areas, while Migueles came and went in the more public parts of the hotel. Migueles went in to work after noon, and when he left at night, Leocadio had already returned home and gone to bed. But even though he saw him less, Leocadio still felt a special camaraderie with his friend. He was amazed at Migueles's self-assurance; there were little tickles in his stomach sometimes, like when he saw Migueles in his waiter's uniform giving precise orders about what to take to tables. Even though he arrived home dead tired, Leocadio tried to stay awake for Migueles, just like before, and listen to him talk about the hotel and his clients. In that way he nourished the special bond that kept him close to his mentor.

Some days, Migueles tried to find a way to spend time with Leocadio during work. Together they would climb up to the roof of the hotel, and from there regard the city, resting awhile as they gazed at its trees and its hidden plazas. Migueles would smoke a cigarette and share complaints about work with his *hermanito*, telling him how the boss was always on his back about something, how he'd correct the way Migueles served the tables or placed the silverware, or get angry because Migueles hadn't checked to see whether the silverware was clean. Other times Migueles would celebrate with Leocadio over how much money in tips and gifts he had collected that week. Leocadio begged him to describe the bar over and over.

"You didn't get enough of it with the scare Stan gave you when he caught you snooping around?"

"Tell me, Migueles, don't be like that. . . ."

"*Pero, Leon,* it's just like any other bar."

"*Que va a ser!* You can tell from a mile away that it's different."

"And how do you know, if you've never even been in it? You sneaked in? If the *jefe* catches you, Leocadio, you're going to get into a lot of hot water and you'll get me in trouble again. Look, I promised you—"

"No, I haven't even taken a peek. But you can tell it's different by the music. They don't play *bachatas* in there, or *merengues* or anything like that. *Pura música americana* is all you can hear downstairs."

"Well, you're right."

"That's why it has to be different. Tell me, Migueles, what's it like? What are the lights like, the feeling?"

"I already told you, *hermanito,* it's like any other bar. Besides, I'm not good at describing things. I tell you what, we'll wait, and one of these days when the coast is clear, I'll take you up to the bar without anyone noticing. And you'll see with your own eyes, so you won't be so curious anymore."

Leocadio tried to make do with Migueles's promise, but he suspected that if he didn't insist, months would pass before he saw the bar. Many Friday afternoons he would hang around the lobby, near the stairs, hypnotized by the commotion, the music, the coming and going of *turistas*. He always kept an eye out for the *jefe* or his manager. He didn't want to lose his job or get Migueles into trouble. But he had to see that bar. Every chance he could, he reminded his friend "Um . . . about the bar." Migueles, getting fed up, would say to Leocadio, "What's your hurry? If I had known you were going to be like this, I wouldn't have promised anything." They would both laugh after the scolding, during which Leocadio would look at his friend with timid resolve and coax a smile out of him with his big gray eyes. Still, Migueles remained firm. "*Hermano,* don't keep bugging me about the bar. I already told you that I would take you up secretly, but it has to be when I have time, not when you want to go." There was nothing Leocadio could do. He had to wait. Or venture on his own.

He got mad at Migueles. He didn't want to hear Migueles tell his stories. And Migueles grew quiet. He didn't even ask Leocadio what had happened. He looked at him for a long time, while Leocadio avoided his eyes and felt his face begin to get hot. He couldn't look at Migueles. He knew that if he raised his eyes, they would fill with tears. One day, his friend stopped him when he was on his way to the bathroom.

"*Vente, vamonos,* come on, let's go," he said.

"Where?" asked Leocadio, without getting a response because Migueles had already opened the door that led to the service stairs to the bar.

It was completely dark when they entered. Leocadio put out his hands, looking for Migueles, because he couldn't see him. Suddenly he heard the little click of the light switch and on came the colored lights around the bar, the little white lights on the ceiling, the spotlights on the dance floor with its shimmering mirrored ball. The walls were covered with murals and mirrors that reflected Leocadio's image and Migueles's, opposite him in his waiter's uniform. Leocadio shuffled over the rug to feel its pile through his shoes, traced the edge of the bar with his fingertips, ducked through the little door and played bartender with Migueles, who asked him to pour a glass of Brugal. He drank it in one swallow and looked around to make sure no one had seen him. Leocadio laughed.

"Why are you so afraid? The only one here who can go running to tell the *jefe* is me. Or some partying ghost, locked up here to pay for his sins."

"A partying ghost who died as a tourist in the Hotel Colón."

"After dancing a disco-merengue."

"With Stan, who scared the tourist to death by telling him he was a *dominicano*."

"*Oye*, Migueles, do men really dance together here and no one thinks badly of them?"

"Why should they think badly of them, if everyone is doing the same thing?"

"And what's that *vaina* like?"

"What *vaina*?"

"Dancing."

"*Pues*, like this." Migueles took Leocadio by the hand, putting his other arm around his waist and pulling him against his body, smiling. At first Leocadio felt uncomfortable in the arms of his friend. But he knew that if Migueles noticed it his visit to the bar would be over. To hide his inner turbulence, he pretended to be a timid *señorita*, batting his eyelashes and dancing with Migueles on that bright dance floor showered by tiny lights blinking on and off. Then he became a little distracted, looking at the reflections of the lights in the mirrors on the walls. The entire floor was covered with reflections, like dancing glowworms surrounding them. Migueles was still dancing rhythmically. Leocadio was trying to swallow it all with his eyes. The sound system was turned off, but Leocadio swore he could hear music playing, some of that foreign dance music he could hear sometimes down in the lobby. Migueles guided his steps, and Leocadio paid careful attention to learning the sound that drove the steps. Eyes shining with happiness, he looked at his friend.

"So one leads and the other follows?"

"That's how it is."

"The bigger one leads the smaller one."

"Not always. Sometimes *el más grande no es el más hombre.*"

"What do you mean, *no es el más hombre?*"

"*El hombre* is the one who leads, the one who decides. The other one is *la mujer,* the woman."

Leocadio grew quiet for a while. He kept watching the lights, but it was obvious from the look on his face that he was concentrating on the words that Migueles had just spoken.

46

Selena steals the light like a thief. Sirena steals the eyes from those who adore her. She wants everything they have. She deserves to be at the top. She deserves a better life than the one she has. That's what she declares on the nights she sings. That's what her voice declares to all those it inebriates. Each time she sings her voice is a hunger, a tumor of hunger, a wanton abandon.

And she can't explain why the audience pays to see her suffering, now that she's losing the self-assurance of what used to be a perfect illusion. Hugo is in the back, embraced by his luxury, watching her dying painfully in front of her host.

Could it be that only through people like Sirena Selena can the audience really feel pain? It's scary to die in front of so many witnesses, really; it's scary to live so close to pain.

The evening's performance is over. Hugo waits patiently as Selena's fans admire her, speak to her, congratulate her. They approach her to see if what they have witnessed is real. Some discover what Hugo knows: it is a *muchachito* who has sung to them that night, a *muchachito* acting like a *mujer*. Others can't see anything, and they congratulate her and go home to sleep tranquilly in their beds, in their ordinary lives. Sirena glides over to Hugo, who is leaning against the bar, waiting for her.

"Let's go get something to eat," she proposes.

"Not tonight. I ordered something special to be delivered to your room."

"Okay." Sirena maintains a silence that can mean many things.

They go up to Sirena's suite and sit down to eat lobster Thermidor. Sirena has never eaten lobster. She is content, sucking on the claws, breaking the shell, licking the melted butter that coats her hands. Hugo looks at her without wanting to speak, because he fears his voice will break the spell and transform her again into her character. They have finished eating and are drinking cognac and talking. Hugo waits for a moment of silence. That's the signal for the beginning of another ritual. He kneels in front of Sirena and she feels a buzz in her chest. She begins to sing softly.

"Don't sing tonight. I only want you to feel me."

The nymph grows quiet. On the outside she refrains from singing, but inside she tries to sing a love song. "Blessed God," she thinks in the midst of the melody, "don't let the script fail me. Holy Virgin," she begs, afraid, "let this man just keep on where he's already headed." But she foresees that Hugo is on the verge of something else. He's already put it in his mouth and is kissing it so voluptuously. He caresses her buttocks and holds them to maintain the rhythm. He lifts her off the sofa and kisses her softly on her small breasts. Now he's biting her ears, embracing her passionately. He throws her onto the bed, undressing her completely and lying beside her. Hugo puts her hand on his pants so she can feel it. He wants her to feel what she has done to him.

"Look what you have done to me, Sirenito."

And he calls her Sirenito. He uses the masculine form he has never used; it disrupts her song. It makes Sirena open her eyes, forgetting about her act.

"*Ay, mi* Sirenito, look, look . . ."

Now it is Hugo who is ready to receive her with all his desires exposed. His flesh jumps from his trousers like a shark out of water. Sirena senses a devouring. She touches it. Hugo is lost in the ecstasy of her touch. He doesn't even hear when Sirena, recovering, opens her throat. He thinks it is another surge of the ocean. His respiration is agitated as Sirena calmly continues singing and caresses him with her hand, wet with saliva, her fake nails still intact. She touches him behind, too, with a wet finger, she sinks her finger until she scratches him inside. Hugo enjoys the pain. He lets her touch him, he would let himself be killed for that *chamaquito* to see if that would prove his commitment, to see if it would convince him to one day let the boy go inside to that place where Hugo was hiding, frightened to death.

I will love you Selena as I have always wanted to love . . .

—his breathing is labored. He falls facedown on the pillow. His *sirenito* scratches him again. Hugo imagines she is burning with desire and looking at him tenderly. The host thinks his *serenito*'s lips are moving and that perhaps she is saying that she loves him, that she has never felt so close to anyone. Hugo tries to say that he feels as if she is another version of himself, as if each one had been waiting on the other side of a very old mirror.

"Look at me, Sirenito, look at me," Hugo repeats as Sirena scratches her host's pink flesh with her fingernail. She watches him turn facedown onto the pillow, and for a moment she becomes tender. The obedient pain of Hugo offering himself up calms her anger. Sirena gazes at his wide back, at the relaxed arms that have sheltered her so many times. She would like to say so many things to those arms. . . . But to speak she would have to let go of who she really is, who it took her so much work to become. And if she goes out there and doesn't come back? Who would she be then?

Hugo feels a drop of warm saliva between his buttocks and then smiles when he feels himself clothed in the pressure of a tiny body climbing on top of his and putting the tip of its mystery in his rear opening. Hugo twists, the warmth of the rubbing soothes him and he no longer knows anything but the sheets on the bed as his *sirenito* rides him slowly, then more and more rapidly. Hugo lets himself be transported by a whisper of flesh, a cold current, as if he were at the bottom of something very blue and deep. Outside, the ocean churns.

The next day, Hugo Graubel awakens, tired. He searches in the bed for Selena's body. She's not there. Maybe she's in the bathroom. He gets up. He goes to see what time it is. He can't find his Cartier watch. He looks for his trousers, his wallet in the pocket. It's not there either. He goes to the closet. Empty hangers; the boxes from the shoes he bought Sirena are also empty. Hugo dresses quickly and goes down to the lobby of the hotel. He asks to speak to the manager. He asks about Sirena.

"I saw her take a taxi this morning and heard her tell the driver to take her to the capital. She was carrying a large bag and a small case. She left the keys to the room. She said you would take care of the bill."

"And she didn't leave anything else, not even a note for me?"

"Not that I know of, Señor Graubel."

"Nothing?"

"No, *señor*, nothing."

47

*T*he bigger one, the smaller one. One is *hombre*, the other is *mujer*, although he can be the smaller one; the man is not necessarily stronger or bigger than the other one, but he's the one who leads, who decides, who rules. There are many ways to rule, many things required to be *un hombre* or to be *una mujer*, for each person can decide for himself. Sometimes you can even be both. Without having to choose one or the other. Money, a big car, the *billetes* to go far away, to go into the best bars, the ones with the most lights. That's what the man has. And if he dances and the other one leads, then he's *la mujer*. And if she decides where to go, then she's *el hombre*, but if he stays there in the arms of Migueles, who is leading, he's *una mujer*. But what if it was she who convinced him to dance, who brought him here with her hot face and her tricks? Then who is *el hombre, la mujer*? If I were the one who led him forward and backward, who knew where the light switch was and turned it on so that the little lights flickered against the walls? And if a tourist takes Migueles by the waist and leads him, and invites him to go for a ride in his big car to the beach, and he is the one with the money? Which is the *hombre*? Migueles speaks with confidence and he stands up to the boss; he finds jobs. He is *el hombre*. The bigger one, or the smaller one, the stronger one, the braver, the smarter one. And if the smarter one isn't the stronger one, and if the one who leads isn't the one with money, but the one who obtains it by being smarter? And if I am here with this music, surrounded by Migueles's arms, which are strong and tender like a tree trunk? And if this tickle is strong, and big, and smart, and forceful? It must be the tickle of *un hombre*, a dance with a bigger one and a smaller one, but a smaller one who is going to be smart and strong. Migueles is *un hombre* and he likes that. Sometimes he follows and obeys, sometimes he doesn't. When he comes upstairs, for example. When he comes to dance, not as a waiter but to dance, to sit at the tables with the *turistas* and dance with them.

If they want to be the ones who lead, let them. If they want to be the ones who snuggle against the chest, let them snuggle. But they can't toy with you, they can't coax you into a corner, making you scared, afraid, your mother calling you, and you seeing a wild animal in her eyes. Not here, here you dance and the lights entertain you and frighten away the beast. And me in his arms and under these lights, shining, I am the smart one, not the coward; the big one, not the little one; the one who has money. And Migueles is my brother who taught me how to dance, and treats me like a man, but he dances with me. Even if I am small and delicate. He respects me and dances with me. I am respectable and when I grow up, soon, I will dress respectably and I will come to dance here, where there are no wild animals, only men.

48

What was it that she saw? That image she glimpsed as she was hurrying down the stairs of the Hotel Colón? To Martha it looked like two boys dancing without music in the hotel bar, in complete silence. They turned, one in the arms of the other, two *muchachos hermosos*, one bigger than the other, his skin the color of copper, the color of thick, pinkish chocolate. But it was the younger one she held in her memory. He was yellow like a cat, with gray eyes warning of a storm and something else, a sacrificial air about him that would make anyone's hair stand on end. *¡Que fuerte era ese muchacho!* Not even he himself knows how strong he is! The other one had better prepare himself, the smaller one is going to get him all tangled up. It's obvious that they are boyfriends. And if they aren't, they'd better get ready, because they're going to be. She knows about these things, she smells them in the air. It's not for nothing that she has been in this world for so long. She has left husbands rotting in hospitals, has managed to flee vengeful parents and thousands of crazy clients and policemen with clubs in their hands. She can recognize the energy anywhere. Maybe it's what spiritualists call an aura. But there aren't colors encircling this person. It is the weight of his steps, the glances, the denseness with which he comes into the world. She knows how to recognize it. She knew it as soon as she saw Sirena. She sees it in that little *muchachito* dancing in the arms of a waiter.

Ay, Señor Santo, la Sirena. She was like that, like that *muchachito*, someone who could never be invisible simply walking down the street, even if she wanted to. A hungry eye always spots them. There will always be those who want to gobble them up and are left with frustrated desires, their hunger half satisfied; they are powerless, because they don't have what it takes to digest that powerful creature. *Ella lo sabe*, Martha Divine knows. And that's why she feels that Sirena is out there, laughing at the world. Because, *así es la vida*, baby. You laugh as you sing about dying, you drug yourself up, but you can still see clearly, and you die as you break into a fit of laughter, because *así es la vida* in this soup of islands stewed in hunger and the desire to be someone else. She hasn't lived what she has lived for nothing, hasn't run the risks she has run, trafficked in what she has trafficked in, all the while knowing how to disguise herself, for nothing. Because she knows that without something to hold on to no one can bear life. Because she knows that without the makeup and the glamour, without the dreams and the memories, the only thing one has left is waiting for the four shots around the corner, or drinking away one's liver alone, or slowly cutting one's veins hoping for a caress. *No, mi amor*, without makeup and high heels, without tricks and betrayal, life isn't life for one who lives with this weight in her belly. And anyone who doesn't like it can just move to another planet. *Que esto es así. . . .* That's why she doesn't blame Sirena. How could she blame her? It wouldn't do any good. Martha will still break her face if she sees her, because she's entitled to. But she doesn't blame her.

But now she has no time for such thoughts. She has to go back, pick up, represent, prepare, send, promote. Go back to her regular life. With bigger and more feasible plans. To see if she can finally make a better life for herself. And still hang on to the tricks that one needs to survive in these islands. *Qué barbaridad.* But she saw what she saw. The image of a wildcat dancing in the arms of a poor boy who didn't even suspect that he would be the first victim of the day. She saw it as clear as daylight; there had to be a reason for living as Miss Martha Divine on the face of this earth. She would love to see that *chamaquito* when she comes back to the República with her entourage. He has something, that boy. Just like what Sirena had. Who knows? Life takes many turns. And she still has energy in her *implantes*. Maybe she can start over again.

49

*G*ood evening, my darling audience. How are you tonight? Better than me, I hope. *Ay sí,* dear God. From the bottom of my little heart I hope that life has treated you better than it treated me last night. I am a wreck. No, seriously. You all see me standing here, so divine, with this sculptured body, but let me confess something: this binding is killing me. I drank too much last night. Even though I keep going to the bathroom, my belly is still swollen. One lives so pressed and so tense these days. Your heels are scratched, the drug-store has run out of shoe polish, the disc jockey 'accidentally' erased the track you had rehearsed and now you have to improvise another Cher song, your husband wants to leave you again and you don't earn enough to pay the rent on your own. . . . Modern life is enough to bring out the monster in anyone.

"Believe what I am telling you, *querido público.* Even though you can't see the ravages on this taut, virginal face, I am what you'd call a mess. Last night I went wild. I sniffed, smoked, swallowed, sucked. I don't even remember what I did most. And all out of disgust. Cuquito, honey, give me another whisky while I tell my beloved audience what happened to me last night. Make it a double, *mi amor.* And don't give me that crap you give the customers that passes for liquor. I've seen you with my own eyes put rubbing alcohol in old liquor bottles to fill them up. No, give me a drink of that fabulous Chivas Regal you're hiding back there. Yes, darling, the one that Amelia and Dulce keep on hand for the VIPs who are visiting us tonight. *Gracias, mi amor.* Well, my distinguished audience, to your health. Oh, what relief!

"As I was saying, last night I dragged myself along life's gutters.

I couldn't help it. My husband left me. Again! And you are all to blame. I was killing myself rehearsing a new routine to entertain you with tonight. So because I was rehearsing, I got home late. I didn't have dinner ready, and he used that as his excuse. But I saw it coming. For a while now he's been looking for a way to start a fight so he could get out of the house. What he doesn't know is that I am fully aware that he has a new lover, one of those young girls who still don't know how to wrap themselves so the binding doesn't pinch their pecker. Yes, because they have little peckers. It still doesn't work very well for them and they clump around in their mother's high heels, looking like cripples in the street. You don't need to tell me how it is, I know all about it.

"Just let me catch her, I'll scratch that tramp's face. Housewrecker. Filthy little hussy. I'll rip her wig off and throw it in a blender, head and all. So she learns that you have to respect marriage, even between *locas*. This world is full of betrayal. I really don't know how people can do these things. . . . And my husband had better watch out, because he's gonna get what's coming to him, too. I'll be out of my heels in a flash and I'll punch him so hard in the stomach that he'll have to ask his mother to give him some air. In fact, he took one of those punches with him last night as a good-bye present. I am a total lady, the living image of elegance and glamour, until you unleash the demon inside me. We all have a little demon inside, don't we, girls? And mine slashes faces and throws punches.

"It's all your fault. Yes, yours and this artist's job which allows me to honorably earn the pills which make me thin and the false lashes that make me stunning. It was the preparation, the search for wardrobe, and the rehearsals—they took a lot of time that I should have devoted to my husband. Yes, honey, what did you say? Why are you laughing? I don't rehearse? Amelia, Dulce, look what these folks are saying. That for this show I offer here in the club the only thing I have to do is stand here under the spotlight and open my mouth. Well, let me tell you, you bunch of ingrates: I kill myself for every production. The details one has to oversee—the music, the lights, the improvisations . . . How little you all know about artistic work, the sacrifices it entails. One even has to be willing to lose one's husband.

"Besides, for your information, let me tell you that everything in this life requires rehearsal. Everything! Even to find a job flipping hamburgers in a fast food joint, one has to practice. And to find a husband! *Ay, niñas!* The weeks of dedication in front of the mirror practicing smiles, winks, giggles of admiration in order to conquer some man. Then it takes more rehearsing to convince them that they had control over the whole thing. Everything in this life requires practice. Listen to me so you don't end up clueless. . . .

"Believe me, *muchachas,* the secret of success lies in rehearsal and a positive disposition. I'm going to give you a little lesson in visualization. I learned it from a cassette called *Positive Thinking* that I bought this afternoon to get me over the loss of my husband. Repeat after me: 'Desire creates ability.' 'He who perseveres accomplishes.' 'Don't go backward even to get a head start.' But, then again, sometimes a little rest for the bones isn't all bad. But anyway, you know what I mean. You have to remain positive. Even though you feel like a dirty rag because life is tearing your heart apart. Even though the police grab you coming out of a club for being a *maricón* and your husband takes off with somebody else. Even though you live in a tiny room filled with cockroaches, and moths are eating the dresses you've sewn so painstakingly in order to enjoy an instant of luxury in this horrid bar. Just keep on looking for your lucky star. It's up there, shining in the firmament, holding a future of luxury and happiness for you. That's why I want to sing you this positive, playful song, to give us the courage to catch our lucky stars. I can already see mine, just beyond my grasp. I can almost reach it. I swear, there are days when I believe I can touch it with my fingertips."